DARK QUETZAL

Read all the books in
The Echorium Sequence

The
—Echorium Sequence—
Dark Quetzal

Katherine Roberts

SCHOLASTIC INC.

New York   Toronto   London   Auckland   Sydney
Mexico City   New Delhi   Hong Kong   Buenos Aires

For Dorothy,
the best mother in any world.

First published in the United Kingdom in 2003 by The Chicken House,
2 palmer Street, Frome, Somerset, BA 11 1DS, UK.

ISBN 0-439-52309-5

12 11 10 9 8 7 6 5 4 3 2 1   3 4 5 6 7 8/0

Printed in the U.S.A.   40

First Scholastic paperback printing, November 2003

Book design by Elizabeth B. Parisi

CONTENTS

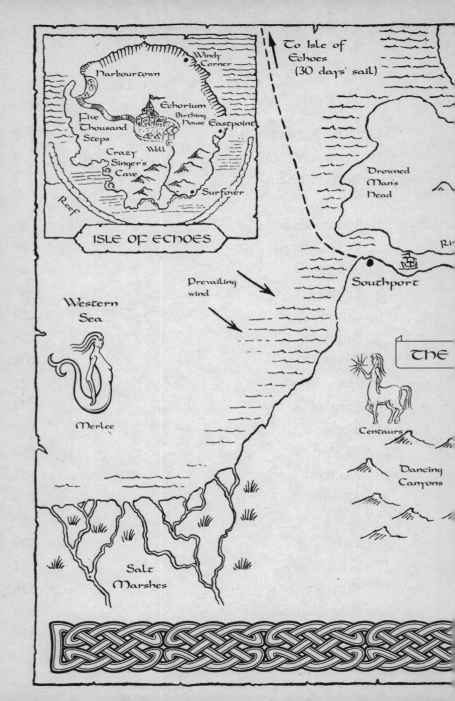

The Echorium sequence

Long ago, before human history began, the world was inhabited by beautiful creatures — half human, half animal — who knew the secret of using the ancient power of Song to control their environment. These Half Creatures lived in harmony with their human neighbors.

But the humans, impatient for progress, began to turn their backs on the old ways. They made tools and built great towns and cities, ships to sail the seas, and wheels to travel the land. They made war on one another, destroying the very things they had built. The Half Creatures fled to the remote regions of the world — deep into the forests, to the bottom of lakes, and far beneath the waves — taking their secrets with them.

Not all humans forgot the old Songs. Those who saw how destructive their way of life had become set out across the sea to find a haven. On an island of enchanted bluestone, they built a school and taught their children the five ancient Songs of Power: *Challa* for healing, *Kashe* for laughter, *Shi* for sadness, *Aushan* for discipline, and *Yehn* for death.

News of the enchanted isle where people were healed by the power of Song quickly spread to the farthest corners of the world. The island became known as the *Isle of Echoes*, the school became the *Echorium*, and the people who lived there became the *Singers*.

The Singers made it their mission to restore harmony to the world. They dyed their hair blue to enhance the power of their Songs and added diplomatic skills to their lessons. Any youngster whose voice could not manage the Songs was trained in self-defense so they could help protect the Echorium. The Singers negotiated treaties with the world's leaders and ensured these treaties were kept. When necessary, they sailed to the mainland to stop wars and put an end to cruelty. Their children were able to speak with Half Creatures and became friends with them. But as the fame and influence of the Singers grew, so did the number of their human enemies.

Eleven years after the events described in *Crystal Mask*, the world of the Singers faces its biggest threat yet.

Echorium Anthem

For healing sleep of lavender dreams,
For laughter golden and gay,
For tears shed in turquoise streams,
For fear, blood, and scarlet screams,
For death of deepest midnight shade.
For these the Songs,
Five in one.
Challa, Kashe, Shi,
Aushan, Yehn.

1

SINGER

The Crazy Singer who lived in a cave on the beach had disappeared, and the whole Echorium was in turmoil. Kyarra couldn't understand why people were so worried. It wasn't as if they'd lost any of the proper Singers who lived in the vast building of bluestone on the summit of the Isle of Echoes and taught the novices everything they knew, from basic hums to history. The woman who occasionally climbed the Five Thousand Steps to visit them no longer even dyed her hair blue, and no one had ever heard her sing on the Pentangle to cure the sick like Singers were supposed to do. But Singer Kherron wanted all the Final Year novices down on the beaches to help look for her.

The rest of that morning was a whirl of preparation for the rare outing. Orderlies ran back and forth with worried expressions. Novices laughed and shouted until the bluestone rang with *Kashe*, while their teachers desperately tried to calm them down. Kyarra kept quiet and avoided catching the eye of any of her teachers. Her skinny build often made people think she was younger than her years and although she was nearly eleven, and had been moved up a class because her voice was so exceptional, this would be her first time outside the Echorium. She didn't want anyone to suddenly decide she ought to be chaperoned.

Singer Renn was waiting for them in the courtyard. He wore a formal robe of flowing gray silk and must have redyed his hair just that morning, because it shone bright blue in the sunlight. Kyarra liked the young Singer, who was serious and quiet and blushed easily. He had amazing gray eyes that changed mood like the sea. Some of her disciplinary Songs had been due to her daydreaming in Singer Renn's class.

His gaze passed over the novices, counting heads. She felt her cheeks grow hot as it reached her and quickly looked away. The gates of the Echorium stood open, showing the Five Thousand Steps that plunged down through sunlight and the blue slate roofs of Harbourtown to the sparkling, dancing sea. She caught her breath, suddenly dizzy.

A boy called Caell, who was the closest she had to a friend in her new class, squeezed her hand and said in a pallet-whisper, "Don't worry, Ky. I expect the Crazy Singer's gone off swimming again with those Half Creature friends of hers. She'll grow a fish tail herself, if she's not careful! She'll be back safe in her cave by the time we get down the Steps, you'll see. Old Kherron's just being paranoid again."

"Shh!" Kyarra stiffened as the Singer he'd named emerged from a door in the wall and strode across to Singer Renn. The whispers and giggles fell silent as he passed. Eyes followed him, but quickly looked away when he turned to address the assembly.

"Pay attention, novices!" he said in his cracked, rough voice. "This isn't a holiday outing, as some of you seem to think. Singer Rialle is missing. She's been gone more than two weeks, and that's longer than she's ever stayed away before. We need to contact the merlee to find out if she's all right, and that means one of you will have to sing to the creatures. So get down those Steps and keep your eyes and ears open! Any novice caught messing around down there, rather than looking for merlee as they should be, will answer directly to me. Understand?"

They understood. The whole Echorium knew the story of how Singer Kherron had lost his voice on his last overseas mission, and how many Songs he'd been given over the years in an attempt to cure him. His temper grew worse with each failure. To be sent to Singer Kherron for a lecture was a punishment worse than *Yehn*. But even the bitter old Singer's presence couldn't subdue so many excited novices for long. Kyarra and Caell found themselves jostled toward the gates, where the two Singers were checking people through. Kyarra pushed to the other side, hoping to avoid being noticed, but Kherron's shadowed green eyes missed nothing. He held up a hand and the whole line stopped. The twisted lips pressed together as he drew Renn aside. The two Singers, young and old, held a swift discussion using pallet-whispers. They kept glancing at Kyarra as they spoke.

Caell frowned. "Singer Kherron seems awfully interested in you. What have you done?"

"Nothing."

But her stomach was jumping. Lianne and some of the other girls in her class were grinning at her. Had they set something up to get her into trouble?

Singer Renn beckoned her across. She looked desperately at Caell, who gave her hand another encouraging squeeze. The girls nudged one another and winked.

Kyarra raised her chin, but couldn't help a shiver as the old Singer's green eyes bored into hers. He didn't speak, though. It was Singer Renn who smiled at her and said gently, with an undercurrent of calming *Challa,* "Kyarra, I know how excited you must be about going down to the beach to see the merlee, but I'm afraid you're going to have to stay in the Echorium this afternoon. You can use the time to practice your breathing exercises. I'm sorry. Someone should have told you earlier."

Kyarra stared at him in disbelief. "Stay in the Echorium? But . . . *why*? What have I done?" She looked longingly through the open gates at the blue Steps leading down to the sunlit beach.

Singer Renn glanced at Singer Kherron. "You're not being

punished, Kyarra, if that's what you think. You've worked very hard, as usual, and your teachers are pleased with you. But being moved up a year means you've still got a bit of catching up to do. We thought you might welcome the chance for a bit of uninterrupted Song practice." He smiled. "After all, you'll be singing on the Pentangle soon, and —"

"No!" The protest burst from her before she could think. "It's not fair!"

The rest of the class had gone quiet. They shuffled their feet and tried very hard to look as if they weren't listening, though of course everyone was hanging on to every word.

Singer Renn frowned, his gray eyes avoiding hers. Singer Kherron grasped her arm and gave it a little shake. "You're going exactly the right way to get sent to the Pentangle for *Aushan*, my girl! Until you've sung on the points yourself, you will address all your teachers as 'Singer' and do what they tell you without question. In my day, a novice who spoke to the next Second Singer of the Echorium like that would have been taken straight to the cells." Renn blushed, but Kherron didn't seem to notice. "We haven't time for this now! Go and do what Singer Renn instructed. I'll speak to you later."

He might have lost his Songs, but his tone was dark enough without them to make Kyarra's legs wobble. Novices didn't get the Fear Song unless they'd done something really terrible. It was supposed to harm their development. Even the information he'd let slip, that Renn would be next Second Singer, made her miserable. That meant Singer Renn would have to give up teaching and spend most of his time overseas. She caught Caell's sympathetic look, though Lianne and her friends and some of the boys whose voices were cracking looked rather pleased. They'd love to see Kyarra put back down a class.

She straightened her shoulders and held her hair off her face so she could look Singer Kherron in the eye. The wind coming through the open gates straight off the sea tugged at the long, blue strands and blew them around her head, wild as her thoughts.

"Thank you, Singer," she said as coolly as she could manage. "I really appreciate the extra time to practice. I'm sure it'll do me a lot more good than messing around on the beach looking for Half Creatures."

Singer Kherron's expression darkened. Singer Renn bit his lip. For a moment, Kyarra thought she'd gone too far. Then she saw the glint in the young Singer's eye and realized he was trying not to laugh.

"Hurry on back inside then, Kyarra," he said. "Tell the orderlies I said you're to have the East Chamber to yourself for two sunsteps."

It was quite an honor. She supposed.

"Yes, Singer," she said. As an afterthought, she added, "Thank you."

She let the wind take her hair and pushed past the others, head high and back straight, meeting no one's eye. They watched her go in silence. But as the blue corridors enclosed her, she heard Lianne mutter, "Good, perhaps now we won't have to baby-sit her all afternoon!" And Caell's swift reply: "Perhaps you should ask to go back with her? *Ky* doesn't need the extra practice."

Eyes still stinging with the unfairness of it all, Kyarra deposited her cloak in the girls' dormitory, climbed a spiral staircase, and walked with a Singer's poise along the wide, curving corridor to the East Chamber. She passed on Singer Renn's message to the duty orderly and quietly shut the door.

Alone at last, she let it all out.

"*I hate him!*" She thumped the wall on either side of the window and thrust her face to the narrow opening. But from here it was impossible to see the Five Thousand Steps or the West Beach. She could only imagine the others laughing, chasing one another through the shallows, putting handfuls of sand down their friends' necks, exploring the caves together, seeing the mer-lee . . . She glared at the clouds massing on the eastern horizon.

"I hate, hate, *hate* him."

She didn't shout. The Echorium was supposed to be capable of transmitting Songs halfway across the world, and the West Beach was only five thousand steps away. Also, no one seemed able to agree whether Singer Kherron had lost his skills of far-listening and truth listening along with his ability to sing. But she did her best to saturate the words with *Yehn*, imagined them pouring down the Steps and drowning the old Singer under a dark wave. *Yehn makes you die.* If a Singer was going to disappear from the Isle, why couldn't it have been Kherron? What could anyone possibly want with the crazy, silver-haired Singer who lived in a cave?

*

Far across the Western Sea, deep in the Quetzal Forest, a vol-cano thrust through the leaf-canopy like a steaming wound. A warm river gushed out of a hole near the crater and flowed in two streams down its wooded slopes. One stream fed a string of lakes, each smaller than the last; the other twisted and tumbled through the trees until it disappeared into the mist that shrouded the forest. In the lakes, Half Creatures — half human, half snake naga; and half human, half fish merlee — were busy tending their underwater breeding grounds. Steam from the surface of the water drifted through the trees.

Beside the largest lake, rainbow quetzal eggs lay in a nest of warm black crystal. The half human, half bird mothers, their tails spread over the fragile eggs, exchanged soft hoots as they cut arrows and fitted them with flights plucked from their own wings. From time to time, one of them would break off from her task to whistle at the young fledglings, whose shrieks filled the clearing as they chased one another in a game of pretend take-off and landing. The older fledglings, who had recently learned to fly, were just as excited as they prepared their bows and pouches for the day's Yellow Flower harvest.

An unusually dark-colored quetzal named Night Plume was in charge of the flock. As ever after a night grounded on the nest, he couldn't wait to lead the others above the forest canopy. He stretched his strong, young wings and playfully pecked his friend Sky Swooper, whose glowing green-and-blue plumage made her the most beautiful of all the young female quetzal. The mist under the trees sparkled with bronze sunlight, and birds filled the forest with music. It was going to be a glorious day, perfect for flying.

But just as the young quetzal were about to take off, two black-robed humans emerged from a tunnel in the side of the volcano. These were two of the priests who served the Starmaker in his underground Temple and looked after the Half Creatures who lived nearby. They walked quickly around the lake to the hatching ground. The fledglings stopped their game to giggle at the little triangles of hair on the priests' chins, while the quetzal mothers hooted for them to come back to the nest. Night Plume's flock stopped stretching their wings and shifted their talons uneasily in the crystal.

The Memoryplace, which contained all quetzal memories since the beginning of time, showed these same two priests yesterday when they were dragging a silver-haired human female into their Temple. In the Memoryplace, the prisoner was bound and gagged.

One of the priests pointed to Night Plume. "There he is. Looks quiet enough. Do you think he's going to behave?"

"Why don't you ask him?" said the other, fingering the black crystal star that all the priests wore on chains around their necks. "They speak, you know." He smiled at Night Plume. "Are you ready to come with us, dark quetzal boy?"

Night Plume looked hopefully at his bow and quiver lying on top of his neatly folded pouch. "I fly now, lead flock, find Yellow Flowers for Starmaker."

The priests exchanged a glance. The one who had spoken directly to Night Plume gave him a sympathetic look. "Sorry, boy. Someone else will have to lead the flock today. Leave your bow. Starmaker wants us to bring you inside." His large fingers closed around Night Plume's wrist.

Night Plume shivered. "Inside?" he repeated, his plumage prickling in alarm.

Rarely did the priests lay hands on any of the Starmaker's Half Creatures. Night Plume had once seen a merlee carried from a boat on the Warm River to the Salty Lake, but she had been carried in a net, not *touched* as the priest was touching him.

The other-priest picked up Night Plume's tail, wrapped it around the young quetzal's wings, and held the end of it in his own hand. "I don't think this one's been in the Temple before," he muttered. "I hope he's not going to panic."

"He should be all right," said the one holding Night Plume's wrist. "He's just spent a night in the nest, remember? It takes time for the effect of the crystal to wear off." He tugged Night Plume gently toward the tunnel. "Don't try to fly," he advised. "You'll be fine."

As the priests took Night Plume away, the rest of the flock took off in a flurry of bright wings, led by a scarlet-and-gold quetzal boy called Sun Glimmer. Some of them waved to Night Plume as they went. Sky Swooper hung back, but she couldn't do anything except hoot in sympathy. Night Plume experienced a moment of wild panic as the rock closed around him. The priests paused, as if they'd anticipated this reaction, and the hand on his wrist tightened.

"Careful," muttered the one holding his tail. "Their bones are hollow, remember? We'll be in trouble if we break his arm."

Night Plume was too busy studying the inside of the Starmaker's Temple to worry about his fragile bones. Despite the horror stories the quetzal mothers told to get the little ones to behave, no fledgling had ever been farther inside than the crater. Gradually, as the priests gave him time to adjust, curiosity replaced his panic, and he stored the new information in the Memoryplace for other quetzal to see. The tunnel had rough walls lit by torches set in brackets of black crystal. More tunnels led off into echoing, unseen chambers, and through an archway he glimpsed a network of glittering tubes like a giant spider's web. Priests crawled like insects in its midst, collecting a steaming yellow liquid in little flasks. A soft hoot of surprise escaped him.

The priest holding his wrist chuckled. "Never seen anything like that before, huh?" he said. "Bet you always wondered what the Starmaker did with your Yellow Flowers, didn't you?"

Night Plume fluffed his feathers, suddenly uneasy. As the priest spoke, a strange vibration came through the rock and a sudden draft brought warm, bitter air from the depths of the Temple. It made Night Plume open his beak and pant.

The priests guided him along a side tunnel and deeper into the mountain until they reached a barrier of black crystal with a little round hole set at human-eye height. One of his escorts peered through the hole, then rapped on the barrier. It swung open, and all the sadness in the world seemed to flood the tunnel.

Night Plume staggered backward, dragging the priests with him, every feather standing on end. Beyond the door, he caught a glimpse of wide gray eyes . . . a glimmer of silver hair threaded with pink seashells . . . several dark-robed humans packed into the tiny space . . . and, dominating the center of the cell on his throne of dark crystal, the Starmaker himself.

The Starmaker had balanced his spear of dark crystal across his knees and was studying the prisoner in silence through the eyeholes of a darkly glittering mask. The hem of his plumed cloak fell down over the edges of his throne to brush the floor in imitation of a quetzal's folded wings. Beneath it, he wore a black robe sewn with lozenges of crystal that hid his arms and concealed the fact that his legs were mutilated and useless for walking. The mask had been fashioned to look like a quetzal's face, complete with crystal beak, crest, and tufted ears. Its chin and cheeks had been threaded with tiny fluffy feathers collected by the fledglings from the hatching ground. The little ones who hadn't yet learned to use the Memoryplace very well thought the Starmaker pushed the feathers into his skin and grew them by enchantment. They said he'd be really handsome one day — like a quetzal. Night Plume blushed to think that, not so long ago, he'd believed the very same thing.

"It'll all come out in the end, Singer," the Starmaker was saying in his rasping voice. "You can sing your little heart out, but your Songs will get no farther than these crystal walls, and I'll have everything out of that head of yours before we're finished. The Quetzal Forest has secrets you wouldn't believe. Moss that glows with the light of the stars, water that steams hot enough to cook leaves, flowers that loosen tongues and open thoughts. You can feel the Yellow Flowers working already, can't you? Dissolving your soul, baring your deepest hopes and fears? I don't need a Pentangle and Echorium Songs to control you, Rialle. I've always been able to control you. You remember the Karch, don't you? How young you were! You thought you could destroy me. But it didn't work, did it? I escaped, yet you remained a prisoner — oh yes, I know! You remembered me so well, you couldn't even bear to close a door after yourself once you were free. How are you feeling now? Can you feel the rock pressing in all around you?"

The prisoner's Song grew louder and *changed,* growing deeper and darker in a way that made Night Plume shiver to the roots of his tail feathers.

But the Starmaker only chuckled. "And don't make the mistake of thinking your voice will work on my priests! They're protected by khiz-crystals, as you can see. And this part of my Temple is lined with khiz-crystal, too. You won't find *this* place as easy to crack as my Khizalace that your Half Creature friends so shortsightedly destroyed eleven years ago! You're powerless in here, Rialle. No one knows where you are. You'll never see your little Isle of Echoes, or your friends, again. Make her drink some more."

There was a scuffle inside the cell and the rattle of metal. The human female choked, spluttered, and let out another hum that filled Night Plume's head with turquoise and tears. He couldn't resist mimicking her. It was quetzal instinct and, like all quetzal, Night Plume had perfect recall. His beak opened of its own accord and the human's Song flooded back out.

The Starmaker looked round. "Ah, my favorite young quetzal!" he said. "Maybe now we can make some progress." He motioned Night Plume's escort to release him, and touched him lightly between the eyes with his glittering spear.

Dark stars fizzed deep inside Night Plume's head, driving out the Singer's voice. Although the touch of the Starmaker's spear interfered with his connection to the Memoryplace, it was a relief to stop singing. When the pain cleared and he could think again, he gathered his tail about his wings and stood straighter. He made an effort not to appear afraid of the small, enclosed space, and must have succeeded because the Starmaker nodded approval. "Curious about our visitor, are you, my dark quetzal?" he rasped. "Well, there she is! One of the *enemy*. Take a good look."

He motioned his priests aside so Night Plume could see inside the cell. The human female had been tethered to the wall with black chains that encircled her slender wrists. She was sitting down, so her arms were stretched above her. Her eyes were unfocused, her head drooped, and her silver hair trailed on the crystal floor. Two more of the Starmaker's priests stood nearby, one of them holding a flask similar to those Night Plume had seen on his way in. The other was wiping blood off the narrow end of a funnel stained with bright yellow juice. The prisoner's lip was bruised as if the flask had been forced into her mouth. More of the yellow juice stained her tattered robe.

She seemed sleepy, mumbling and humming snatches of things under her breath like a fledgling singing to itself in the nest. But when she saw Night Plume, she stiffened. Her gray eyes stared at him as if they could see straight into the Memoryplace itself. With a struggle, she used the chains to pull herself to her feet.

Softly, she began to hum, and the dark cell seemed to fill with lavender light. Night Plume hummed as well, unable to help himself mimicking her. The Starmaker watched through his mask.

Shh, calm, I'm your friend, the human's Song seemed to say.

The Starmaker chuckled. "You've lost none of your spirit, I see! But this is one of *my* quetzal, and he has more to thank me for than most. See his beautiful dark plumage? Quetzal are suspicious of colorless eggs like the one he hatched out of. He'd never have survived in the wild. But when the quetzal mothers rolled his egg out of the nest, my priests put it back again, nice and safe in a bed of khiz-crystal. He can't help you, even if he wanted to. Tell the Singer who I am, boy."

Night Plume glanced uncertainly at the Starmaker. Was this some kind of test? He fluffed his feathers and repeated the familiar memory, exactly as it appeared in the Memoryplace. "Starmaker make blackstars in nest and blackstars in lake and blackstars in river. He be my father and father of all creatures that hatch from eggs in places protected by blackstars. He love us all equally and he teach us how to make bows and arrows so we can stop enemies from destroying nests."

The Singer made a peculiar sound in her throat and clung to her chains for support. Still staring at Night Plume in disbelief and horror, she shouted at the Starmaker, no music at all in her voice. "This is a violation of the Half Creature Treaty! You can't teach quetzal to talk and make weapons! What have you done to the naga to make them bring you their treasure? What have you done to my poor *merlee*?" The shouting seemed to exhaust her. A violent shivering came over her. She slumped to the floor with a clank of her chains and stared at the dark walls. "They'll come looking for me," she whispered. "Singers will come, and this time we'll take you to the Pentangle. I'll dye my hair again and sing on one of the points myself. I haven't forgotten how."

The Starmaker looked down at her from his throne and shook his head. "You don't know when you're beaten, do you, Rialle? How are they going to find you? You ran to those dear little merlee of yours at their first distress call, didn't you? You didn't stop to wonder if they might be lying to you, not even after they led you to my men's ship so you could be captured. I've shoals of merlee out there who love and obey me exactly like this quetzal boy here. They'll tell your friends any tale I want them to. It's taken me some time to get them ready — you can't expect instant results from a breeding program, as well you Singers know. But I've learned patience in my old age. You stole something from me, and now I want it back."

The prisoner frowned. "Singers don't need to steal. We trade Songs for everything we need."

"Except children."

This seemed to penetrate her confusion. Her shivers eased a little.

"No one owns a child," she said, looking pointedly at Night Plume, "whether human or Half Creature."

The Starmaker thoughtfully stroked his spear. "You admit my child lives? That's a start."

The Singer shook herself, as if trying to clear her head of dark stars. "You'll never get into the Echorium and out again with an unwilling child!"

"Unwilling?" The Starmaker sighed. "Oh yes, I was forgetting. I suppose you'll have fed him on years of Singer lies?"

"They're not lies! She's nearly a Singer, she's got a good voice — surprised us all. We moved her up a class . . ." The human female started to cry. "She thinks she's a normal child of the Echorium. She thinks her parents were Singers like everyone else's. We haven't told her what happened. She's nearly eleven years old! You can't just go in there and snatch her away from everything she knows . . ."

"She?" The Starmaker smiled. "I have a daughter?" The thought appeared to please him. "What's her name?"

But the prisoner closed her mouth and refused to answer.

The Starmaker turned to the priests. "She hasn't had enough Yellow Flower juice. Give her the rest."

As the two priests used the funnel to force the remains of their yellow potion down the Singer's throat, the Starmaker turned to Night Plume. "Yellow Flower juice is an excellent tongue loosener, but my previous experiments have shown me that the results tend to become rather erratic as the subject loses control of their reason. I've more important things to do than stay here and listen to the Singer ramble on about the boring details of her pathetic little life, so you can do the listening for me and store everything she says in that phenomenal memory of yours. A day or two should be enough to empty her of everything she knows. Listen carefully, my faithful dark quetzal! I want to know everything there is to know about my daughter. Her name, what she looks like, what she's afraid of, the names of her friends, where her mother is being kept, how they're guarding her . . . everything. If you report what I want to hear, you can fly again. I might even let you lead your flock to the edge of the forest. You're curious to know what lies beyond, aren't you? The time is coming when I'll need you to fly over human lands."

A thrill of pride rippled through Night Plume. He almost forgot that, in order to listen to the Singer as the Starmaker instructed, he would have to remain inside the tiny, dark cell with her.

The Starmaker addressed his priests, who had finished dosing the prisoner. "Give her another flask of the juice at noon, another at sunset, another when the moon rises, and another at sunrise. At noon tomorrow, bring the dark quetzal up to the crater so I can hear his report."

The priests glanced at each other. "Five flasks in two days, Lord?" one of them ventured. "Won't that make her ill?"

"I don't care how sick it makes her, as long as she keeps talking." The Starmaker indicated they should carry him out. He didn't look at the prisoner again. "Singers wrecked my life and stole my daughter, and now they're going to pay."

2
MERLEE TALES

Normal classes had been canceled for the afternoon because of the search for Singer Rialle, and none of the other Singers seemed to realize Kyarra had been sent back inside. When her two sunsteps of practice was up, she made her way back to the dormitory.

There were some advantages to being small and skinny. By piling five pallets on top of one another and balancing on top of them, she could lean out of one of the windows and see over the courtyard wall. She watched clouds pour their rain into the sea and the sun sink slowly toward the west, embroidering the sky with gold. But she still couldn't see the cove where the Crazy Singer's cave was supposed to be. She laid her head on her arms and stared at the sea, wondering what it would be like to sail across it and if there had ever been a female Second Singer.

A sudden rush of feet and excited voices in the corridor interrupted her daydreams. Before she could scramble down from the wobbly pallets, the door burst open and salty-haired girls with stained cloaks streamed in. They stopped when they saw Kyarra and burst into giggles.

"What are you *doing,* Kyarra?" Lianne shrieked.

The others pushed forward. "Spying on us, isn't she? For all her high-and-mightiness out there, she wishes she'd been allowed to come! What was it again, Ky? 'Messing around on the beach'?" They laughed and pushed playfully at the pallets. Kyarra gripped the windowsill in alarm as the pile swayed.

Lianne smiled and shoved harder. "Get off, Kyarra! That's my bed you're standing on."

Someone said, "Stop it, she'll fall —"

Too late. The pile wobbled dangerously, and the topmost pallet slid beneath Kyarra's feet. She half jumped, half fell in a pile of splintering wood and screaming girls. Lianne snatched her pallet out of the wreckage. "Now look what you've done! You've broken one of the slats, you stupid baby!"

Shakily, Kyarra picked herself up. She scowled. "You shouldn't have pushed me then, should you?"

"Oh, stop it you two!" said the girl who'd warned she would fall. "Put the mattress over it, Lianne, no one will notice. We'll all get sent for a disciplinary Song at this rate."

Lianne was still glaring at Kyarra. "She should swap. She was the one hanging out the window like a homesick First Year."

"It's not Ky's fault she got sent back inside, is it? Wait till you hear who could hear the merlee, Ky!"

"Who?" she said, before she could stop herself.

Lianne made a face. But the other girls gathered around, full of their adventure. "You'll never guess. Old Kherron's such a spoilsport! Do you know, he wouldn't even let us go in the caves together? We had to go in one by one with Singer Renn, while *he* stayed outside to make sure we didn't have any fun at all."

This reminded Kyarra of Singer Kherron's threat to "speak to her later." She hoped he'd forgotten. She looked at the girls' windburned faces, then at the door, and lowered her voice. "Did the merlee come, then? What did they say?"

Giggles. "Shall we tell her?"

"Don't know if we should."

"Who cares what a bunch of stupid Half Creatures say, anyway?" Lianne said. "Everyone knows *proper* Singers don't hear them — only babies who haven't sung on the Pentangle and Crazies like Singer Rialle. I'm glad they didn't try speaking to *me*."

Kyarra ground her teeth. She wanted to fling herself on Lianne and shake her. But that wasn't how Singers handled things. Trying to look as if she didn't care, she brushed off her skirt and dragged her own pallet back into place. She did a quick breathing exercise to calm herself. She'd get the whole story out of Caell at supper time.

But Lianne hadn't finished. Leaning close to Kyarra, she whispered, "I always knew your boyfriend was a Crazy — would have to be, to hang around with you so much. Now Singer Rialle's gone, maybe he'll take over her cave. Then he can talk to his precious little Half Creatures whenever he wants."

She stared at the girl. "Caell? *Caell* heard the merlee?"

Lianne waved a hand. "Doubt you'll see him again. Singer Kherron dragged him off so quick, he didn't even get a chance to kiss us all good-bye."

The afternoon's frustration, barely contained, swelled inside Kyarra and burst out in a furious hum. *Shi. Shi makes you cry*. She leaped on Lianne and thumped her with her pillow. Hard. "Where is he? What did Singer Kherron do to him?"

The other girls laughed. Mistaking the fight for a bit of harmless fun, they joined in, and soon feathers were flying down the length of the dormitory. Lianne's face twisted. She dragged the pillow from Kyarra's hands, gripped her bony wrist, and twisted her arm up behind her back. "Think you're better than us, don't you?" she hissed. "Always batting your eyelashes at Singer Renn so you'll get good reports! Think he even notices you? Well, he'll be off on the *Wavesong* soon with Caell, and you'll still be stuck in here — but not as a Singer! I heard them talking about you down on the beach. Soon as you're old enough, you're to be given a Song to make you forget all you've learned and put to work in the Birthing House. That'll take you down a few steps!"

Her arm was on fire, but Kyarra would not give her the satisfaction of tears. "That's not true! I wouldn't have been moved up a class if my voice was that bad."

"Wouldn't you? Maybe they just want to get you out of the way as fast as possible. People have to be Final Years before they can be made into orderlies."

The pain was making her feel faint. She hummed *Aushan* to make Lianne let go, but the noise had attracted the attention of the duty orderly who banged open the door and bellowed at them with Singer-trained lungs. "Settle down, everyone! Excitement's over. It's almost supper time, and you've still got to get changed and take your clothes down to the laundry for washing. Final Years are supposed to set a good example for the younger ones. You're a bit beyond pillow fights, don't you think?" His gaze passed over the mess and stopped at Kyarra, full of a compassion she'd never noticed before. Could it be true, what Lianne had said?

Lianne released Kyarra's arm and snatched up her cloak. "Better have my bed cleaned up by the time I get back, crybaby!" she hissed. "Might as well make yourself useful while you're still with us." With a final glare, she hurried after the other girls.

The orderly shook his head. "What was that all about?" he asked in an undertone, helping Kyarra stuff feathers back into the pillows. "They picking on you again? You should report them, you know. First Singer will send them for *Shi.*"

Kyarra eyed him warily. "Do you know where Singer Kherron took Caell?" she asked.

The orderly grinned. "So that's it, huh? The boy's safe inside the Pentangle with the First Singer and Singer Renn. And the pentad leader, Lazim, is in there as well — he and Singer Kherron go back a long way, so he'll help keep Kherron's temper under control. Don't worry. Your friend will be out telling you all about it before you've finished supper, see if I'm not right."

He tweaked a blue curl. "Run along and grab yourself something to eat before the others get there. A bit of flesh on those skinny bones of yours would soon stop that girl bullying you."

Kyarra almost asked if he knew the real reason she'd been moved up a class. But the orderly straightened, and the moment was past. "Lianne wanted so much to hear the merlee sing," he muttered, staring after the girl. "No excuse for her behavior, of course, but those creatures are uncanny, the way they know. They only ever contact the best of the young Singers. You know they used to speak to Singer Renn, don't you? He lost the knack of it when he grew up, unlike Singer Rialle . . . it's strange for her to stay away from the Isle for so long, though. I hope she's all right."

Kyarra made her way downstairs, her head spinning. Singer Renn had heard the merlee when he was younger? She wasn't really surprised. Nor was she surprised Caell had heard them, too. His voice was sweet still and showed no sign of breaking. Then a colder thought struck. If her voice was as good as it was meant to be, why hadn't the merlee contacted *her*? Or did you actually have to be in the water to hear them? Was that why Singer Kherron had kept her inside the Echorium? Because he didn't want her to hear merlee?

She shook her head. If no one would tell her the truth, she'd find out for herself.

At the bottom of the stairs, the blue corridors forked. Kyarra checked that no one was watching, turned her back on the laughter and chatter coming from the dining hall, and hurried toward the Pentangle.

The big double doors were closed and a pair of orderlies stood guard outside. Kyarra hesitated, straightened her shoulders and marched straight on, her Singer-trained ears tuned to whatever was going on inside. She meant to make a slow pass, then pretend she'd forgotten something and walk back for a second listen. Songs sometimes leaked out through the crack that ran diagonally across both doors — earthquake damage, people said. But the orderlies stepped out into the corridor to block her way.

"Where are you going?" demanded one.

Kyarra waved a vague hand. "Past."

"Why? Only the teaching chambers are that way, and nobody's got classes now till tomorrow morning."

If only they'd shut up, she might be able to hear. She sidled closer to the doors. "Er, Singer Renn said . . ."

"Just a moment!" said the second orderly, smiling at her. "You're the girl who got moved up a class, aren't you?"

"Yes, sir," Kyarra said, smiling back.

"Special class, huh?"

"Y-yes." She glanced again at the Pentangle doors. It was no good. They must have blocked the crack. Not a sound leaked through.

"Who's your special class with? Singer Renn's in there with the others."

"I . . . er . . ." Her mind had gone blank. Desperately, she tried to think of someone not important enough to be called into a special Pentangle session. "Singer Ollaron!" she blurted out, thinking of the ancient, half-deaf Singer who once a week tried to drum into the Final Years a lot of boring stuff about battles with long-dead mainlanders.

"History? At this time of night?"

Now the orderly was standing in front of her, arms folded, giving her an amused look.

"Yes!" Kyarra said, tilting her chin to meet his eyes. "And the First Singer will be angry if you make me late."

"The First Singer will certainly be angry if we let a novice wander about this section of the Echorium unsupervised," he corrected. "Particularly one who's clearly got no special class to go to. You picked the wrong name, girl. Singer Ollaron's in there with the others. Seems history's suddenly in favor again."

"So, back you go, Kyarra." The other man smiled and patted her cheek. "And if you want my advice, you'd do better concentrating your energies on your singing, rather than spying on things that don't concern you."

Kyarra stiffened. She eyed the orderly uncertainly. Did everyone in the Echorium know her name?

She reluctantly made her way back toward the dining hall. But before she rounded the corner, the Pentangle doors gave a deep chime and swung inward. The orderlies snapped to attention. Kyarra ducked into the nearest stairwell. Heart thumping, she pulled her hair across her face and crouched so her white uniform wouldn't show in the shadows.

Singer Kherron emerged first, scowling, and swept off toward the Singers' quarters, his robes tugged tightly around him. The First Singer, an old woman called Graia who had been in charge of the Echorium since before Kyarra was born, hurried after Kherron using a sun-bleached stick to help herself along. There was a pause before Singer Ollaron came out. Grumbling under his breath and squinting in the dim corridor, he turned the opposite way and headed for the dining hall, passing not two paces from where Kyarra crouched. Finally, Singer Renn emerged with Caell and a dark-skinned orderly who wore bones in his hair. One of Renn's hands rested on Caell's shoulder. The boy's blue curls hung in his eyes, and his tunic was stuck to his back. He looked exhausted.

Singer Renn gave him a small push along the corridor toward the dining hall and said, "Have something to eat and then get some rest, Caell. You did well today. I'll make sure you're let off morning hums tomorrow."

Caell mumbled something that might have been thanks and shuffled down the corridor like someone walking in their sleep. Kyarra waited until he was level with the stair then hissed in a pallet-whisper, "Caell!"

He gave a start and his eyes opened wide.

"Don't look at me!"

Caell never needed much prompting. He recovered quickly,

pretended to stumble and whispered back, "I have to talk to you! Meet you in the toilets." Then he was gone.

Kyarra itched to follow her friend. But Singer Renn was still in the corridor talking to the fierce-looking orderly. "It's as I expected," Renn said. "Mother decided to go off and live with the shoal for a while, that's all. It's not as if she hasn't gone off like this before — even the caves get too much for her sometimes. Too many walls, not enough air. She'll be back before the winter storms, you'll see. Kherron makes such a fuss over nothing. It's embarrassing." He closed the Pentangle doors, one by one.

"So you don't think it's strange what the boy said about the different merlee stories?"

"Not really. Merlee have short memories, don't they? One of the creatures probably forgot what Mother told it to say. It was Caell's first attempt at communicating with the merlee, after all, and I know how obtuse they can be. We'll get him to try again tomorrow when he's rested, maybe take him down to the cave again."

The dark-skinned orderly smiled and promised to prepare the pentad guard in case the Singers needed to sail from the Isle in a hurry. Kyarra tensed, ready to rush after Caell the moment the corridor was clear. But one of the orderlies who had been guarding the doors whispered something to Singer Renn, who turned his head and frowned at her hiding place.

"Kyarra?" he said. "Come out of there."

Her face burned. She considered pretending she hadn't heard, but the thought of being dragged out in disgrace by the orderly who had betrayed her was worse. She crawled out, straightened her back and faced the gray-eyed Singer, desperately searching for an excuse. "I . . . I was just going past, and . . ."

"It's all right, Kyarra," Renn said gently. "I understand. It's been a long day for all of us. Go and find your friend. I expect he's bursting to tell you about the merlee."

Kyarra didn't need telling twice. Flashing a grateful smile at Singer Renn, she escaped around the corner, only to hesitate again when she heard her name mentioned behind her.

"Kherron was wrong to keep her in today," Singer Renn was saying in an undertone. "She's an intelligent girl. Anything out of the ordinary is bound to arouse her curiosity. What trouble could she have got up to on the beach with the others? It's one thing to rush her up a class so she can be made completely ours, quite another to punish the poor girl for things that aren't her fault."

The dark-skinned orderly mumbled something about Singer Kherron, but Kyarra hardly heard. *One thing to rush the girl up a class so she can be completely ours.* Coupled with what Lianne had said earlier, it sounded very sinister.

She held her breath and listened for more. But their voices faded as they climbed the stairs to the Singers' quarters, and anything else they might have said about her was lost in the echoes of old Songs.

*

Kyarra raced down the worn steps to the foundations of the Echorium that served as its toilets, hoping Caell had waited. She shivered as she looked around the deserted, rough-walled cavern. Down here, vertical tunnels carried their waste through the rock of the Isle all the way to the sea and strange drafts blew back up, bringing the smell of salt and unexplained echoes.

A hand closed on her arm, making her jump. She let out her breath in relief as Caell pulled her into a cubicle and shut the door.

"Where did you get to?" he hissed. "I thought you weren't coming! I'm missing supper for this, you know, and I'm starving after climbing all those steps up from the beach."

Kyarra scowled. "Got trapped in the Pentangle corridor, didn't I? Singer Renn and that orderly with the bones in his hair were talking about me."

"They're not the only ones." Caell checked outside the

cubicle door and whispered, "Listen, Ky, I think something's going on."

"You don't have to tell me!"

"Not so loud. Singers might be listening."

She knew what he meant. Since the Echorium was built entirely of bluestone, a conversation in one chamber could, in theory, be listened to at the other side of the building. In practice, their teachers only used the technique to listen to patients in the treatment levels, or to pick up messages directed at them personally — though she wouldn't have put it past Singer Kherron to spy on people.

They changed to pallet-whispers.

"I heard the merlee." Caell paused, searching her face for a reaction.

"I know," Kyarra said. "Lianne told me. That's why you were in the Pentangle, wasn't it? What happened?"

"They . . ." Caell licked his lips and stared at the wall, as if seeing through it to another place. His voice softened. "The merlee sang to me in my head. They called me *stone-singer*, but they were excited and they all spoke at once, a bit like First Years in the dining hall, so it was hard to tell what they were saying. I think some of them were trying to tell me about Singer Rialle. How she swam with them, and how she cared for them when they were hurt, how she made strings of shells that sang in the wind." His eyes sparkled as he turned to look at her. "Their songs were so beautiful, Ky! But the First Singer and the others weren't interested in hearing them. They wanted me to ask the merlee what had happened to Singer Rialle. Except by the time we were in the Pentangle, the original merlee I'd heard on the beach had gone, and some others told me Singer Rialle was safe with them. But it wasn't quite the same." He shook his head. "I can't really explain. They sang, too. It's just that, somehow, they didn't sound so . . . innocent."

Kyarra sighed. If all Caell wanted to do was brag about how he'd sang with the merlee, they might as well talk at supper.

Seeing her glance at the door, he sighed. "I know this isn't making much sense. You wouldn't understand unless you'd heard them yourself. I tried to explain to the Singers that there were two sorts of merlee with different memories, but they just thought I meant two different shoals. And Renn said using the Pentangle wasn't the same as communicating with them at close quarters as I'd done in the cave, so that was why they sounded different. Anyway," he went on as Kyarra started to fidget again, "that's not why I wanted to talk to you. The second lot of merlee told me something about you." He broke off and stared at her.

"What?" Kyarra said, forgetting supper.

"I probably shouldn't be telling you this. It's so silly. I didn't tell the Singers."

"Caell!" She gripped his salt-stained tunic in her fists. "Tell me! I know something strange is going on. Lianne said the First Singer only moved me up a class because they wanted to make me forget the Songs and send me to work in the Birthing House."

"That's just Lianne being nasty. You know what she's like."

"And Singer Renn said I'd been rushed up a class because they wanted to make me completely theirs."

Caell frowned at her. "He told you that?"

"No, stupid! It's what I overheard in the corridor just now. Then there was the way old Kherron kept me in when you all went down to the beach, almost as if he was afraid to let me go with you. If you know anything, I want to hear it! And I want to hear it now, before I get dragged off to the Pentangle to have my head cleaned out."

"Afraid to let you come with us?" Caell repeated. "I suppose it makes a sort of sense." He took a deep breath, hesitated, and gave an embarrassed cough. "I don't know whether to believe this or not, but the second lot of merlee told me your mother wasn't a Singer. They were pretty specific. They mentioned your name."

She blinked.

Caell rushed on. "They said you were born in the Birthing House like everyone else, but apparently your mother was brought to the Isle against her will. After you were born, she was given *Yehn* and sent to live in Windy Corner. She was pregnant when she was brought here, which probably means your father wasn't a Singer, either, though the merlee were a little vague about that. They kept going on about your poor mother wanting to see you and not being allowed to, and how I had to tell you so that you could do the right thing before the ship came for her. There's supposed to be a ship, you see, coming to take her away, but the merlee said if I told the Singers it was coming, they'd make sure you weren't allowed to see her before she went, and . . . oh, I know it sounds silly! Except if she really is living in one of the Isle villages, that might explain why Singer Kherron kept you in today. The ship's not supposed to be coming until tomorrow night, anyway, so I've still got time to warn the Singers. But I thought it only fair to tell you first."

Kyarra felt the blood drain from her face. The cubicle spun, the hole in the floor behind them moaned as if in sympathy, and her ears roared.

"Ky! Don't faint on me, please!"

She realized she was slumped against Caell's salty tunic, virtually in his arms. She stumbled out of the cubicle, needing air. He came after her, reached out to steady her, then drew his hand back as she leaned against the wall and took deep breaths.

"Ky? It's just a silly Half Creature story. I wish I hadn't told you now. It's ridiculous to think your parents weren't Singers. You might be just a bag of bones, but you've a better voice than anybody in our class — that's why Lianne and the others tease you so much. You must have Singer blood."

"But my mother," she whispered, refusing to respond to his grin. "What if it's true she had been given *Yehn*?"

"Even if it is true, it obviously didn't work," Caell said brightly. "Otherwise she wouldn't still be living in Windy Corner after eleven years, would she?"

Kyarra pushed herself from the wall. "What's her name? Did the merlee tell you her name?"

Caell sighed. "They don't seem very good at human names."

"You said they told you mine."

"That was different, like they were repeating something without understanding it . . . You mustn't tell anyone about this, Ky! Even if it is true, we're not supposed to know who our parents are. I don't know who mine are."

"Yours were Singers."

"Maybe."

"Definitely. You're going to be a brilliant Singer, Caell. That's why the merlee sang to you. But this proves I'm different! If no one knows who my father was, and my mother was given *Yehn*, what hope is there for me? I'll be an orderly, for certain. Lianne's right! I'll spend the rest of my days in the Birthing House delivering Singers' babies. I hate blood. I wouldn't be able to stand it."

"Oh, Ky, no, I'm sure they won't make you work in there if you don't want to. Even orderlies get a choice, you know. And they can leave the Echorium if they want, once they've done their required years of service. I asked. Most of them stay, though."

"See? Even you believe I'll be an orderly now! My poor mother . . . I've got to find her, Caell! Now. Tonight. Before it's too late."

"Ky . . ." Caell touched her elbow. "You're not allowed."

"Just try to stop me." Kyarra set her jaw. "If Singer Kherron wouldn't let me go out with you, then he shouldn't be surprised if I go out on my own. There won't be a chance tomorrow with classes and everything, and then your ship will be here, so it has to be tonight."

"Same old impulsive Ky." Caell smiled, but his eyes betrayed his concern.

"I'm going, Caell. If you want to come, fine. If not, I'm going alone."

"You don't know the way out. You can't just walk out of the front gate."

"I'll climb over the wall."

He shook his head. "You'll get caught. Then you'll get sent for a Song. *Aushan*, probably, for breaking such a serious rule. *Aushan* makes you *scream*, Ky."

They stared at each other. Kyarra's stomach was fluttering, but she didn't want Caell to know that. She still felt light-headed. More than anything, she wanted to get out of the Echorium to spite Singer Kherron, and this search for her mother was the perfect excuse at the perfect time. If she turned out to be living in the village as the merlee had said, that was fine — and if not, well then that was fine, too. Novices grew up not knowing who their parents were. It was perfectly normal and, deep down, she didn't even believe the crazy story. But what if —? No, she wouldn't think about it. Not yet.

Shrieks on the stairs warned them of the after-supper invasion. Caell glanced up and sighed. "I'd better come with you, I suppose," he said calmly. "You won't know how to get to Windy Corner, even if you do manage to find the way out without getting caught by the orderlies. Then afterward, if there's time, I can show you Singer Rialle's cave and her shell-strings that sing in the wind. I think you'll like them. The merlee might want to talk to me again, anyway." A strange glimmer came to his eye. "Meet me here at midnight. Bring your cloak."

3

WILD QUETZAL

Getting all the details about the Starmaker's daughter out of the prisoner had taken much longer than the two days the Starmaker had predicted. The silver-haired human kept breaking off to sing the wordless songs Night Plume couldn't resist echoing, and this in turn seemed to help her resist the Yellow Flower juice. When the Starmaker finally touched Night Plume's forehead with his spear and told him he could fly again, Night Plume almost knocked over the attending priests with the first joyful beat of his wings. It was such a relief to escape, he was out of the crater and halfway across the lake before he realized that, for the first time ever, there had been no burst of blackstars in his head when the Starmaker's spear had touched him.

Dizzy with the excitement of being allowed to fly again, he retrieved his weapons from the nest and flapped strongly in circles, gaining height until the lakes shrunk to tiny glimmers beneath him. The volcano with its underground Temple was soon lost in its own smoke, and the forest stretched as far as he could see into a green mist on all sides. The weather wasn't good for flying. Clouds were massed on the horizon, rearing into the sky like mountains. Beneath them, flashes of distant lightning warned of a storm to come. But all the colors of the forest seemed more brilliant than before, every leaf and petal freshly unfurled. Scents he'd never noticed filled him with curiosity. Birdsong and the cries of unseen animals were sharper, and even the trees whispered secrets as the breeze ruffled their branches.

He opened his beak and let out a joyous hoot.

Sky Swooper answered, somewhere down the Warm River. Night Plume shifted his bow into a more comfortable position and glided downstream, calling occasionally to check his direction. The flock was spread out too far for safety, but he didn't call them together just yet.

He dived at Sky Swooper out of the sun, wings folded against his back and the air rippling through his tail. She gave a shriek and dodged aside, but he caught her in his arms and carried them both in a dangerous, leaf-tearing dive through the treetops before their combined wing beats regained control of their descent and landed them safely in a cloud of feathers.

"You crazy, Night Plume!" she shrieked, pushing him off and shaking out her beautiful wings so she could preen the flight pinions back into place. "What matter with you?"

"First fly for long time," Night Plume said without apology. He attended to his own wings, glancing in admiration at the brilliant blues and greens in Sky Swooper's plumage. "You molt while I inside Temple?"

"Not be silly," Sky Swooper said, flicking her wings into place. "You not inside that long!"

Night Plume opened his beak and hooted. The shadows of the Starmaker's Temple had obviously made him forget how bright quetzal plumage could be. "Inside too long," he said with feeling.

Sky Swooper finished with her wings and turned her attention to the arrows in her quiver, checking them one by one until she was satisfied they weren't broken. She checked her pouch, too, although today it held only one small Yellow Flower bloom because Sun Glimmer didn't know the best places to tell the flock to search. Finally, she looked up at Night Plume and gave a little whistle.

"What it like inside Temple? What happen to human female?"

Night Plume closed his eyes as he told her how the priests had escorted him up to the crystal-lined crater every day so he could report to the Starmaker what the prisoner had said; and how the Starmaker had then used his crystal spear to transmit the important details about his daughter to his shoals of merlee out in the Western Sea. He told Sky Swooper how the prisoner had cried as the words tumbled out of her, as if she knew she was betraying her friends. Even without looking into the Memoryplace, Night Plume could still hear her sad Songs. Without meaning to, he hummed a few bars softly, and the trees around them seemed to hum as well. When he opened his eyes, Sky Swooper was staring at him.

"What that sound?" she whispered. "Do again."

Night Plume supported himself against a tree. As it had whenever he'd echoed the prisoner in the Temple, the humming made him dizzy. Birds and animals nearby had fallen silent. The shaft of sunlight faded. A coldness invaded the forest. He looked up uneasily. "Storm come soon," he said.

Sky Swooper shook her head. "Sun Glimmer say not for ages. Not need go back yet."

Night Plume's plumage was prickling. Yes, he wanted to tell her. We go back now! But he needed to talk without the Starmaker or his priests listening, so he pushed the storm warnings to the back of his mind.

"Human female say many strange things," he said. "She have Yellow Flower juice, so not tell lies. Starmaker warn me not to put what she say in Memoryplace, so I need tell you in clumsy human speech."

Sky Swooper whistled in sympathy and settled in the roosting position to listen.

"She say about when she young human girl. She born on island in the sea where many merlee are. But she go on journey to cold mountains, where she find wild quetzal inside cavern of ice with feathers plucked out and wings cut off."

Sky Swooper's eyes widened. She hooted her horror, reminding Night Plume of how he, too, had shuddered in horror, and how the prisoner had reached out to touch him, singing her calming song, until the priests had knocked her hand away and tightened her chains so she couldn't reach him.

"Like old Dawn Crest?" Sky Swooper asked, naming one of the quetzal mothers whose flight pinions had been clipped by the Starmaker's priests so she couldn't leave the nest — as if a quetzal would ever abandon her eggs!

"Think worse. Think their whole wings cut off."

There was an uneasy silence. Sky Swooper grew very still. She hooted again, this time in confusion. "Why this not already in Memoryplace? Human female must tell lie."

Night Plume shook his head. "She tell truth! I ask Memoryplace, too. Memory hazy, but it there when I look hard enough. She say long ago humans in cold place worship our father Starmaker, though they call him by different name — Khizpriest. And . . ." Night Plume hesitated. "She say those humans boil quetzal to eat."

Sky Swooper abandoned words and let out a cry that was echoed by quetzal in several parts of the forest.

"Not true! Not true! She enchant you!"

Night Plume remembered how he'd felt when the prisoner spoke of these horrific events, how he'd immediately asked the Memoryplace, and how the images had slowly formed like shadows in smoke, growing clearer as the prisoner sang to him. He huddled close to Sky Swooper, pressing against her as if they were fledglings back in the nest, while he struggled to explain it in words.

"She say some quetzal set free, and others from forest help in big battle on the sea with merlee and human Singers who live on the Isle of Echoes where she born. She also say Starmaker in battle, try to destroy island. He escape, but later he try to destroy Singers again and hurt her boy fledgling." He hooted his own confusion. But at the mention of the battle, Sky Swooper gained control of herself.

"Humans enemy!" she said firmly, shrugging him off and fingering her bow. "We put arrows in them. Wild quetzal enemy! Put arrows in them, also. Not matter if wild quetzal get wings cut off, be boiled and eaten. Not same as we!" She pushed him away. "Starmaker not destroy things. He father of all. Human female put lies in your head. Enchant you, Night Plume."

"No, she not! You know how Memoryplace often have blackstars? Now it have answers when I look, but they strange." Desperate for her to understand, Night Plume opened his beak and echoed the prisoner's turquoise sadness song. "I think all she say is true. I think her Songs affect me because my egg rolled out of nest so much before I born. It like . . . she . . . *un*enchant me."

But before he had a chance to explain his suspicion that the Starmaker's dark crystal had somehow tampered with what they saw in the Memoryplace, a massive crack lit up the sky above the forest. The clouds thundered like the Starmaker's Temple on an angry day, and rain hissed on the leaves above them. Sky Swooper let out a little shriek and spread her wings for takeoff. Night Plume grabbed her arm.

"Not fly in this! Shelter, quick!"

He pulled her deeper into the undergrowth as the rain broke through the canopy and splashed and pattered all around them. Sky Swooper was on the edge of panic, but Night Plume discovered he was amazingly calm. "Find wild nest," he said. "Be safe there."

"You crazy?" Sky Swooper said. "Wild quetzal kill we!" She was close to tears. "We ought go back earlier instead of listen to stupid lies about humans!"

Night Plume resisted the temptation to remind her that she was the one who'd scoffed at his storm warning. Holding tightly to her wet hand, he waited for a break between the crashes of thunder and let out a shrill hoot.

"What you *do*?" Sky Swooper cried. "Not call! Wild quetzal hear, know we grounded, vulnerable, long way from Temple. Where Sun Glimmer? Where others?"

"Expect they get wet, too," Night Plume said. That would teach Sun Glimmer. When he found shelter for his flock, they'd realize he was the better leader. He called again, his feathers prickling in excitement. It was stupid to be so wary of the wild quetzal, he knew that now.

"Night Plume! Don't call! Please!" Sky Swooper sounded frightened as she tugged at his hand. "We stay here, stay quiet, hide. Dry out when storm stops, then fly back — oh!"

She stared wide-eyed over his shoulder, snatched her hand free, and whipped an arrow out of her quiver. Before Night Plume had finished turning, she'd nocked it to her bow and fired into the gloom under the trees.

"No!" Night Plume shouted, knocking her hand aside as she fitted another arrow to the string. "Not shoot!" The arrow spun off into the undergrowth. Sky Swooper swore like a priest and reached for another.

Before she could fire again, the leaves around them exploded with wings. There was a blur of color, and a whistle pierced Night Plume's head. It was more painful than the touch of the Starmaker's spear. Sky Swooper must have suffered the same, for she dropped to her knees and clutched at her crest. Feathered hands grabbed their wrists, took their bows and the quivers from their shoulders, stretched out their wings and held their flight pinions in firm fingers until they didn't dare struggle for fear of damaging the vital feathers. When they were still, a large green quetzal examined their pouches. Sky Swooper hooted in protest as she took her Yellow Flower bloom, but it did no good.

"We friends —" Night Plume began, only to get his head struck from behind by a feathered fist. From the corners of his eyes, he could see others of the wild flock examining their bows and arrows, running the flights through their beaks as if trying to preen them. The green quetzal cocked her head and glared at Night Plume.

-you-take-too-much-yellow-flower-from-forest-

Night Plume crouched, absolutely still. Had those words really whispered inside his thoughts? He glanced across at Sky Swooper, who drooped between her captors as the rain saturated her plumage. She showed no sign of having heard the wild quetzal.

-female-not-hear-we-
-she-too-full-of-blackstars-
-but-your-head-open-as-fledgling-
-we-not-know-before-about-daughter-of-blackstarhuman-
-very-interesting-information-

Night Plume raised his head and looked around at the flock. They were watching him, curious and a little amused. The rain didn't seem to worry them. It glistened like jewels in their crests.

Could he talk back to them the same way? Tentatively, he consulted the Memoryplace. The memory of how to do it was there in the smoke the prisoner had taught him how to see through. Simple, but very strange.

We your friends, he tried slowly.

-friends-not-come-to-forest-with-human-weapon-
-female-throw-feathered-killing-sticks-at-us-
She scared, she not mean it.

He was getting the hang of the wild-speech now. He let out a little hum of pleasure, unconsciously echoing one of the prisoner's Songs.

The quetzal flock put their heads on one side and hummed back, beaks open in delight.

Sky Swooper whistled softly. "Night Plume? Be careful."

"It all right," he whispered back. "I talk to them. Explain later."

He switched back to wild-speech. *We need shelter until storm finish, promise not hurt you.*

This seemed to amuse them. The entire wild flock hooted with laughter.

-we-hurt-<u>you</u>-maybe-

-send-dark-quetzal-back-to-blackstar-place-without-wings-

-like-blackstarhuman-do-to-quetzal-ancestors-

-long-time-ago-

Had they been listening to what he'd told Sky Swooper? Night Plume's heart began to thud uneasily. *Starmaker not do those things. Other humans do them.* But then he remembered Dawn Crest's mutilated wings, and suddenly he wasn't so sure.

The green quetzal opened her beak again.

-you-very-confused-quetzaaall-

-still-think-blackstarhuman-god-

-we-remember-truths-about-blackstarhuman-even-stone-singers-
  not-know-

-take-you-back-to-nest-

-roll-you-out-like-colorless-egg-before-hatching-

-teach-you-lesson-

"No!" Night Plume said aloud, forgetting to use wild-speech. Sky Swooper stiffened and gave him a frightened look.

By now, their wings were saturated and heavy with rain from being held open — which, of course, was exactly what the wild flock had intended. The quetzal holding their flight pinions let go, shook their own wings dry in a glittering shower, and opened their beaks in another laugh.

-confused-quetzaaall-

-not-hurt-us-with-soggy-wings-

-and-broken-weapons-

"No, don't!" Sky Swooper made a lunge across the little clearing, but she was too late. The quetzal who had been examining her bow snapped it in his powerful beak. Another took care of Night Plume's in the same way. They tossed the broken pieces at their talons and threw the arrows on top. Then they were gone into the rain with the same flurry of wings and blur of color as they'd arrived.

Night Plume tried to see which way they'd flown, but it was impossible. The leaves splattered and dripped, green shadows shifted, and the forest whispered all around, confusing Night Plume's sense of direction.

Sky Swooper picked up the two halves of her bow and stared at them. With her beautiful wings bedraggled and her tail trailing in the leaf mold, she shook the broken weapon at Night Plume and said in a furious voice, "Look what your wild friends do, Night Plume! And they take my Yellow Flower! See what come of listening to human female lies? Now Starmaker punish us."

Night Plume was more worried about something else the wild flock had done during that first dizzy burst of wild-speech. They'd accessed his recent memories as easily as if he'd defied the Starmaker and put them in the Memoryplace for all to see. The wild quetzal now knew everything about the Starmaker's plans for his daughter.

4
EVIL PLOT

As the sun sank into a rapidly thickening mist over the Western Sea, Kyarra started to worry about the plan to creep out of the Echorium that night. A lot of things didn't make sense, such as how did the merlee know her name? And how could they possibly know so much about her mother? Was Caell playing an elaborate joke on her? Sweating with last-moment nerves, she almost told him she didn't want to go. Then she remembered the way Singer Kherron had embarrassed her before the entire Final Year and set her jaw with renewed determination. Besides, Caell wouldn't joke about something as important as this.

It seemed midnight would never come. The mist coiled in through the windows and muffled everything outside the Echorium in thick silver. When the orderlies finally ushered them to their dormitories, she meekly swapped pallets with Lianne to avoid arguments and feigned sleep, the broken slat digging into her back. Even when Lianne gave her a suspicious look, huffed, and said loudly, "Being kept in today has obviously done the girl some good. She might make an acceptable orderly, after all," Kyarra refused to rise to the bait.

Keeping her eyes closed, she *listened.*

Lianne settled on her new pallet with much creaking and thumping of the pillow. The breathing of the other novices grew gradually slower and deeper as, one by one, they dropped off. An orderly padded along the corridor outside, paused at the door, then moved on. The bluestone quietened as the Echorium slept.

Kyarra reached for her cloak and rolled carefully off her pallet. She paused to check she hadn't woken anyone, then crept to the door. Someone turned over and moaned as she opened it. She froze. Lianne was staring straight at her, blinking in the light that leaked from the corridor.

"Need the toilet," Kyarra explained in a pallet-whisper.

The girl rolled over with a groan and hid her head under her arm.

With a sigh of relief, Kyarra hurried along the deserted corridors, past the night-lamps with their lavender shades. She stopped at every junction to listen. If she got caught here, she had a plausible excuse, but never had the journey to the toilets seemed so long.

Caell was waiting for her. Finger to his lips, he led her through twisting corridors she hadn't realized existed, along a tunnel that must have taken them under the patients' cells, and out through the kitchens. The courtyard was filled with thick, moonlit mist. They hurried across until they came to the outer wall, where Caell used a key to open a small gate.

"Where did you get that?" she asked.

But he hissed, "Shh!" and dragged her through, shutting the gate carefully behind them. "I'll leave it unlocked," he whispered, threading the key back on a thong around his neck where it chinked against a small blue stone she hadn't noticed him wear before. "Then if we get separated, you'll be able to get back in all right."

"Separated?"

Kyarra's voice squeaked. She was trying very hard to act as if midnight trips outside the Echorium were something she took part in every day, but she hadn't counted on the mist. Out here, with no walls to focus on, it destroyed her balance and confused her ears. They'd emerged on the east side of the Echorium, where a steep hillside dotted with rocks and spiky grass disappeared a few paces in front of them. The cold and damp crept under her cloak. She shivered.

Caell took her hand. "Just in case we lose each other in this mist, that's all. I'm not going to abandon you, don't worry. Windy Corner's not far, but it's on the cliff. Go carefully — we don't want to fall over the edge." He was already pulling her out into the strange, silver night.

The village had been well named. Its squat houses clung to the cliff like nesting gulls huddled together for warmth. Slates were missing from most of the roofs. The mist breathed along the narrow streets, soaking everything it touched. All the windows were dark.

They crouched behind a rock. Kyarra looked doubtfully at the village.

"Are you sure people live here?" she whispered to Caell.

"Course they do," said Caell, but he didn't sound very sure and he wasn't even looking at the village. He was staring instead at the path that twisted down the cliff toward an invisible sea.

Kyarra examined the houses more carefully. "Which one do you suppose my mother lives in? Can you ask your merlee again?"

Caell shook his head and said in a tight voice, "Ky, I don't like this mist. I think we should go back."

She stared at him. "Go back? But we only just got here." She studied the village again. "I'll ask someone. This place is so small, they're bound to know everyone who lives here." Before he could stop her, she'd climbed over the rock and was hammering on the nearest door.

"No, Ky!" He leaped out after her and grabbed her arm. "I think someone's coming! Hide!"

The tension in his voice reminded her how much trouble

they'd be in if they were caught out here. She glanced nervously over her shoulder, checking for orderlies. But the Echorium was a dim, dark shape in the mist behind them, and Caell was looking the other way. Now Kyarra could hear them, too. Clumsy feet knocking stones over the edge, muffled curses, and a man's voice saying, "Quiet, you fools! Do you want to wake the whole island?"

Caell dragged her back behind the rock, which suddenly seemed very small and exposed. "I *thought* I heard someone down there! Ky, we have to go back. That ship the merlee told me about must have come early! We have to warn the Singers."

"No, wait."

As the unseen invaders climbed closer, she could hear them grumbling under their breath. "Hope the woman's where she's supposed to be, that's all. I don't fancy searching the whole stupid island for her in this weather." "This better work, 'cause I'm not breaking into any Singer stronghold, whatever his Lordship says." "Shh!"

The men had reached the top of the path and were working their way through the village, crouched low, running from shadow to shadow. Kyarra counted four of them. They wore scarves wrapped around their faces. Long, curved blades swung at their hips, and daggers were thrust through their belts. Two of the men carried sacks. As she watched, the leader pointed across the hillside. "You two get that stuff into the well," he whispered. "We'll get the woman." He and a burly man headed for the far side of the village, while the two with the sacks ran off along the cliff and vanished into the mist.

Caell clutched Kyarra's hand. "Now's our chance. C'mon."

She let out her breath. "Wait a bit longer, Caell, please."

"Are you crazy? Those men are attacking the Isle!"

"There's only four of them. If we go back now and you tell the Singers about the ship, I'll never get to see my mother. She must be the woman they were talking about."

Caell hesitated, dividing his attention between the hillside where the first two men had vanished and the two who had stayed in the village, as if he was trying to decide which party presented the greatest threat.

"We'll both get *Aushan* when we go back," she reminded him. "Then you won't get another chance to see the merlee again." She was beginning to suspect that seeing the merlee might be the real reason he'd agreed to come with her. But a new excitement was growing in her belly. It looked as if Caell's merlee-tale had some truth in it, after all.

Before he could answer, the door she'd knocked on earlier creaked open. A woman's face, nervous in the glow of her lamp, peered out. "Who's there?" she called.

The two men who had remained in the village swung around and stared at the open doorway. The leader motioned with his head. His burly companion pulled something small and dark from the folds of his scarf. It glittered in the mist as he ran back toward the house. Caell pushed Kyarra to the ground so she didn't see exactly what happened next. There was a muffled scream, cut off short. When she next looked, the man was emerging from the house, tucking the dark thing back under his clothes. He shut the door softly and rejoined his friend.

"He just did something awful to that poor woman!" Caell whispered, eyes wide. "Come *on*, Ky!"

Kyarra felt sick. "But my mother —"

"Forget your mother! This was a mistake. Oh, echoes, I got it all wrong! The merlee tried to warn me, but I didn't listen properly . . . I should have told the First Singer about that ship straightaway! Hurry, before they come back. We can't do anything to help your mother now."

Which was the wrong thing to say. Kyarra shrugged him off, tears in her eyes, and raced after the men. She saw them disappear into a hut at the far side of the village and sprinted faster.

"No, Ky!" Caell called behind her. "Don't!" He was coming after her, but too late.

Kyarra burst through the door of the hut . . . and time slowed.

A plump orderly in Echorium gray lay unconscious on the floor. The leader was helping a tall woman, with long, thick hair the color of midnight, out of her bed. He looked up in surprise . . . nodded to someone behind her . . . a scimitar hissed out of its scabbard and ended up at Kyarra's throat.

She skidded to a halt, realizing with the kiss of that blade how stupid she'd been. But at the same time, she couldn't take her eyes off the beautiful, midnight-haired woman whose night-dress swirled around her ankles like an elegant gown. "Mother?" she whispered.

The woman did not react. Her face was slack, utterly vacant of expression. Her dark eyes stared straight through Kyarra as if they were seeing a far-off place.

The man holding the woman's arm looked Kyarra up and down, finishing at her blue hair. He chuckled. His clothes were as scruffy as the rest of his men's, but he had a proud, upright bearing and wore a ring on his left thumb set with a large crimson jewel. Red hairs escaped from under the scarf.

"Both targets together," he said. "How convenient! I thought we'd have a long wait down on the ship for you to pluck up the courage to come after your dear sweet mammy, yet you almost beat us to it." He appraised her again. "You're even skinnier than I thought you'd be, but the description fits, and you've obviously got spirit. That's good, because you'll need it where you're going." He twisted his hand in the woman's hair and pulled her head around. "Say hello to your long-lost daughter, your Ladyship."

The woman didn't even blink.

All Kyarra could think was: *It's true. Mother's here. It's all true, and she's had a Song like the merlee said.* Then she saw how some of her mother's hair had come away in the leader's hand. "Stop it!" she shouted, tears springing to her eyes. She hummed *Aushan,* aiming the Song at her mother's tormentor. *Aushan makes you scream.*

The leader scowled. "Be quiet, Princess, or I'll have to ask Blackbeard here to silence you."

The man holding Kyarra pressed his scimitar harder against her throat and reached beneath his scarf with his other hand, reminding her how he'd silenced the villager she'd woken. "Let's get them out of here, Asil!" he growled. "We don't want a horde of Singers on our tail all the way to the mainland."

"Don't panic," said the leader, still looking thoughtfully at Kyarra. "His Lordship's tame fish-people will sing us up another nice thick mist and a storm or two to keep the Singers harbor-bound. With our honored guests on board, they'll probably give us a favorable wind all the way to Drowned Man's Head as well."

"I don't care what sort of wind they give us! If we get caught on this rock, none of us'll be goin' anywhere. The others are takin' too long, I don't like all this relyin' on Half Creatures — *What was that?*"

Something outside the door fell over with a clatter. Asil let go of the woman's arm, which flopped unresisting to her side, and drew his scimitar.

Kyarra turned cold. "CAELL!" she shouted with Singer-trained lungs. "RUN!"

"I thought Asil told you to shut up? Or do you want me to use this on you?" Blackbeard dangled the object he'd used on the villager before her eyes. It was a five-pointed star fashioned of black crystal.

Kyarra shuddered.

The leader checked up and down the street, then went down on one knee and squeezed Kyarra's chin. "Who's Caell?" he demanded. "Who were you shouting to?"

"No one!" Kyarra spat back. She looked desperately at the woman who was supposed to be her mother. Why didn't she try to escape? She simply stood there, staring at nothing. She didn't even seem to notice the Echorium orderly lying unconscious at her feet.

Asil sighed. "Have it your own way, Princess." He nodded to Blackbeard.

Before she realized what they were going to do to her, the big man pressed his crystal to the back of her skull. There was an instant of terror, as if someone had just pushed her over the edge of a bottomless pit. Then darkness invaded her head.

*

In the crater of his volcano Temple, the Starmaker was in an unusually good mood. He sat on his throne with his crystal spear resting across his knees and studied Night Plume and Sky Swooper through the eyeholes of his mask.

The two quetzal were being punished for letting the wild flock break their bows. After being touched by the Starmaker's spear, they had been forced to roost in the volcano's crystal-lined crater for a day and a night in the rain, while the Starmaker went back underground to deal with more important matters. All this time, Sky Swooper had crouched miserably with her beautiful tail trailing in a puddle and her head full of dark stars, while Night Plume spread one of his wings over her bedraggled plumage and tried to cheer her up. Thanks to the lasting effect of the prisoner's Songs, his own head was free of enchantment. He was fairly sure that he could have defied the Starmaker and flown out of the crater any time he wanted — except, of course, he couldn't leave Sky Swooper.

As the two young quetzal waited nervously to see if the good mood meant they would be released to fly again, the Starmaker raised his spear to Sky Swooper's forehead and sent her back into a trembling crouch. He watched Night Plume carefully as he did this, as if daring him to protest. Night Plume made himself stand still and say nothing, but he stored this unfairness in the Memoryplace so no quetzal would ever forget.

The Starmaker lowered his spear and smiled. "Come with me, my faithful dark quetzal," he rasped. "I think it's time we showed our guest that her pathetic attempt to use her Songs to turn you against me has failed. I admit I wondered after all that nonsense with the wild flock, but no quetzal roosts a night in the rain unless it hasn't any choice. Wrap your wings and follow me." He gestured toward the tunnel that led into the depths of the volcano, and the four priests who bore his throne carried him to the dark opening. None of them looked back to check if Night Plume was coming.

Night Plume's wings lifted in alarm. Go inside the Temple again? No, he couldn't. He glanced wildly at the circle of sky above the crater, then remembered Sky Swooper and forced his wings back down. Picking up the end of his wet tail and suppressing a shudder, he hurried obediently after the Starmaker's throne.

They went to the prisoner's cell. The silver-haired human was still chained to the wall, though it hardly seemed necessary. Her lips bubbled a little, as if she wanted to vomit but there was nothing left to come up. Night Plume thought she was too sick to care. But when the Starmaker touched her with his spear, she stirred and opened her eyes. Seeing Night Plume, she tried to stand. Her legs wouldn't support her, and after a short struggle she gave up and flopped back against the wall.

"Not feeling too good, Rialle?" the Starmaker rasped. "Yellow Flower juice has that unfortunate side effect, I'm afraid. You shouldn't have resisted it. I might not have needed to give you so much. I've better uses for the flowers than wasting them on you. But you'll be pleased to know your information was correct and I've taken all I want from the Singers. My faithful merlee in the Western Sea just confirmed that the men I sent to the Isle of Echoes have got the child you stole from me. They got her mother as well, so my daughter will have plenty of time to study the results of your Songs before she gets here." He smiled. "You were even right about her friends. Apparently, she was with a boy who can hear Half Creatures and tried to follow her with the aid of a wild shoal — I've instructed my merlee to make sure he drowns. The Singers have outlived their usefulness. I've sent them a little present that should keep them busy for a while, and as soon as my daughter gets here I'm going to change history. I know how to do it. All I need is enough Yellow Flower to access the quetzal Memoryplace, and then I'll simply replace it with my own version. History is only what everyone remembers, after all. Very soon now, your Singer friends and their little blue island will no longer exist." He chuckled.

All the while, the prisoner's gray eyes stared at Night Plume, making him dizzy. It was as if he were back in the forest and the wild quetzal were —

. . . know you can hear me. Don't show it. Just listen.

Night Plume stiffened, distracted from the unsettling things the Starmaker had said. *How you use wild-speech?*

Don't react! I hoped my Songs would take effect sooner, but I could always speak to the merlee, it's just a little harder to reach quetzal. The Yellow Flower helps, I think. But we haven't much time. He'll find out soon and stop bringing you here. I can't reach you through his khiz-crystal, can't reach anyone —

The Starmaker, seeing her staring at Night Plume, laughed again. "You're wondering why my dark quetzal is here, aren't you? I brought him to show you that there's no hope of him helping you. You can have no secrets from me, Rialle. Did you really think your Songs were strong enough to break the power of the Khiz? This quetzal was born on my hatching ground, surrounded by my crystal. He has khiz-crystal in his blood and khiz-crystal in his head. He's my creature, Rialle, and will be until the day I order him to die for me — which, of course, he will do without question when the time comes. He's a fine leader, cares for his flock in an uncannily human way. But if I tell him to lead them to their deaths, then he'll do it."

Only part of Night Plume registered what the Starmaker was saying. Talking to the prisoner in wild-speech made him see her differently. She was no longer merely a human. He felt almost as sorry for her as he did for Sky Swooper.

Help you? he asked. *Get you out?*

Briefly, her eyes filled with hope. But she shook her head very slightly. *If you try to help me, little one, he'll know my Songs have freed you from the enchantment of the Khiz. Then you won't be able to help my friends and their children. You have to fly to the Isle of Echoes, across the Western Sea. Warn the stone-singers. Warn them . . .* Her wild-speech faltered as she clutched at her stomach with another groan. But when she looked up again, her expression was fierce. *Tell them Frazhin is alive and plans to destroy the Echorium. They must-n't trust the merlee unless they're sure the shoal hasn't been corrupted by Frazhin. They must be wary of all Half Creatures until they know which ones are free and which ones are Frazhin's. Tell them, little one, please! Fly fast!*

Night Plume blinked. The new Memoryplace that the prisoner had helped him see yielded hazy memories for *Isle of Echoes* and *Western Sea*. But how could he possibly fly there, as she wanted him to?

Sky Swooper still enchanted, he said. *Not leave her.*

The stone-singers will help your little friend when they get here. But you've got to tell them about Frazhin before it's too late!

Not know way.

Follow the river to the coast. Ask a wild merlee shoal to guide you across the sea. Go now.

Night Plume shook his head, and the prisoner's eyes dulled as the burst of strength left her. "Please," she whispered aloud. "Please help me. If you don't, they'll die. All the Singers will die, all the children, everyone . . ."

The Starmaker leaned down from his throne and prodded her with his spear. "That's enough, Singer. He's not going to help you. No one's going to help you. And you can't do a thing about it, not this time. Your Songs are no good to you, your attempt to turn my dark quetzal against me has failed, and you've betrayed your friends. You can think about that while my daughter's on her way here. You're probably wondering why I'm keeping you alive now that you've told me everything I want to know? I'll tell you. When my daughter arrives, I'm going to let her have the pleasure of killing you — of killing the last Singer in the world. She'll hate you enough to want to do it by then, I promise you. I hope she'll be inventive, but that's up to her. You Singers made a big mistake when you gave her mother *Yehn*."

He gestured that the priests should carry him out of the cell. Almost as an afterthought, he brushed Night Plume lightly with his spear on his way out. "You can go back to your flock now, dark quetzal," he said. "Get them back out into the forest. I want a lot more Yellow Flowers by the time my daughter gets here, and while you're out harvesting I want you to brush up your archery skills. You can use the wild quetzal as target practice — they're getting much too bold and need a lesson. When my mer-lee tell us the ship has arrived, I want you to lead your flock to the edge of the forest and wait for my daughter. You'll protect her and the men she's with until they reach my Temple. And if the wild quetzal get so much as within hooting distance of her, I'll clip your mate's wings like that old quetzal mother's out in the nest. Your sweet little mate will stay here in my crater, enchanted, until my daughter's safe. That should give you an added incentive to be vigilant."

Night Plume's heart sank as the priests escorted him from the Temple. Very faintly, he could still hear the prisoner's desperate plea. *Fly, little one! Fly!* But, until Sky Swooper was free, he knew he couldn't risk doing what the silver-haired human wanted.

5

PIRATES

Her pallet was moving — a horrible, swaying, sideways motion — and someone was crouched nearby, giggling. Kyarra groaned and turned over. "Go away, Lianne," she mumbled, hiding her head under the covers. "Leave me alone."

"I know you're awake," said a girl's voice. "So you might as well get up. Father's put me in charge of you, and I'm warning you now, I'm not standin' for no high-and-mighty nonsense, so stop moanin' and get on up!"

The covers were dragged off her, and something cold and wet landed on her chin. "Here — mop your face. Make you feel better."

Kyarra struggled up and peered in confusion at her tormentor. A grubby face framed by tangled red hair swam into view. Interested eyes studied her, reminding her of another pair of eyes that had studied her in exactly the same way as their owner had crouched before her, squeezed her chin, and asked who she was shouting to.

"Where's Caell?" she demanded. "What did they do to him?"
The girl frowned. "Who?"

The rest of it was slowly coming back now. Creeping out of the Echorium, the mist, the men with their faces hidden behind scarves, the poor villager and the orderly they'd knocked out . . . Kyarra stared around in panic. Her bed wasn't a pallet on the floor, but a type of sack suspended from the ceiling by chains. And this wasn't the dormitory in the Echorium, but a tiny wood-paneled room that tipped and swayed around them.

"Where am I? What happened to my friend? Where is he?"

"Ain't no boys here."

"He was with me in the village. He saw me go into the hut!"

The girl shrugged. "Then I expect Father silenced him."

Kyarra struggled to get her legs out of the sack. It was difficult at first, then suddenly the whole contraption tipped sideways and deposited her with a painful thud on the floor at the girl's feet. She was wearing scuffed boots and boy's trousers. Thrust through her belt was a little dagger with a glittering blue handle.

The girl laughed. "Never slept in a hammock before, huh? You're not what I expected, I must admit. Do you always wear a skirt? Is your hair really that color?"

"Get off me!" Kyarra batted her curious hand away and used the hammock to pull herself to her feet. "If you've hurt Caell, I'll . . . I'll . . ." She couldn't think. She clung on to the chains, swaying with the motion of the cabin. Her head throbbed. She raised a hand to the back of her skull, felt a little star-shaped weal, and shuddered. "Where are you taking me? I remember now — that bully your father called Blackbeard knocked me out!"

The girl sighed. "What's the matter? You never been stunned before? Stop makin' such a fuss! I don't know what happened to your friend. I wasn't even on your stupid island. Father made me stay on the ship." She pulled a face. "Don't you even want to know my name? I know yours. You're Ky-aahra." She pronounced it funny, with a long, drawn-out "a."

Kyarra scowled. "Ky*arra*," she corrected, eyeing the dagger in the girl's belt. It looked more decorative than useful, but if she could get hold of it she might have a chance.

The girl shrugged. "Whatever. I'm Jilian. I'm the only girl in Father's band who's allowed to go on raids!" She tossed her hair over her shoulder and smiled. "Last year I stabbed a man. Bet you've never done *that,* huh, Kyarra?"

Kyarra's stomach twisted with anxiety for Caell, and anger at herself for being afraid. The cabin had a small, round window. Through the glass, she glimpsed spray and the open sea. She quickly looked away, tightened her jaw and picked up the wet cloth Jilian had thrown at her earlier. She pressed it to the sore place on the back of her head and tried to think.

"Singers don't need to stab people," she said. "Our Songs make fighting unnecessary. This one, for instance . . ." Softly, she began to hum.

Aushan, Aushan makes you scream.

Jilian quickly reached beneath her tunic and pulled out a thong on which a familiar-looking star of black crystal was threaded. She dangled it before Kyarra's eyes and laughed when Kyarra shrank back. "I know what you're trying to do! Father said you might try your enchantments on me. You've already seen one of these, haven't you? They don't just knock people out, you know. This is a magic black crystal star from the Lord of the Forest himself. Your Songs won't work on any of us while we're wearing these." With a little smile, she pushed the star back under her tunic. "But don't you try takin' it off me, mind! I might just stab you by accident." She fingered her dagger and giggled again.

Kyarra's head was still hurting. She looked at the door. It didn't seem to be locked. As Jilian chuckled to herself, Kyarra tested her balance then suddenly let go of the hammock and barged past the girl. The door opened more easily than she'd anticipated. She stumbled through, but tripped over an unexpectedly high step and sprawled across the passage outside.

Jilian was on her in an instant, her sharp knees pressing on

Kyarra's arms, a hand tugging at her hair. Used to similar fights with Lianne, Kyarra made herself go limp. When she felt the girl begin to relax, she twisted out from under her, got an arm free and made a lunge for the star pendant. Her fingers caught the thong. But Jilian's teeth sank into her wrist, and she had to let go. The dagger appeared at Kyarra's cheek, suddenly not so small and pretty. She froze, the fear returning. Had this girl really killed a man?

Panting, Jilian glared down at her. "I told you, Kyarra, I'm not standing for no high-and-mightiness! Try that again and I'll tell Father to tie you up for the rest of the voyage like he had to do to that woman we picked up from the fish-people on our last trip out this way. She was all sorts of trouble, real stupid. I thought you had more brains. We're doing you a favor, you know, rescuing you from that Singer island. So you'd better start actin' grateful!" She put the dagger away, climbed off Kyarra, and planted her hands on her hips. "Get up. And let that be a lesson to you. Next time, don't try messing with Jilian of the Hills!"

Kyarra gritted her teeth and did as she was told — but slowly, as if dazed by the fight. She used the time to study the passage. There were two more doors like the one to the cabin she'd woken in, and a ladder at the end leading up into a gray mist. Was her mother behind one of the other doors? If the way she'd acted in the hut was anything to go by, they wouldn't even have to lock it to keep her inside.

"Where's my mother?" she demanded. "Is she here, too?"

Jilian put her head on one side, watching her with interest. "So that's who you were running to, is it? You're wasting your time. She can't help you. Singers did her in proper. Why don't I show you?"

Kyarra looked at the girl suspiciously, but it didn't seem to be a trick. Seizing her hand, Jilian led her along the passage to the farthest of the two doors. She didn't bother to knock, simply opened it and pulled Kyarra inside. "Mind the step!" she said, grinning.

Kyarra stepped carefully over the ledge, her heart beating hard. The woman Asil had taken from the village lay in a hammock similar to the one Kyarra had woken in. Her beautiful hair trailed over the edge in a thick, dark waterfall and the fingertips of one hand brushed the floor as the hammock swung to and fro with the motion of the ship. Her eyes were open but stared right through Kyarra without seeing her, just as they had done back on the Isle. Her expression was so blank, it made Kyarra shiver.

"Mother?" she whispered, going down on one knee beside the hammock and taking hold of the trailing hand. It was warm, not cold as she'd expected, but it didn't so much as twitch when she held it. "Mother? Can you hear me?"

"Father says she can't talk," Jilian said. "But she does what you tell her. Watch." She picked up a jug and poured some water into a cup, which she held out to the woman. "Drink!" she ordered.

The hand pulled itself out of Kyarra's grasp and obediently took the cup. The woman roused herself, drank without spilling a drop, then held out the cup for Jilian to take away from her. Only when Jilian had done so did she lie back in the hammock. All the time, her eyes stared unblinkingly at the wall.

"See?" Jilian said. "But she'd never have drunk without being told to. If I didn't come in here and see to her regular like, she'd soil her hammock and starve to death. Nice work, huh? Your precious Singers did that to her."

Tears sprang to Kyarra's eyes. "They gave her the Death Song, but when the merlee told Caell she was living in Windy Corner I thought that meant it hadn't worked. She's so young . . ." She picked a black curl off the smooth cheek and pushed it behind a delicate ear. "They didn't tell me."

"Wouldn't, would they?" Jilian took her hand again and tugged her back out of the cabin. "Wanted you to grow up like them, didn't they? Grow into a good little Singer, so's you could help them turn other people into zombies like her."

Kyarra shook her head. "She must have done something awful. Singers wouldn't have given her *Yehn* otherwise. Hardly anyone ever gets the Death Song."

"What's bad enough for *that*?" Jilian's expression was fierce as she shut the door behind them. "Better to have killed her and got it over with!"

Kyarra closed her eyes. It was too confusing to work out just now. But at least her mother didn't seem to realize she was a prisoner. She took a deep breath. "Where's As — I mean, your father?" she demanded. "I want to talk to him."

Jilian grinned at her. "Up on deck, communicatin' with the fish-people, and he don't want to be disturbed. You're to stay down here with me."

Kyarra blinked at her. "The merlee, you mean? But I thought only novices could talk to them. Caell said —" She bit her lip, remembering something Asil had let slip in the hut. *His Lordship's tame fish-people*. And Caell had said there were two different kinds of merlee. It was all starting to make a chilling sense.

"Proves your Singers lied to you, then, don't it?" Jilian said. "His Lordship's fish-people tell Father lots of interesting stuff. Where there's a ship in trouble, or a wreck just happened with treasure for the taking. Me, I prefer a good ambush in the hills — much more exciting! But Father says there's no harm in easy pickings once in a while to replenish funds."

"So you're pirates, then?" Kyarra said, glancing along the passage to where the ladder led up into the mist. From above came the smell of salt and the faint cries of sea birds. She eyed Jilian and took a sideways step.

"Not just pirates. We work the trade routes on the coast, too."

Kyarra feigned admiration. "You must be very brave! Don't the people you attack fight back?"

The girl giggled, pleased. "Oh yes, they try! But Father's men are the best robbers this side of the Purple Plains. People tell stories about us as far north as Silvertown, you know. They even

named the hills beside the trade route after Father. Asil's Hills
— good, huh?"

"And you really stabbed a man, all by yourself?"

"Well, he didn't actually die . . . I only scratched him, really,
but — oy! Come back here!"

While Jilian was boasting, Kyarra had been quietly edging
toward the ladder. Judging herself close enough, she made a
dash for it. Jilian grabbed for her hair, but missed. Kyarra leaped
up the ladder, kicking as a hand closed on her ankle. Her heel
connected with something soft and there was a yelp of pain
behind her. The hand let go.

As she scrambled out of the hold, a blast of spray caught her
in the face. She wiped her eyes and hugged herself against the
chill. On all sides, the sea vanished into a mist full of echoes and
half-heard songs. Her cloak was back in the cabin and her
Echorium uniform was much too thin for such weather. Sails
snapped and creaked above her, water hissed under the hull. Up
in the bows stood Asil. He had something dark and glittery
pressed to his forehead. His eyes were closed and he'd obviously
been standing there some time, since the spray had soaked his
clothes. The burly man who'd knocked Kyarra out stood beside
him. His scarf blew loose, showing the black beard that gave
him his name.

Kyarra rushed toward him and shouted, "What did you do to
Caell?"

Before she could reach him, rough hands caught her from
behind. She struggled, but the man who'd caught her held on
grimly. Blackbeard turned his head and grinned at her in an
unpleasant manner. Asil's trance broke. He focused on her with
some difficulty and dropped the thing he'd been holding to his
forehead. As it swung back against his chest, Kyarra saw it was
another black crystal star.

"I'm sorry, Father!" Jilian gasped, climbing out of the hold
behind Kyarra. "She tricked me. It won't happen again."

Kyarra noted with some satisfaction that one of Jilian's cheekbones was turning purple.

The girl drew her little dagger and started toward her, a dangerous glint in her eye, but Asil held up a hand. He studied Kyarra in silence and motioned to her captor to let her go.

"So, our little sleeper is awake at last," he said. "Glad to see you're feeling better, Princess. Now, who's this Caell you keep talking about?"

"He's my friend!" Kyarra glared at the pirate leader. "And if you've hurt him, I'll never do anything you want me to do. Ever!" She transferred her glare to Jilian. "And I'm not afraid of your silly little knife. I don't believe you've ever stabbed anyone with it!" She raised her chin and held down her skirt, which the wind was threatening to blow around her ears.

To her surprise, Asil laughed. "Looks like my daughter's met her match! Jilian, put that thing away. Doesn't matter if she comes up on deck now we're away from the Isle. She's not going anywhere, is she? I'm sure she's got more sense than to dive over the side in this weather." He smiled at Kyarra. "As you can see, Princess, we're days away from the nearest land. But you're welcome to swim for a bit, if you like. We'll just wait till you've used up some of that fierce energy of yours before we tell his Lordship's fish-people to bring you back." He gestured at the gray water.

Kyarra shivered at the very thought. She didn't tell him she couldn't swim.

Asil smiled again. "You look cold. Why don't you go back down below with Jilian and let her show you where the galley is? We could all do with some hot soup, I think." He glanced at the others. "This sea mist gets into a man's bones. Rusts his brain."

"First, I want to know what you did to Caell!" Kyarra said through gritted teeth.

The pirate leader sighed and loosened his scarf. Beneath it, he had a surprising copper beard, the same bright color as Jilian's hair. "Your friend tried to swim out after us when we left the island. Fish-people lost him underwater. They think he drowned. I'm sorry, but it was his own fault."

Numb and cold through to her bones, Kyarra let Jilian take her below. She stared, unseeing, at the steaming mug of soup the girl put into her hand. Caell dead? Tears rolled down her cheeks and dripped into the soup. Jilian was watching her, but she didn't care.

"It wasn't Caell's fault," Kyarra whispered, squeezing the mug so tightly that the contents slopped over her skirt. "It was mine! If I hadn't made him take me to Windy Corner, none of this would have happened and he'd still be alive! Why do you work for this Lord of the Forest, whoever he is? Why did you have to kidnap me and my mother? What have we ever done to you?"

Jilian seemed embarrassed by Kyarra's tears. "His Lordship pays well," she mumbled. "Jewels the size of your fist, that's all I know. His snake-people, the nagas, find them in the deep places, but Father don't care where they come from. There's some things we wouldn't do, even for jewels, but his Lordship said you'll be happier away from the Singers. Go to bed, Kyarra. In the morning, I'm sure you'll see I'm right."

*

Kyarra cried herself to sleep, so thoroughly miserable she considered throwing herself overboard to join Caell at the bottom of the ocean. But by the time she woke, her misery had dulled and she'd begun to think more clearly. Asil might have been lying to her so she wouldn't try to escape. Even if he weren't lying, he hadn't actually seen the body. Caell might have made it back to the beach. Besides, throwing herself into the sea wouldn't help her mother. She'd do better finding out more about her captors and where they were taking her.

She climbed out of the hammock, washed in the bucket of seawater Jilian had left for her, straightened her uniform, and hammered on the door until someone came. Slightly relieved it wasn't Blackbeard, she pushed her hair behind her ears and gave the man who unlocked the door a big smile. "I'm hungry," she said firmly. "And I expect my mother is, too. I'll see to her if Jilian isn't awake yet. Don't worry, I won't try to escape. I can't even swim."

So it was that she got the job of looking after the strange, midnight-haired woman for the rest of the voyage. Remembering what Jilian had said about her fellow prisoner not being able to do anything for herself, she had her hammock moved into the same cabin, even though it was cramped. Jilian looked in on them occasionally, but seemed content to let Kyarra deal with things, particularly the mess in her mother's hammock each morning. She tried her best to get the silent woman to talk, but her mother gave no sign she even realized anyone was in the cabin with her. Kyarra tried gentle questions. She tried talking to her through the long nights when she couldn't sleep. She tried Songs, humming them softly to reach only as far as the cabin walls so no one else would hear. Once, she lost her temper and screamed at her in frustration, shaking her in an attempt to get a reaction. Nothing made the slightest difference. In the end, Kyarra resorted to imagination, inventing the things they might have done together when she was small. There was a lot of time for such dreams, and soon her fantasy childhood, where the beautiful, midnight-haired woman sang to her and sat her on her knee so she could tell her stories of the sea, seemed almost as real as her life in the Echorium.

If the weather was fine, she guided her mother up the ladder on to the deck and told her to hold tightly to the rail while she searched the horizon for signs of land. Asil's men watched, but did not interfere. Most of them gave her mother a wide berth and made superstitious signs in the air if they had to pass too close. The only one she didn't trust was Blackbeard. Every time he walked past he fingered the ends of her mother's hair, baring his teeth when Kyarra warned him — with undercurrents of *Aushan* — to keep away. "I'll tell Asil you did that!" she yelled after him.

But when she reported Blackbeard's behavior, the pirate leader merely chuckled and told her not to worry because all his men had strict orders to leave them alone. "You're precious cargo, Princess," he said. "You and your mother both. But maybe it's best if you keep her below till we land. Your mother's an attractive woman, and my men have been at sea a long time."

Though it was claustrophobic in the cabin, Kyarra took his advice. She brushed her mother's hair until it rippled like black water, stayed at her side every possible moment to make sure Blackbeard didn't touch her again, and tried not to think of Caell.

"He's alive," she told her mother between strokes of the brush. "I know he is." Then she'd burst into tears because it all seemed so hopeless and she didn't really know.

The voyage seemed endless. But after about twenty days at sea, the lookout sighted land and everyone rushed up on deck to see it. Kyarra's heart beat with excitement and renewed fear. But the "land" was a mere smudge on the horizon ahead of them, and the ship was sailing at an angle to it. Too early yet to see if there would be a chance to escape.

She was about to go back below when Asil took out his crystal star and pressed it to his forehead. She glanced at the hatch. But she'd left her mother sleeping safely in her hammock, and this might be an opportunity to find out what had happened to Caell.

She sidled along the rail until she was near enough to see the deep furrows in Asil's forehead. Jilian stood next to him, bending over the rail, her red hair flying in the wind as she stared into the water. Her own star pendant swung free, glittering darkly in the sunlight. The rest of the crew went about their tasks, trimming sails and adjusting course, ignoring Kyarra.

She took a step closer. There was a strange song at the edge of her hearing, very faint and wild. She closed her eyes and concentrated, but it became no clearer. Then, there was a loud splash below and a gasp from Jilian.

"There they are, Father!"

Kyarra opened her eyes in time to see a multicolored fin break the water beside the ship. She caught her breath. A whole shoal of merlee was down there. She was close enough to see the ridge of scales where their human halves joined their fish tails. Their skin glowed luminous green and the spray glittered with rainbows as they surfaced, dived, and surfaced again. One male with a curly turquoise beard reared out of the water directly beneath Asil and stared up at the pirate leader.

Kyarra rushed to the spot and leaned over the rail. "Where's Caell?" she shouted at the creature. "What did you do to him?"

Asil grunted and let his star drop back on his chest. "Get her away from here," he said through gritted teeth.

Jilian grabbed Kyarra's arm and dragged her away. "Don't interrupt, Kyarra!" she hissed. "Talkin' to the fish-people ain't easy for Father, you know!"

Kyarra wrenched her arm free. "I only want to know what they did to Caell. They're supposed to be our friends, the Singers' friends . . . they should have saved him . . ."

"He drowned, Kyarra. Stop kidding yourself." Jilian's expression softened a little. "Look, I know this ain't easy for you, but —"

The merlee were leaving, slipping into the depths, mysterious untouchable shadows. Kyarra ducked under the girl's arm and put a leg over the rail. Jilian came after her and grabbed her tunic, all sympathy gone. "*Now* where are you going? Not plannin' to swim for it, are you? 'Cause I wouldn't recommend it. Where we're headed ain't called Drowned Man's Head for nothin', you know." Kyarra aimed a kick at the girl's shin and Jilian let go with a yelp. "Ow! That hurt! All right then, jump in an' drown yourself! Tell you the truth, I'm sick of nursemaiding you." She let go.

Kyarra shut her eyes. She had just worked up the courage to let go of the rail when something else distracted her. Her gaze flew around the deck. Under Asil's orders, the crew were preparing the ship for the final approach to land. But one man was missing.

Another faint thud sounded below her feet, followed by a chuckle — not loud enough to be heard, except by Singer-trained ears. She slid off the rail and raced to the hatch, heart thumping, while Jilian stared after her, shaking her head. She went down the ladder so fast, she lost her footing and slid the final few rungs, landing in a heap. Up again, she raced along the passage. The door of the cabin she shared with her mother was open, banging with the roll of the ship. From inside came a whiff of the brew Asil's men drank when they were off duty.

Blackbeard had lifted her mother out of her hammock and was kissing her. He had one arm around her and his other hand held her wrists together, though of course she wasn't fighting him. She hung limply in his grasp, her eyes blank of expression.

"Get off her!"

Kyarra flew through the door and fastened her arms around the big man's neck. She was dizzy with fury. A Song burst from her, louder and with more passion than she'd ever put into any Song before. *Aushan, Aushan makes you SCREAM!*

The man grunted. At first he didn't seem to notice her. Then her weight made him lose his hold on her mother, who slipped to the floor. Kyarra clawed at the big man's face, still singing. But she'd forgotten about the star that protected him. His eyes glittered as he threw her off. She staggered against the wall and banged her head. When her vision cleared, he was laughing at her, his breath stinking of the brew he'd drunk.

"So you've got some fight left in you, after all, Princess!" he slurred. "I thought you were actin' too quiet lately — pretending to be a good girl, were you, so you could escape when we sighted land?"

Kyarra blinked the dizziness away. She scrambled to her feet and lunged for the star around his neck. "You leave my mother alone, or I'll sing *you* to death! I'll . . . I'll make *you* helpless like her!"

"Oh, I don't think so, Princess." He chuckled, holding his star out of reach and pushing her away easily with his other hand.

"I said, STOP IT!"

Kyarra tried to kick him. Then suddenly the cabin was full of men, pulling Blackbeard and Kyarra apart, staring at her mother lying serenely on the floor with her clothes awry. Jilian shoved through, scowling and yelling. She frowned when she saw the woman on the floor, pulled her skirt straight and ordered two of the men to lift her back into the hammock. Finally, she turned to the ones holding Kyarra and Blackbeard, and frowned again. "Bring them on deck," she said. "Father will deal with this."

Kyarra fought the men who held her. "I'm not leaving my mother! You saw what he tried to do! How could he? She's . . . she's . . . look at her."

Jilian looked, and a coldness replaced the brief pity in her eyes. "Singers did that to her, not us."

Kyarra stared at the girl in disbelief. "Why, you little —"

The blue-handled dagger appeared at her cheek. "Shut up, Kyarra," Jilian hissed. "I told you, I ain't standing for no high-and-mightiness. Father'll deal with it."

Kyarra spat at her. Jilian stepped out of range and motioned to the men to take her up on deck.

Asil was waiting for them. At first, Kyarra was so upset that nothing else registered. She fought the hands on her arms and yelled at the pirate. She didn't remember what she said, only that it was full of all the helpless frustration and anger that had been building up inside her throughout the long voyage. Asil let her shout. Then she noticed two things.

Behind him, the dark strip of land with spray crashing over rocks was much closer than before. And Blackbeard was being bound to the mast, his eyes uncertain as they lost some of their drunken glitter and focused on his leader.

Asil stepped aside and gestured toward the bound man. "If I tell my men to release you, what will you do to him?"

Kyarra blinked. "I'll make him pay for what he did," she said in a tight voice.

Asil motioned with his head. The hands left her arms. "He

wronged your mother," he continued in the same calm voice. "It's your place to decide his punishment. I don't accept that kind of behavior among my men."

Kyarra glanced at Jilian. The girl was still scowling. "Hurry up an' do it, then, Kyarra!" she called.

She looked at the faces around her. Was it a trick? But the others seemed ashamed, not meeting her eye. One of them spat in the direction of the man tied to the mast. "If you want him flogged, I'll do it myself," Asil offered. Blackbeard looked defiant, but said nothing.

Kyarra took a deep breath and pushed her hair out of her eyes. She faced the pirate leader. "Take his star away," she said. "And let me sing to him."

Blackbeard's eyes flickered to her. For the first time, she saw real fear in them. The rest of the crew glanced at their leader. Jilian fingered her own pendant, frowning at Kyarra.

Asil gave a nod. "Remove his crystal," he said.

Blackbeard heaved against his bonds, but one of the crew cut the thong from around his neck and held it carefully.

Motioning his men back, Asil looked at Kyarra. "Go ahead," he said.

She took a deep breath. It wouldn't work without the Pentangle, a trained Singer on each of the five points, and the Song Potion to relax him. And, anyway, she was only a novice so it was doubtful her voice had the power. But Blackbeard didn't know this. He began to struggle as she stepped closer and did her breathing exercises. Jilian's eyes brightened. She leaned forward with gruesome interest and fixed her eyes on the big man's face. Some of the crew left to attend to the sails because the boat was drawing dangerously close to the rocks. But the rest stayed to watch.

Kyarra hummed a few bars of *Yehn*, then thought of her mother and closed her eyes. Even this man didn't deserve that. She changed to *Shi, Shi makes you cry*. And then, when she couldn't stand the big man's sobs any longer, to *Challa*. She tried to imagine she was singing for Singer Renn, note perfect and with every tiny nuance correct.

Shh, calm, Challa makes you dream.

One of the men cursed under his breath. "I don't believe it — look at 'im!"

"Shh, you fool!" someone else whispered. "Let the girl finish."

Kyarra kept humming for as long as she had the breath. The pure Songs were hard work, and she was out of practice. When she opened her eyes, she was surprised to see Blackbeard slumped in his bonds, snoring with the tears still wet on his cheeks. The other men stared at her, something between awe and fear in their eyes. The one holding Blackbeard's pendant squeezed it tightly without seeming to realize what he was doing. Jilian stepped forward and prodded the prisoner with her dagger. Asil snapped at her to leave him alone. Looking thoughtfully at Kyarra, he held out his hand for the pendant, walked to the rail and dropped it over the side. The crew was so quiet, they could hear the tiny splash as it slipped into the sea.

"And if anyone else thinks what this man did was clever, they can hand over their own star right now," he said. "Otherwise, back to your stations! The fish-people have given us all the help they can. We don't want to run aground now."

The crew shook themselves and hurried to their posts, still whispering about what they'd just witnessed. Asil gave Kyarra another hard look, then told her to go below and see to her mother.

"That was well done, Princess," he said quietly as she passed him. "But don't get any ideas. The rest of us are still protected, and we'll be leaving that one behind when we land." He looked back at the snoring man still tied to the mast and pressed his lips together. "I think you both learned a valuable lesson today."

6
COUPLING

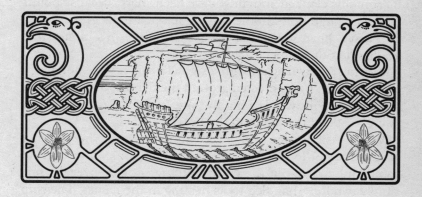

Drowned Man's Head was well named. At first, the deserted stretch of coastline with its waves breaking a ship's height over the rocks seemed unapproachable. But Asil's crew expertly steered their ship into a narrow crack in the cliffs, where the wind stopped and the water was deep and still like a dark green jewel. They dropped anchor and lowered a boat over the side. As promised, they left Blackbeard behind on the ship, though Kyarra felt his eyes on her back all the way to the beach.

The cove was ringed on three sides by sheer purple cliffs. The only way out of it seemed to be by sea. Kyarra's heart sank as Asil helped her and her mother out of the boat and guided them to a pile of rocks, where he told them to sit and wait. He left Jilian to watch them while he went off to supervise his men, organizing a fire and unloading the bundles that had come off the ship.

Jilian took out her dagger and used it to clean her fingernails, giving Kyarra sly little smiles. "No point thinking about tryin' to climb that," she said, seeing her glance up the cliff. "You wouldn't get halfway up before we caught you."

"Do we have to climb out of here, then?" Kyarra asked. "How are you going to get those sacks up? What's in them, anyway?" She watched Asil's men drag another bundle up from the boat. Its contents clanked and must have been sharp, because points poked through holes in the sacking and left trails in the sand.

"Nosy!" Jilian waved her dagger, grinning. "It's pirate stuff. You'll find out soon enough."

Kyarra sat down again with a sigh. The men were building a large fire with rocks erected around the flames to make it hotter and the light was leaving the sky. It looked as if they were going to spend the night on the beach.

When Asil finally beckoned Kyarra to bring her mother across, she got to her feet eagerly enough, looking forward to something to eat. But there was nothing cooking over the fire, simply two long-handled tools heating in the flames. The ship was still at anchor — a dark silhouette out in the inlet. Her steps slowed. She glanced uncertainly at the pirate.

"Let's get this done," he muttered. He seized her mother's hand and pulled her closer to the fire. Kyarra started after her, then stopped in horror as she saw what lay on a flat-topped rock beside the flames. Two open manacles, joined by a short length of chain.

Asil told her mother to kneel, which she did in the same dreamy way she did everything she was told. He lifted her left arm and laid it across the rock. When he let go she didn't move, though she was very near the fire and the flames must have been hot. Asil picked up the manacles and fitted one of them around her wrist. Another man took one of the tools from the fire, revealing a glowing red pin at its end, which he slid through the holes in the manacle and hammered closed.

"Why are you chaining her?" Kyarra said, her legs beginning to unfreeze. "You know she can't run away!" She stared desperately at her mother as someone poured sea water over the manacle. The metal cooled with a hiss of steam. The woman didn't so much as flinch.

Asil looked up and smiled. "The chain's not for her sake, Princess."

Cold rippled up Kyarra's legs. She backed away from the fire. But the men had been expecting this reaction and there was a ring of them behind her, cutting off her escape. Jilian shook her head. "Didn't think we'd let you run off alone in a wild place like this, did you? It's for your own good. If anything happened to you out here, we'd be in trouble for lettin' you get hurt. You hardly left your dear mama's side on the ship, anyway. This way you get to stick close to her till you're both safely where you should be."

Asil moved her mother's arm to the edge of the rock, picked up the second manacle and looked expectantly at Kyarra. "Give me your right hand," he said.

She shook her head, tears in her eyes. Asil nodded. The men dragged her to the fire, forced her arm across the rock and held it firmly.

She shut her eyes as the manacle went around her wrist, but it was not followed by the heat she expected from the pin. Instead, Asil cursed. "The girl's skinnier than a plucked quetzal! Better fix this first, or she'll slip out of it like a fish through a hole in the net."

Kyarra opened her eyes to see the pirate frowning at the manacle. She almost laughed. It was too big for her.

The man presiding over the fire looked uncertainly at her mother. "That chain's pretty short. Shouldn't we—?"

"No time," Asil snapped, his expression tight. "The spare pins are on the ship. By the time we get them, the fire will be cold. I've been told the woman can't feel anything. Just get on with it and be as careful as you can."

Still shaking, Kyarra watched while her mother's left hand was wrapped in rags soaked in seawater. She only realized what they intended when the man working the tools used one of them to pick up the manacle that had been intended for her and plunged it into the heart of the flames, dragging her mother's arm after it. Another man grimly worked some bellows. The heat they'd built up between the rocks turned white.

"No! You're burning her!" she yelled, struggling against the man who held her. "Stop it! You don't have to do this! I promise I won't try to run away . . . *please*!"

The smell of singed flesh rose into the air, making Kyarra's head spin. She yelled louder. But it seemed Asil spoke the truth. Her mother simply knelt there, her hand at the edge of the fire, not a flicker of pain on her face.

Asil ordered his men to put more wet rags around her arm and told the others to take Kyarra away from the fire. Weak with sobs, she didn't have the strength to resist. Even Jilian, who had been watching the chaining process with interest, seemed sickened and came after them. She crouched in the shadow of the cliff and scraped at the sand with her dagger. "It's your fault for bein' so skinny," she said in the end. "Father didn't realize, or he'd have fixed the manacles first. He don't want to harm her. But his Lordship wants you kept safe, and this is the best way."

Kyarra glared at her. "You didn't have to chain us! I wouldn't have run away and left her with you!"

Jilian looked at her sideways and said, "I'd not leave *my* mother with strange men, but everyone knows Singers don't care that much about their folks. I heard you talkin' to her on the ship. You don't really believe she *is* your mother, do you? You're a tricky one, Kyarra. I reckon you'd be gone, first chance you got."

"Shut up," Kyarra hissed, because Jilian's words struck too close to the truth. "Just shut up!"

By the time the manacle had been suitably beaten to fit her wrist and Asil ordered her brought back to the fire, she had regained a measure of self-control. She shrugged off her escort and walked to the rock, chin high. She knelt in the warm sand, laid her right arm beside her mother's left and tried not to look at the blisters on the soft skin. She stiffened as the hammer fell on the hot pin to lock the metal around her wrist, but forced

herself not to move until the cooling water rose in a great hiss-
ing cloud of steam, hiding her tears.

*

After the coupling was done, the men settled down to play a
game with pebbles, ignoring Kyarra and the black-haired
woman who sat beside her staring blankly at the sea. They knew
Kyarra wasn't going anywhere. Asil and Jilian walked along the
shore together, the daughter a smaller version of the father.
Kyarra eyed the boat pulled up on the shingle and wondered
what their chances were of getting away by water. Maybe she
could row with one arm while her mother rowed with the
other? It would have to be later, though, when the men slept.

But when the first stars appeared, a soft whistle sounded
above. The men immediately abandoned their pebble game,
kicked sand over the remains of their fire and ran to the base of
the cliff, where ropes came swinging down out of the night. The
bundles they'd unloaded from the ship were quickly tied to
these and sent up. Next, came a platform, which Jilian jumped
on to and motioned Kyarra to follow. Clumsily, not yet used to
having her right hand chained to a woman who needed telling
to put one foot in front of the other, Kyarra followed with her
mother. When the three of them were kneeling on the platform,
Jilian flashed her a white grin in the gloom and tugged on one
of the ropes. The platform jerked, tipped alarmingly at one side,
then began to rise up the cliff. Kyarra caught at the edge with
tight fingers as the beach and the watching men faded away into
the shadows.

"This is my favorite part!" Jilian said when they were halfway
up and the wind had begun to catch the platform. She spread
her arms and tipped her face to the sky, her red hair blowing
around her in the drafts off the cliff.

Kyarra eyed the girl's feet, so close to the edge. Jilian wasn't
holding on. One good kick . . . She shook her head. "You're
rocking us," she warned.

"Not scared, are you?" Jilian grinned. But she sat down again and contented herself with trying to snatch eggs from the gulls' nests in the cliff as they creaked past. She only got one, which slipped out of her fingers and smashed on the dark rocks below.

At the top, they were met by six men as raggedly dressed as Asil and his crew and similarly armed with scimitars and knives. They grinned at Jilian and swung her from man to man, laughing when she threatened them with her little dagger. The platform, Kyarra saw, had been towed to the top of the cliff by a scruffy pony with a tail that trailed in the dust. She stepped off in relief and stood on shaky legs, her mother silent beside her. The pony was backed up and the platform sent down again. Almost as an afterthought, Jilian put her hand on the chain that linked Kyarra to her mother and pulled them away from the edge.

"This is Princess Kyarra," she told the men. "I know she don't look like much, but you'd better all keep your stars on and watch your tongues, because back there on the ship she sang old Blackbeard half to death for daring to lay a hand on her mother!"

The men looked at Kyarra and laughed. But Kyarra's thoughts were churning too much to be angry about the fun they were making of her. She'd thought Asil called her Princess as a joke. Only the way Jilian had introduced her, it didn't sound like one.

There was more waiting around while the pony was prodded into action and the platform brought up again with Asil on board. By this time it was fully dark. A crescent moon shone on the foam below and the boat could be seen as a black dot returning to the ship. Inland, hills rose dark against the stars. There was no sign of civilization. Kyarra shifted her sandals uneasily on the stones and looked at her mother's slippers. Neither of them would last long over this terrain.

Asil must have read her mind, for he broke open one of the bundles and produced two pairs of well-worn boots, which he tossed at her feet. "Put them on," he ordered with a frown.

"They're the smallest we've got. If they don't fit, you'll have to stuff the toes with grass. Jilian, help her. We've a long way to go tonight."

Kyarra pushed the girl away and sat down. Awkwardly, she completed the task herself, putting her mother's boots on for her and bruising both their wrists with the manacles despite her best efforts not to. She suspected her feet would soon look like her mother's blistered hand, but the leather was soft and they were an improvement over sandals. She stood up, pulled her mother up beside her, and tested them. "Thank you," she said.

Asil grunted. "Don't thank me, Princess. I just don't want you falling behind, that's all. Let's march!"

A nightmare. That was the only word for it. They marched through the night, up and down and up again, following stony tracks that seemed to lead nowhere in the dark. Kyarra's mouth was full of dust, her hair thick with it, her Echorium uniform as dirty and colorless as the pirates' rags. Her mother was just as filthy, and the beautiful hair Kyarra had brushed so carefully on the ship was matted and stuck to her cheeks. Both of them had rings of dirt around their wrists where the sweat under their manacles had mixed with the dust to form a thick crust. Her feet felt as if they were on fire. She suspected they were bleeding inside her boots. She almost envied her mother, not being able to feel pain.

Asil led the way, striding tirelessly over the hills as if he did, indeed, own them. Jilian led the pony behind her father, stumbling from time to time and catching herself on the mane with a quick look around to make sure no one had noticed. Kyarra stared at the pony's long, tangled tail and wondered if the girl really was as accustomed to this kind of journey as she claimed to be. Two men walked behind, prodding their captives in the back whenever they slowed down. The others spread out on both sides of the trail, their hands resting warily on the hilts of their scimitars.

Finally, Asil called a halt and crouched behind a boulder, staring down at something ahead. He waved a man over and they exchanged whispers. Jilian put a hand over the pony's nose, her eyes bright in the moonlight. Kyarra was just glad of the chance to stop. She sank onto a nearby boulder and pulled her mother down beside her. One of the men brought them water in a skin. She gulped thirstily, then put the skin to her mother's lips and instructed her to swallow. If they were going to have any chance of escape at all, she'd have to make sure her mother was as well fed and rested as she was when the time came.

"What's happening?" she asked.

"Shh!" Jilian scowled. "Great South Trade Route's down there. We got to cross it, but someone's coming."

Kyarra eased her finger under her manacle and picked out a crust of dirt. "What's the problem? I thought you just robbed them and stabbed them with your dagger?" She laughed. It came out sounding slightly hysterical.

This earned her another scowl. "You know nothin' about robbin', Kyarra! And you better be quiet, if you don't want me to stab *you*."

"That's enough, girls." Asil came back down from the ridge. He wiped his forehead with his scarf and settled himself on a nearby boulder. "We'll wait for them to pass."

"And let them go, sir?" one of his men said in an incredulous tone. "They're a small party. We could take 'em, easy!"

"No," Asil said. "They might have the fighting horses, and we've more important things to do tonight." His eyes rested on Kyarra.

The men grumbled. But they let the caravan pass without further argument before creeping across the Trade Route and up into the hills on the other side. Kyarra stared curiously at the road as they crossed. It wound along the valley through steep-sided passes, obviously well traveled. There were fresh hoof-prints in the dust, maybe six or seven horses. A green glimmer showed in the distance. How far had the caravan gone? Could she and her mother catch up with the horses before Asil's men caught them? She lifted her arm to test the weight of the chain, saw Jilian watching her, and let it drop again with a sigh. Their best chance would be to slip away when the men were asleep. They'd surely have to camp soon.

But they marched a lot longer than she thought possible, up into more rocky hills and down again toward what her tired eyes at first thought was another sea, but turned out to be a vast forest spread beneath the brightening horizon. Waves of leaves, eerie and dark, rippled under a layer of green mist.

As they drew closer to the trees, the men fell silent. Kyarra's steps slowed. These trees were nothing like the scrubby bushes on the Isle of Echoes. Huge trunks rose like gigantic pillars to a canopy of tangled branches. Strange scents leaked out, together with a sticky heat. Under those branches lurked a darkness so thick, it seemed alive. And there was something else. A dark song that crept out of the forest and wound itself around her thoughts.

The small hairs on the back of her neck rose. She pressed closer to her mother, slipping her hand into the woman's limp one, all thought of escape gone.

The pony sensed something, too. As they passed into the shadow of the first trees it planted itself and with a frightened snort jerked the rope out of Jilian's hand.

"Watch it!" Asil warned.

Too late. The pony twisted on its haunches, barged through the men, and galloped back the way they'd come, the packs on its back bouncing and scaring it into further speed.

Asil cursed under his breath and gave Jilian a glare that clearly said what he thought of her. "You told me you could control it."

Jilian flushed, nursing her rope-burned hand. "I'm sorry, Father. It must have heard something."

"I should send you back after it, might teach you to hold on tighter next time. Would do, too, if I didn't need you to look after our guests." He shook his head at her, turned to the men and pointed. "You and you! Go after the stupid beast and see if you can catch it. If it's still spooked, carry the stuff back yourselves. The rest of you, find some dry wood and keep a good watch. We'll camp here."

"Here, sir?" one questioned, his voice rising an octave.

"Yes, here! Unless you want to carry our guests yourselves? The pair of them are dead on their feet, and we've been instructed to wait for an escort before we go any deeper into the trees."

The men he'd ordered to chase the pony exchanged questioning glances, then jogged back into the hills, following its hoofprints. The others reluctantly went in search of firewood. They drew their scimitars before they ventured under the trees.

Asil touched Kyarra's cheek. "Hear them, do you, Princess? This place spooked the last Singer we brought here, too. I hope you're going to be more sensible than she was."

Belatedly, Kyarra realized whom he must be talking about. *The woman we picked up from the fish-people.* So Singer Rialle had been brought here as well? The merlee had told Caell a lie. What else had they lied about?

With an effort, she dragged her eyes from the darkness under the trees and shook the strange song out of her head. "What's in there?" she whispered.

Asil smiled. "Can't you guess?"

Jilian sidled closer. She seemed to have recovered from her scare with the pony. "Tell her, Father," she urged.

"I think she already knows." He turned Kyarra and her mother around until they were facing the forest and spoke softly, as if afraid someone would overhear. "This is where the quetzal live. You'll be seeing some of them soon when they come to escort us into the forest. They worship his Lordship, who they call Starmaker — probably because they've seen him make the black crystal stars we wear, though quetzal are strange creatures and it's a mystery to me what goes on in their heads. Anyway, his Lordship must get lonely in there with only Half Creatures and priests for company. A dying man should have his wife and daughter by his side. It's the natural way of things. He's been waiting for you, Princess. He's been waiting a long time."

7

AMBUSh

When the message came from the merlee saying that the Star-maker's daughter had arrived on the mainland, Night Plume knew he had to do something. It had been easy enough to fool the priests into thinking he was still obedient to the Starmaker's spear, and he'd managed to avoid shooting down any wild quetzal by leading his flock to another part of the forest whenever he felt their wild-speech at the edge of his thoughts. But the night the message came, the Starmaker sent his priests out hunting. The next morning, when Night Plume flew out of the crater where he'd been roosting with Sky Swooper, he found three wild fledglings hanging upside down by their talons from a tree at the edge of the clearing.

Night Plume joined the rest of his flock beneath the tree and stared upward in horror.

The captives' feathered hands had been bound behind them and their beautiful tails trailed through the branches, floating gently back and forth in the mist. They were dead. But that was not the worst of it. Their half-grown wings had been cut off and nailed to the trunk. Blood from the wounds dripped onto the leaves below, where the Starmaker sat on his crystal throne with his spear resting across his knees.

"As you can see, I've given the wild quetzal something to think about," he said. "So they shouldn't bother you for a while. Bring my daughter back safe, my faithful dark quetzal. Fly, fly, fly!"

Night Plume would have liked to put an arrow in each of the Starmaker's eyes. But thinking of Sky Swooper, he made himself sling his bow over his shoulder and lead his flock into the air.

Sun Glimmer flew alongside Night Plume. "Wild quetzal our enemies," he said with a soft whistle, as if he were trying to convince himself. "They attack you and Sky Swooper. Need lesson. It right."

"It right!" echoed the others, and one of the younger blues got excited and loosed an arrow into the nearest dangling body.

Night Plume's head whirled. He folded his wings and dived at the blue youngster, snatched the bow out of his hand and beat up above the canopy. The youngster followed, hooting in protest.

"You do that again without order, I snap it!" he threatened, lifting a knee and holding the bow across it. He had to stop himself from snapping it anyway. The others went quiet.

Sun Glimmer frowned. "You act strange since you go inside Temple, Night Plume. We worry."

Night Plume almost told him how the prisoner's Songs had changed something in his head so he could see the truth in the Memoryplace. Then he thought of Sun Glimmer reporting his words to the Starmaker and said, "You act strange, too, if you been inside Temple." He took a deep breath and handed the youngster's bow back with a sharp whistle, wishing he could manage the piercing inside-whistle of the wild quetzal. "Waste of arrows," he said. "Might need them. Follow!"

Refusing to look again at the bodies displayed below, he led his flock above the trees and set off briskly toward the edge of the forest. The others were soon stretched out behind him, unable to keep up, but Night Plume was too upset and worried to care. "Faster!" he called, beating his strong black wings. "Faster!"

He knew he wasn't being a good leader, but all he could think of was getting the humans they were supposed to meet back to the Temple as soon as possible so that Sky Swooper could be free. The wild quetzal would want revenge for what the Starmaker had done to their fledglings, and Night Plume had a horrible feeling he knew what form that revenge would take. The Starmaker didn't realize how much they knew about his plans. If the wild flock got to the Starmaker's daughter first, he dreaded to think what they might do.

*

In the permanent twilight at the edge of the forest, the pirates and their two prisoners huddled close to the fire. There were so many questions Kyarra wanted to ask. But Jilian didn't know the answers and Asil was busy organizing the camp. The pony had made off with their food. But luckily the men had been carrying their water skins, and while they were collecting wood they found some berries and a species of twisted root that they roasted over the flames. The berries were bright purple and tasted bitter, but Kyarra made herself swallow some and instructed her mother to chew and swallow the rest, before lying down in the pile of leaves that the men had collected for them. Jilian lay wrapped in her cloak nearby, seemingly asleep. Asil and his men sat talking quietly by the fire. The two he'd sent after the pony still hadn't returned.

Kyarra closed her eyes and focused her Singer-trained ears on their words.

". . . must have had the fighting horses. They wouldn't dare travel through Asil's Hills at night otherwise."

"Think it was a trap?"

"No. They'd have had more armed men."

"They might've had more men hiding in the hills."

"We'd have seen them. It was only a small caravan, anyway, hardly worth the bother — shh! You hear that?"

Their conversation cut off as they stared into the trees.

Kyarra eyed the brightness that showed between the trunks back the way they'd come. Somewhere out there, the sun was shining. Very slowly, she eased herself into a crouch, giving her mother instructions in pallet-whispers. The men were still staring at the trees. Jilian did not stir. Kyarra led her mother carefully around the girl and slipped behind one of the thick trunks.

She risked a look back. The men were on their feet now. She saw Asil draw his scimitar. Then one pointed at the treetops and said in a relieved tone, "It's the quetzal! They got here quick."

At the same time Jilian woke up, blinked at the flattened leaves beside her and yelled, "Father! They've escaped!"

Kyarra turned and tugged her mother after her. "*Run!*" she hissed in a pallet-whisper.

They followed the line of trees, keeping the brightness to their left, moving as quietly as possible. After staring around wildly, Jilian raced back along the path, dagger in hand. Kyarra smiled. She'd counted on her captors expecting them to flee that way. If they kept to the edge of the forest, they could hide until their pursuers gave up, and maybe creep out later.

But she hadn't reckoned on the quetzal. As she and her mother dodged through the trunks, there was a soft whirr in the air above the trees. Kyarra's neck hairs rose. A heartbeat later, the canopy overhead exploded with color and piercing whistles.

She swerved and tugged desperately on the chain. "Run!" she shouted, abandoning pallet-whispers. A huge bird — except it wasn't a bird — dived at Kyarra's face, talons extended and beak open. She caught a glimpse of intelligent black eyes in a face covered with red and gold feathers, enormous wings like flames, a long tail streaming in the gloom . . . Her breath stopped in terror. Then the chain attached to her manacle tightened as her mother, lost without constant instructions, tripped over a root and sprawled facedown in the leaves. Kyarra stumbled over her and fell also. The quetzal streamed over them, so close she felt the wind of its passage in her hair. It regained height and disappeared back through the canopy, whistling wildly.

Kyarra staggered to her feet, yelling at her mother to get up. Her heart missed a beat. The quetzal had returned silently through the canopy for another dive. This time it was followed by a second creature, blue and purple. They turned together, perfectly synchronized, cocked their heads at the two humans crouched on the ground, opened their talons, and dived from two different directions at once.

Somewhere off in the trees, a man was yelling. "Those aren't his Lordship's quetzal!" Screams and thuds came from the undergrowth, interspersed with desperate shouts. "Whose are they, then? Where'd they go?" "Quick, Asil! Where's the girl? Can't you get her to sing to 'em like she did to Blackbeard?" "Look out — behind you!"

Sing to them.

Kyarra raised her head and stared the red-and-gold creature in the eyes. Somehow, she gasped enough breath and let out a shaky hum.

Aushan, Aushan makes you scream.

The quetzal shook its head and swerved at the last moment. Its talons thumped into the leaves by her hand, and it beat up through the canopy again, hooting wildly. The purple one followed, leaving Kyarra with a long gash down her arm. She hardly felt the pain. She dragged her mother to her feet, looking desperately for the sunlight between the trunks. But all directions were dark and green. She couldn't remember which way the camp lay, let alone which way they'd come in. Throat sore from singing, her wrist bruised from tugging her mother after her, her arm on fire where the quetzal's talons had ripped it open, she stumbled more and more often. Her vision blurred. Her mother fell again and she sank to her knees beside her.

Suddenly, Jilian was there. Hands pulled at her blood-spattered uniform. "Get up, Kyarra!" she shouted. "This way!

They won't follow us out of the forest! Come on, your Ladyship, get up! Run!" She dragged the unnaturally calm woman to her feet and kept hold of her other hand.

Kyarra blinked. The pirate girl had twigs in her hair and was brandishing a fullsized scimitar at the sky. The quetzal shrieked furiously, circling, looking for an opening to attack. She let the Song fade. "I thought they were supposed to be tame?" she croaked.

The quetzal whistled. The red-and-gold one dived.

"Keep singing, you idiot, or they'll kill us all!" Jilian screamed, pulling them both into a stumbling run. The quetzal thumped into the leaves where Kyarra had been kneeling, one of its talons making a hole in her boot. Trembling, she ran after her mother and Jilian, singing as loudly as she could.

They stumbled through the remains of their campfire. A man lay beside it, his heart torn out. Kyarra's stomach heaved. The *Aushan* faltered. "Run!" Jilian yelled. "He's dead. Keep singing!"

Something whistled through the leaves overhead and thudded into the ground behind Kyarra, giving her an extra spurt of speed. It was an arrow with a black flight feather. The quetzal hunting them whistled wildly, and there were more whistles above. Feathers floated down as more arrows sliced through the branches above. But sunlight showed through the trunks ahead. Her legs found new strength.

Then they were out in the open, racing up a rocky slope with the quetzal cries growing fainter behind them. They ran as far as their legs would take them before they stopped. Neither of them had any breath left for talking, though thankfully Jilian proved right about the quetzal not following them out of the forest so Kyarra was at least able to stop singing. They stumbled into a patch of shade beneath an overhang and sank to the ground, too exhausted to do anything except stare at one another and pant.

Kyarra examined the purple streak down her arm where dust had clotted the blood. It hurt, but she dared not touch it in case it started bleeding again. At least the boot had saved her ankle. Now that they'd stopped, she realized her companions looked nearly as bad as she did — their clothing torn, their faces scratched from twigs and thorns, their hair disheveled. "Were those the quetzal who are supposed to worship my father?" she said, catching her breath at last. "They've a funny way of showing it."

Jilian put down the scimitar, eased her shoulders, and winced. "They must've gone mad! I don't understand it. They were supposed to escort us through the forest. Father got a message from the fish-people to wait for 'em."

"At least you could fight them off. This stupid chain nearly killed me and my mother in there!"

Jilian bit her lip. "One of them knocked me over. I couldn't see a thing, except feathers everywhere. When I got back to the clearing, Grossi was dead —" She swallowed in memory. "I grabbed his scimitar to keep the quetzal off him, but I couldn't find Father. Then I heard you singin' and saw the quetzal chasing you. My head went kind of funny. I knew I couldn't fight 'em all off on my own, but I wanted to kill them, Kyarra! I wanted to kill them so much."

Kyarra stared at her. "Thanks for coming back," she said grudgingly.

Jilian shrugged and gave a little grin. "Couldn't let 'em peck *your* heart out, could I? Father said I'm supposed to look after you." She picked up the scimitar again and tested the edge. "Needs a sheath. I'll slice me own leg off if I carry it around like this much longer."

"You'd have done better bringing the water," Kyarra said.

Jilian scowled. "Didn't see you stoppin' to get any water skin, either. Shut up and let me think."

Kyarra eyed her mother. She'd stopped panting now and sat staring into the distance, leaves and twigs sticking out of her hair. They could escape now. Jilian wouldn't be able to stop them.

"We'll have to go back to the cave," Jilian decided. "Tell the others what happened. They'll know what to do. We're not supposed to take strangers back there, but I can't leave you out here."

Kyarra frowned at her. "What cave?"

"Where we live, silly! Don't think we build little blue houses like yours out here in the hills, do you? Authorities'd soon find us! *Hey, everyone, here's where the famous pirate Asil lives! Come* and arrest us!" While she was speaking, she was hacking strips off her cloak. She used one to wrap around the scimitar and tied the other around Kyarra's arm.

"Ow!" Kyarra protested, pulling away. "That hurts!"

"It's only to stop you bleedin' all over the place. Don't be such a baby. Mother'll see to it properly when we get to the cave."

Kyarra pushed her off. "I'm not going to any robber's cave with you, so you don't have to bother. I'm taking my mother back to the Isle. The Singers will heal my arm with *Challa*." She stood up, pulled her mother up beside her and took two determined steps back down the path. "Don't try to stop us."

Jilian laughed. "Oh? And how far do you think you're goin' to get with no water? I bet you don't even know the way back to the coast from here. These hills are pretty big, you know. We came the shortest way last night. Or are you thinkin' of going back into the forest for a drink?" She laughed again.

Kyarra set her jaw. "I'd rather die of thirst than go a step farther as your prisoner."

"And you choose for your mother as well, do you?"

Jilian's words stung. She glanced at the midnight-haired woman. She showed no sign she was thirsty, but she had to need water — or did she? No one had actually withheld her food to see what happened. She kept walking.

"Go on then," Jilian said. "Go back to your precious little island! Go back to your Singers who steal people's souls. Aren't you even a little bit curious about your real family, and why the Singers did that to your mother? I know I would be."

Kyarra kept walking.

Jilian ran up behind her on soft feet and touched the manacle about her wrist. "You're angry 'cause Father chained you, aren't you? I can understand that. I would be, too. We have fire back at the cave and tools. If you come with me, I could get someone to take this off."

Kyarra stopped. She was dizzy and thirsty, and she wasn't sure she could find the way back to the coast alone. "Why do you keep calling me a princess?" she said.

Jilian grinned and thrust the scimitar through her belt to join her blue-handled dagger. "Because that's what Father says you are, and Father's never wrong."

"He was wrong about those quetzal," Kyarra pointed out, wondering if being a princess would make up for her parents not being Singers.

A flicker of uncertainty crossed Jilian's face. But she pushed back her tangled hair, straightened her shoulders, and started up the trail. "Half Creatures aren't like us. They do weird things sometimes. Are you comin' or not? It's this way."

Kyarra's heart sank at the thought of climbing more hills. But before they'd climbed very far, they saw the two men who had been sent after the pony leading the animal back down the trail toward them. It still had most of its packs, now covered in purple dust, and it kept flattening its ears and snorting as they led it slowly back toward the forest.

Jilian, who had lapsed into a worried silence, broke into a grin. She waved and ran toward the men.

One of them looked up. His eyes widened. "Go back!" he shouted. "It's a tra —" Something green glimmered beside his ear and he fell silent.

Kyarra frowned at the pony, which continued to sidle and snort. The other man was standing stiffly, shaking his head at Jilian. Something was wrong. Jilian skidded to a stop and frowned at the air beside the man who had shouted. There was another green glimmer and a curved blade slid out of nowhere and came to rest at his throat. Jilian's eyes widened. She fumbled for her weapons. But the scimitar was tightly wrapped, useless in an emergency. As she freed her dagger, the air behind her glimmered green and a hand appeared, closing about her wrist. She screamed once and vanished into the green light.

Kyarra stared at the spot where Jilian had disappeared, her head spinning. It's the thirst and lack of sleep, she decided. I'm seeing things.

"Jilian?" she whispered, her throat too sore to shout. The men with the pony were staring past her at the rocks as if expecting someone else. When no one appeared, they looked at Kyarra and her mother and frowned.

There was another green glimmer beside the first one's ear. "Where's Asil?" he said roughly, as if the words were being torn from him.

Kyarra slowly began to back away, whispering instructions to her mother. She didn't have the first idea what had happened to Jilian, but she knew one thing. She wasn't going to let the men get close enough to use their strange weapon on her as well.

"They're alone," said a new, strong voice from the air behind her. "Do it quickly."

She whirled in alarm, but before she could see who had spoken the hills dissolved into fizzing green sparks.

*

Night Plume's day was going from bad to worse. As he'd feared, the wild quetzal had beaten them to the meeting place and been attacking the humans when his flock arrived. Night Plume had spotted the Starmaker's daughter and another girl running out of the forest and flown after them, only to see them vanish before his very eyes. He circled the area in stunned disbelief, his gaze fixed on the spot where the girls and the woman had been standing only moments before. A human weapon that disintegrated people with green light? The Memoryplace told him nothing, but the Starmaker had threatened to cut off Sky

Swooper's wings if Night Plume so much as let his daughter get scratched!

His head roared. He flew down and wasted five arrows shooting at shadows, before realizing that he was likely to be disintegrated by the green-light weapon as well if he remained exposed. For the first time in his life, he was alone. The others had turned back at the edge of the forest, unable to follow when he'd flown after the human girls. His shadow rippled over the empty ridges and gullies below, sharp and black, mocking him. The sunlight, reflecting from all the bare earth, made his head spin.

A wave of hopelessness came over him as he turned back to the forest. He found Sun Glimmer circling over the clearing where the dead human male lay with his heart missing. Some of the younger members of the flock had landed nearby and were poking curiously at the body. Night Plume whistled at them to come away. The others returned from driving off the wild quetzal, breathless and hooting their triumph.

"I kill two!" boasted a green-and-scarlet girl.

"I injure one!"

"I frighten three with feather-ruffling arrows!"

"We save humans from heart-tearing death."

"We fierce patrol! We report to Starmaker and get rewards!"

Night Plume still felt faintly sick. He'd had to kill three of the wild quetzal to drive them away from the human girls. Their bodies were caught in the canopy, wings and tails snagged on branches as if they'd been nailed there like the ones back at the Lake of Stars. All for nothing. The girls had gone.

Sun Glimmer was staring at him. "You fly beyond edge of forest, Night Plume," he hooted softly. "How?"

Night Plume didn't answer straightaway. He checked for traces of wild-speech, and indicated that his flock should land in the clearing.

"Good work," he made himself say. "Sun Glimmer, you take

others. Find surviving human men. Keep them safe from wild flock. If I not come back before sun sets and rises again, escort human men to Starmaker and report. Say I bring daughter safe to him, soon. Remember to say this. It very important."

Sun Glimmer gave a soft whistle of confusion. "You leader, Night Plume. We follow you."

"You not follow this time. I go that way!" He pointed in the direction of the hills.

More confused whistles. "But why?" Sun Glimmer said. "Nothing out there."

Night Plume counted his arrows. He was running out. He looked at the others' quivers, but few had as many left as he did. Sun Glimmer's quiver held a single scarlet flight.

"I give order!" he said firmly. "You do as I say."

He put a hand on Sun Glimmer's arm and led him a short way off into the trees, where the others wouldn't overhear. The scarlet-and-gold quetzal looked at him, puzzled.

"How many wild flock you kill, Sun Glimmer?" he asked.

"Five," Sun Glimmer said without a trace of regret.

"You feel sad?"

Sun Glimmer shook his head, but must have seen the glitter in Night Plume's eye for he omitted to say they were the enemy and it was right.

"What you see when you fly to edge of forest?" Night Plume asked.

"Nothing. Only darkness, like Memoryplace say."

"I see hills and Starmaker's daughter running with other humans in the sunlight." He didn't mention the weapon.

Another stare.

"Something happen to me in Temple, Sun Glimmer. I see different things in Memoryplace, things that were hidden by blackstars before, like what lie beyond edge of forest and what human Singers do. I not sure yet which memories true and which memories false, but go to find out more. Starmaker know this when you report where I fly, so important you not go back to Temple until sun sets and rises again. You roost here in clearing tonight. Find food for others. Preen wings. Collect arrows. Watch for wild flock. Give men excuses. Make sure they not talk to Starmaker or come out of forest until I return. Give me chance, Sun Glimmer. Or Starmaker angry and cut off Sky Swooper's wings like priests do to wild quetzal."

Sun Glimmer hooted in horror. "He not do that to Sky Swooper!"

"If I not come back, important you get Sky Swooper out of Temple and tell her to hide from priests before you report. You do this, Sun Glimmer?"

His nestmate was still shaking his head and hooting his protest. "Starmaker not hurt us, Starmaker father of us all. You not fly beyond forest, Night Plume, it wrong —"

Night Plume seized him by the shoulders and tried for the inside-whistle that the wild quetzal used. He must have partially succeeded, because Sun Glimmer stiffened and stared at him in shock.

"I tell you it right! I tell you Starmaker not father of us all. Since I go inside Temple to listen to silver-haired human, I see same things in Memoryplace that wild quetzal see. Starmaker human behind mask! Not god."

Sun Glimmer's eyes widened still farther. "Night Plume! You enchanted!"

"No, I not. Silver-haired human break enchantment of blackstars with her Songs."

He released his nestmate and shook out his wings. He felt a bit better. "Promise?" he whispered. "You do what I ask? Help Sky Swooper?"

The scarlet-and-gold quetzal stared at him a moment longer, then unexpectedly hooted and pressed up close like a fledgling. "I try," he whispered.

Night Plume's eyes smarted as he whistled good-bye to his flock and headed for the hill where he'd last seen the human girls. He fitted an arrow to his bow, glided lower and examined the ground carefully. But the girls, the woman, the men, and their pony were gone as if they'd never been. Their footprints led up to the place of disintegration, where they were lost in a confusion of hoofprints and churned-up dust. He shrugged his bow back on his shoulder and set his face to the wild, alien smell that came across the hills on a stiff headwind.

Sea, whispered the prisoner's wild-speech from the Memory-place. *Ask a wild merlee shoal to guide you across the sea.*

8
DILEMMA

Night Plume had thought the Warm River in the forest was wide, but the Western Sea went on forever like an endlessly moving canopy with nowhere to perch or rest. He followed the sun until it grew huge and red and slipped into the watery horizon. The stars came out and the sea turned black and glittered like the Starmaker's crystal. Night Plume hoped he'd find the Singer island soon because he wasn't sure he'd make it back without a rest. Every ten wing beats or so, he closed his eyes and sent out wild-speech.

Merlee? You hear me? Stone-singer need help!

There was no reply from the black sea. Sometimes, he saw pale glimmers of foam and changed course in excitement, only to find they were waves breaking over submerged rocks. He considered trying to land on one of the rocks for a breather, but the thought of the Starmaker's merlee finding him and dragging him off his perch into the sea frightened him. His plumage would get wet, and if he couldn't take off again he'd drown. A bit farther, he promised himself. Then I'll try for a large rock . . . when I'm really tired . . . if I haven't found the island. . . . With a start, Night

Plume pulled himself back from the edge of sleep to find his tail trailing in the waves and his wing tips heavy with water.

Help! he called, climbing higher in panic. *Please help me!*

. . . merlee . . .?

The query was faint and tentative. At first, Night Plume thought he'd imagined it. But the scare of nearly drowning himself must have given his wild-speech extra range because it came again, tickling the edge of his thoughts. Better still, the contact had no trace of blackstars, so it was unlikely to be coming from any of the Starmaker's merlee. Relieved, he changed course and flew in the direction of the wild-speech.

Need help! he sent. *Stone-singer say you guide me across Western Sea to Isle of Echoes. You wild shoal?*

The voice from the sea went quiet. Night Plume searched the dark water, looking for fish tails and human hair like the merlee back in the Starmaker's Salty Lake. He back-winged in surprise. Almost directly below him was a large boat with tattered gray sails, ghostly in the starlight. Foam glimmered around its bows. Three humans stood on deck — two grown men in long gray robes, and one young boy in a ragged tunic and breeches that might once have been white. All three were staring intently at the waves. The boy was clutching something that looked suspiciously like one of the priests' crystal stars, and with a start Night Plume realized the wild-speech had come from the young human.

He hesitated, circling the boat at a safe height. It was quite a bit bigger than the boats the Starmaker's priests used on the Warm River and it had long masts from which the sails flapped. A little hatch below one of the masts led into darkness. He shuddered.

The humans had been silent as they searched the waves. But now the older man straightened and said in a rough, cracked voice, "Forget it, Caell. The merlee have gone crazy, anyway. Trying to drown a novice who has the gift of hearing Half Creatures! Whoever heard of such a thing?"

"That was the other sort of merlee," said the boy. "The real merlee saved me. Anyway, what I just heard was different —"

The older man scowled. "It was us who saved you, you young idiot! If that girl Lianne hadn't raised the alarm, and we hadn't set out after you in the *Wavesong* immediately, your body would have been discovered floating in on the next tide! Forget the merlee. Let's concentrate on getting to Silvertown before the stupid creatures take it into their heads to sing up another storm. Meanwhile, I'm going back to bed. I'm getting far too old for these midnight escapades. I'd suggest you take the boy back below and do the same, Renn. We'll need all our wits about us when we land."

He started toward the hatch. But the younger man — the one he'd called Renn — put a hand on his arm and said, "If Caell thought he heard the merlee, I believe him. What exactly did they say, Caell?"

"I'm not sure — I was asleep," the boy admitted. "At first I thought it was just a dream. Then I got my bluestone and focused like First Singer Graia showed me. They're near, I know they are. Only . . . they sound different." He frowned.

Curious, Night Plume circled lower. Now he could see the thing in the boy's hand was not a black crystal star as he'd first thought, but a smooth blue stone that reflected the starlight like the moon plucked out of the sky.

The human called Renn hummed low in his throat. "Try singing to them," he said gently. "That always worked for me."

The boy clasped his bluestone tighter and picked up the hum with his sweet voice. Night Plume's head filled with lavender light. Briefly, he was transported back to the prisoner's cell inside the Temple. His beak opened instinctively. Before he could help himself, the Song flooded out.

The three humans on the boat snapped as straight as if the Starmaker had suddenly appeared for a surprise inspection. Their pale faces searched the sky. The boy stared straight at Night Plume, but didn't seem to see him. Heart thudding, Night

Plume shut his beak, wishing he could control his quetzal instinct to mimic.

As he flapped his wings to gain height, the boy saw the movement and pointed. "There!" he said, following Night Plume with his finger. "It's coming from up there!"

The other two looked long and hard. The older man grunted. "Looks like a quetzal! What's it doing all the way out here?"

"See if you can get it to land on the ship," said Renn.

Night Plume's heart beat faster. Could he trust these humans or not? They weren't on an island, but they sang the same songs as the silver-haired prisoner had done. And his wings were so tired. At least their ship would be a place to rest.

He quietly fitted an arrow to his string. Before the boy could clasp his stone again and send the wild-speech, Night Plume glided lower and landed on the raised deck at the back of the ship — a little heavily, for it was moving up and down. The humans whirled, saw the arrow aimed at them, and froze.

"It's armed," breathed the one called Renn.

"And it's black!" grunted the older man, taking a step closer and squinting up at Night Plume. "I've never seen a black quetzal before."

"Careful," murmured Renn. "Let Caell talk to it first."

Shh, calm, nothing's going to hurt you, sang the boy. *Can you hear me, dark quetzal? What are you doing out here?*

Night Plume replied in wild-speech.

Need help. Stone-singer prisoner in Temple say find Singer island. You know where?

Caell's eyes went wide. He'd obviously understood. But when he started to report this to the two men, Night Plume realized only the boy could hear his wild-speech. These human Singers obviously didn't have the wild flock's skill of reading the thoughts of other creatures even before they were formed, and speaking their own at the same time.

This made him feel a little safer. When the boy turned back to him and started to repeat in wild-speech a question the older man had asked aloud, he lowered his bow and said, "Can talk, you know. Use human speech."

For the second time that night, the three humans stared at him in shock and disbelief.

"Echoes!" the older man whispered, his voice cracking. "Did you hear that?"

"I thought you said quetzal only mimicked?" Renn whispered back.

"It's not mimicking, is it? Someone's taught it to talk."

"Who?"

"Whoever has Kyarra! You heard what Caell said. Stone-singer who is prisoner in Temple! Don't let it take off again — get behind it."

"Can hear good, too," Night Plume said, raising his bow again and glancing behind him, just in case. "My name Night Plume. Nestmate Sky Swooper enchanted. Other quetzal enchanted, too. Prisoner say go to island across Western Sea, get help. Are you from Singer island? Will you help?"

Still eyeing the quetzal's weapon, the boy took a step closer. "Have you seen Kyarra?" he asked eagerly. "Some men took her away on a ship and we're following her. Is she the prisoner you're talking about? Have they hurt her? Is she all right?" His face was alight with hope and fear.

Night Plume frowned and looked in the Memoryplace. "Star-maker call prisoner by human name Ri-al-le," he said.

Renn drew a quick breath. "*Mother!*"

The two men whispered furiously to each other. ". . . can't tell . . . quetzal are not like humans, impossible to truth listen . . . could be lying . . ."

The boy stared at Night Plume, biting his lip. "Who is this Starmaker?" he asked.

Night Plume opened his beak and shut it again. How to reply? *Starmaker father of all who hatch from eggs* . . . wasn't right anymore, not now that he could see in the Memoryplace what had been hidden before by blackstars. But he wasn't sure he understood all the things the Memoryplace said about the Star-maker, either. Something about a dark boy and blackstars and shame. He searched for something that would give these humans a better idea. Then he had it. He mimicked in the Star-maker's raspy voice, "*You can use the wild quetzal as target practice — they're getting much too bold and need a lesson.*"

"That's Frazhin's voice!" With frightening speed, the older man leaped across the deck and hauled himself up the steps to where Night Plume perched. Before Night Plume could draw his bowstring, the human's fist closed on his arrow. "What's he done with Rialle, you talking freak?" He wrenched the bow out of Night Plume's hands and brandished it at him. "What's this for? Did Frazhin send you? Who were you supposed to kill? Talk, quetzal, or I swear I'll put this arrow in *you*!"

Night Plume took off in alarm, but the man caught the end of his tail and held on tightly.

"No!" cried Renn. "Don't frighten it! Frazhin's dead — we saw him drown, remember? The quetzal's just remembering his voice from years ago."

"Don't be so soft, Renn!" the older man shouted back. "Frazhin's obviously still alive. The naga we thought were attacking him must have helped him escape, after all. We have to find out where this quetzal came from. It's our best chance of finding Rialle."

He wound the tail feather around his wrist for a better grip. It was like being on the end of a tether. Night Plume beat his wings in panic. There was a horrible, tearing pain at the bottom of his spine — then sudden release. He circled higher, the panic giving way to steadier wing beats. Gradually, his head stopped spinning and his heart slowed.

Don't go, Night Plume! called the boy in wild-speech. *Because Singer Kherron lost his voice, he takes it out on everyone. He didn't mean to hurt you, he's always like that. Please come back, or he'll be in a terrible mood.*

Night Plume had no intention of landing again. Down below

in the darkness, his tail feather trailed like a tattered black rope from the angry Singer's fist. The base of his spine still hurt. But the boy's wild-speech made him want to laugh.

Poor human fledgling, he sent back, circling again.

Renn had joined the older man on the raised deck. He had a hand on his arm and was speaking very fast. His voice was full of songs. Kherron threw the tail feather into the sea in disgust and turned his back.

Renn sighed and peered in Night Plume's direction. "Try singing to it again, Caell. Use the bluestone. Say we're sorry. See if you can get it to come back for its bow."

"It's a he, Singer," the boy said. "And he's still up there, but I don't think he's going to land again in a hurry."

"Tell it — tell *him* no one will try to hurt him again. We have to find out more about Singer Rialle and see if the quetzal knows anything about Kyarra."

The boy started to hum again, filling Night Plume's head with lavender and golden swirls. Peace, he sang. They didn't mean to pull out his tail, didn't really mean to hurt him . . .

Against his will, Night Plume found himself circling lower. He landed near the boy, folded his wings and echoed the song, note for note.

Where did you learn to sing like that? Caell said in wild-speech. *I've been learning those Songs all my life and I can't sing them as well as that!*

Sing only what you sing. Voice beautiful. Not stop.

The boy giggled. "Sorry, but singing's hard work for us humans, you know." He glanced at the raised deck. "Singer Renn wants to ask you some questions. Can he come down if he promises not to pull your tail?"

Night Plume nodded. The younger man had gray eyes, like the eyes of the silver-haired prisoner he'd called his mother. Night Plume felt he could trust him. He saw now that the face and arms of the boy Caell were covered in little bruises and cuts.

What happen to you? Night Plume asked. *Singer Kherron punish you?*

The boy gave him a distracted look, then smiled. "Oh, these bruises you mean? They're from when the merlee tried to drown me. Dragged me under the rocks beneath the water. If the other shoal hadn't come and got me out, I'd be dead for sure." He sobered. "Some of the merlee have gone crazy, I think. What's happening, Night Plume? What do you know about Singer Rialle and Frazhin? Are you sure you haven't seen the girl we're looking for? She's called Kyarra, Ky for short."

Before Night Plume could answer, Renn came down the steps to join them. Night Plume told them everything the prisoner, Rialle, had told him to say about Frazhin destroying the Echorium and not trusting Half Creatures until they knew which ones had been enchanted by khiz-crystal — though of course he couldn't use her voice because she'd spoken in wild-speech. He told them what the Starmaker had done to her, forcing her to drink the Yellow Flower juice that made her talk but also enabled her to use wild-speech to communicate with Night Plume.

By the time he'd finished, it had started to rain. Singer Renn looked up at where Kherron leaned over the rail. "Frazhin's trying to change history. Do you think that's got anything to do with me not being able to contact the Isle?"

Kherron shook his head. "The bit about destroying the Echorium, you mean? He's tried that before, remember? Frazhin won't get near the Isle this time, don't worry."

But Caell was staring at Night Plume in horror. "The sacks!" he whispered. "The sacks the men who took Ky were carrying . . . they said something about putting the stuff in the well. I didn't think at the time, but what if it was poison or something, and that's why you couldn't contact the First Singer when you tried to tell her you'd found me? What if they've drunk poisoned water and they're already dead? All the novices, the

Singers, everyone!" His voice rose in anguish. "Oh, why didn't I go straight back to the Echorium and warn everyone instead of trying to swim after Ky? I should have told you about that ship straightaway —"

Renn dropped a hand on the boy's shoulder. "Steady, Caell," he said quietly. "There are lots of reasons why First Singer Graia mightn't be answering the bluestone." But his eyes were worried. He exchanged another glance with Kherron. "The boy has a point. Maybe we'd better turn around?"

Kherron, however, scowled at Night Plume. "Poison capable of killing the entire population of the Echorium? Don't tell me you actually believe that? And in the next breath, the quetzal himself tells us not to trust Half Creatures . . . It's obvious this is one of Frazhin's plots to delay us. We can't turn back now. What about Rialle? And the girl? If Frazhin gets his hands on Kyarra, echoes only know what he'll do with her. Besides, if Rialle really did tell the quetzal to say that, why didn't he repeat it in her voice so we could truth listen and be sure? I'd say that's as much proof as we need it's a lie."

"I'll try to contact the First Singer again before this storm blows up," Renn said, still looking worried. "Looks like we're in for another bad one." Pulling his robe tight against the weather, he ducked through the hatch.

Kherron cursed under his breath and pointed a finger at Night Plume. "You stay right there, quetzal! We've a lot more questions to ask you. Caell, you get below before you catch your death of cold. Don't worry, your feathered friend's not going far in this." With a grim smile, he hurried after Renn, taking Night Plume's bow with him.

Night Plume fluffed out his plumage and realized how lucky he'd been not to blunder into rain like this on his way across the open sea. He picked up his dropped arrow, preened the flight, and slipped it back into his quiver — though what good it would be without his bow, he didn't know. As the storm worsened, more humans came up on deck, but they were too busy reefing the sails to pay him more than a passing glance.

That left the boy, Caell. Despite the order to go below, he hesitated and blinked at Night Plume through a dripping blue fringe. "You were telling the truth, weren't you?" he said, frowning.

"Why I lie?" Night Plume said. "Prisoner say fly to island, find help. She very brave with gray eyes like young male Singer, and she wear shells in hair. She not young, but she sing sweet like fledgling, and she cry for merlee."

"That sounds like the Crazy Singer, all right." Caell wiped the rain from his eyes and smiled. "You know, that's the first time I've seen truth listening fail. Our teachers use it on us all the time — we can't get away with anything back in the Echorium! But even grumpy old Kherron couldn't tell if you were lying." He sobered. "Do you know what sort of poison Frazhin sent to the Isle, Night Plume? Is it really strong enough to kill the Singers?"

Night Plume whistled sadly. "Not know. Might be Yellow Flower like priests use on prisoner — Starmaker make us harvest many blooms from forest canopy so he can use them to help him change history. But Memoryplace say Yellow Flowers take long time to kill humans, and not all humans die when they eat them . . . it strange, I not understand." He whistled again.

"The same flowers he gave Singer Rialle? You didn't say they might poison her as well! I'd better tell Singer Renn." Caell frowned at him and sneezed. "Night Plume, are you *sure* you haven't seen Ky? She's got blue hair like mine, only longer, and she's not much bigger than you. Real skinny, even for a girl."

Night Plume froze as the image sprang from the Memoryplace.

Long blue hair, streaming behind the smallest human girl as they ran up the hill and vanished into green light . . .

"Not see her in Starmaker's Temple," he said carefully to give himself time to think. Would these human Singers still help him if they knew the truth?

Caell sighed. "That's something, I suppose." He wiped more spray from his eyes and considered Night Plume. "What's Frazhin — er, your Starmaker really like? Singer Renn and Singer Kherron say he's the most evil man in all the world. Singers have done battle with him twice before, apparently, and he's supposed to be the one who destroyed Singer Kherron's voice. Put a crystal down his throat, or something."

Night Plume closed his eyes. "Starmaker like quetzal who cannot fly. He pretend to be father, wear dark crystal mask, and change our Memoryplace with blackstars so we think he god. But Rialle help me see through his enchantment, and Memoryplace say Starmaker come from across the sea as fledgling and fall under blackstar spell because he have darkness in own head. He act like father. Sometimes angry, sometimes gives rewards. But not kind to human prisoner or wild quetzal." He shuddered in memory. "Cut off wings."

"He cuts off your *wings*?" Caell whispered in horror.

"Wild quetzal wings, not ours — except maybe Sky Swooper's, if I not get back to forest before sunrise." He looked anxiously at the sky. But with the storm, it was still too wet to fly.

The boy bit his lip. "We'll never make Silvertown before dawn in this weather. And if Singer Renn decides to turn around and go back to the Isle, we'll be even longer. I'm sorry, Night Plume. I don't think we'll make it in time."

*

Singer Renn failed to contact the Echorium that night, but Singer Kherron persuaded him to continue on their course, saying that as soon as they landed they would send a ship from Silvertown with physicians and an emergency supply of clean water in case the Isle stream had been contaminated as well. It made sense. The *Wavesong* had barely enough fresh water on board for the voyage, and they were much closer to the mainland than they were to the Isle. But the decision put the whole

crew on edge. Even Caell, who seemed relieved they were con-
tinuing after Ky, was uneasy.

"I hope they're all right," he kept saying. "The only person
who deserves to get sick is Lianne, but even she doesn't deserve
to be poisoned. It's horrible, not knowing." Night Plume whistled in sympathy. The storm had kept him ship-bound, and it
was dawn on the third day before the *Wavesong* limped into Silvertown harbor with torn sails — two days too late to stop Sun
Glimmer and the rest of the flock from reporting back to the
Starmaker.

To make things worse, the harbormaster was posting quar-
antine signs, and sick-looking people were camped out on the
quay clamoring for fresh water. "The whole town's been poisoned!" warned the sailors on board the other ships. "Don't
touch a drop unless you know where it's come from!"

Looking grim, the Singers rushed off at once to investigate
this new threat and to organize the rescue mission back to the
Isle, leaving the two youngsters on board with strict instructions
to stay put until they returned. Before he left, Kherron scowled
at Night Plume. "I know you're hiding something, quetzal. Your
speech pattern isn't all that different from a human's. Seems
your poison tale might be true considering what's going on
here, but I'll learn what you're keeping from us soon enough.
Meanwhile, you behave yourself." He handed a bucket to Caell
and whispered something to the boy.

Night Plume was too disturbed by the Singers' escort to
notice the threat in his words. The five men in gray uniforms
were led by one whose skin was almost as dark as his own
plumage, and who wore bones in his hair. The Memoryplace
whispered of similar dark-skinned humans who nested in the
forest and had some strange connection with the wild quetzal
and the Yellow Flowers.

Who dark human? he asked Caell in wild-speech as the men
hurried down the gangplank and struggled through all the
people begging for water.

Caell looked up, distracted. "Oh, that's Lazim. He's Singer Kherron's friend — only friend he's got, mind you! They met when they were my age, if you can believe Kherron was ever young. Lazim was born in the Karch — that's in the mountains near here — but his mother came from the forest, which is why he's so dark-skinned and has such a way with animals. The pentad was Lazim's idea, so he gets to lead them. They're supposed to die for us Singers. Rather him than me."

"Like I lead Starmaker's flock," Night Plume said softly.

Caell gave him a sharp look. "Why *are* you so dark, Night Plume? Did . . . did Frazhin make you that color?"

Night Plume opened his beak in amusement. "Even Starmaker not have power to change colors of quetzal! I hatch from colorless egg. Quetzal usually lay rainbow eggs, so think colorless egg unlucky. In wild nest, high in tree canopy, mothers push colorless egg to edge and it falls, long way. Smashes on ground. Unborn quetzal flows out with yolk and forest animals come to eat him. But Starmaker's nest on ground because priests not climb good. Mothers push my egg out, and next morning priests come to put it back in again. They keep doing this. My egg roll out of nest many times before I hatch. I only dark-colored quetzal in forest!" He fluffed his damp feathers in pride.

Caell laughed and put his bucket down.

The Singers and the five orderlies of the pentad, trained in swordsmanship to protect them, were gone all day. Meanwhile, the sailors left behind to look after the ship questioned the other crews about the people camped on the quay and got the whole story in gruesome detail.

The lake outside the town, Lake Plume, had gone bad. The river it fed, that flowed under the wall and provided the town's water through a clever system of pipes, was therefore contaminated. Half the town had been taken ill before they realized what was causing it. Many old people and babies had died. The ragged people who were camped on the quay had left their homes to beg for clean water from the ships that sailed into the harbor. Most of the crews guarded their on-board supply jealously, though the more mercenary captains had begun sailing along the coast to fill their empty wine barrels at the River Rush a short way to the north, returning to sell this safe water to the citizens of Silvertown at an exorbitant price.

Caell listened gravely. "Only their old people and babies died," he said. "So if it's the same poison Frazhin sent to the Isle . . ." He shook his head. "What's he trying to do, Night Plume? Why did he try to poison Silvertown as well?"

Night Plume searched the Memoryplace. "Not know. Starmaker not say anything about Silvertown. Maybe it accident."

"I bet it wasn't!" Caell said bitterly. "I bet he sent his evil merlee to do it."

"He send his naga. Naga travel better than merlee in rivers and lakes."

"Whatever. He's corrupted all the Half Creatures, and now they're trying to poison the whole world!" Caell frowned at a woman weeping on the quay with a sick baby in her arms. "Oh, I wish Singer Renn would come back! What are they doing? It'll be dark soon."

Night Plume kept quiet. His plumage was nicely dry now and he'd preened it carefully to get rid of the salt. There was no reason to stay with the humans any longer. Only Caell's songs had kept him on board the ship this long. He planned to leave as soon as it was dark, whether the Singers had returned or not.

But as the sun touched the sea in a blaze of scarlet and gold, there was a commotion at the end of the quay. Hooves clattered on the cobbles and a bugle note split the evening air.

"Make way for the Karchlord Azri!" called the bugler. "Overlord of the Silver Shore, Prince Among Men!"

As the echoes died away, a bunch of shaggy ponies trotted along the quay and milled around the *Wavesong*'s gangplank. Night Plume spread his wings in alarm. The slender human in the lead wore his dark hair in braids fastened with bones. He sat atop his pony with ease, his feet nearly touching the ground.

Red metal bracelets flashed on his bare arms. Behind him, mounted less happily on two more ponies, were Singer Renn and Singer Kherron. Near them rode Lazim, whose bone hairstyle matched those of the strangers. All the men looked fierce and carried short swords and daggers.

Caell jumped to his feet and rushed to the rail. The sailors stiffened. But when they saw the Echorium pentad was still armed, they relaxed slightly. The slender man swung a leg over his pony's withers and slid to the ground. He strode up the gangplank, his braids lifting on the breeze, looked Night Plume up and down and said with a thick accent, "A black quetzal — how unusual! And you say it can talk sense?"

The two Singers had followed the man on board, Lazim close behind. Singer Kherron grabbed Caell's arm. "You let it dry out! I thought I told you to keep its wings wet so it couldn't fly away until we came back?"

"I sang to him instead," Caell stammered. "He was wet enough, it's cruel . . ." He said something else, but Night Plume was too occupied with the man standing before him to hear. The Memoryplace was thick with old memories.

"I am the Karchlord Azri!" announced the man. "I owe a large debt to your people, quetzal. They brought me back from the dead when I wasn't much older than this boy here." He patted Caell on the head, making him blush. "Though they had a little help from the Singers, of course," he added with a glance at Kherron.

"Careful, Lord Azri," Kherron said. "We think it's Frazhin's creature."

"Why not let the quetzal speak for itself?" Azri said, his sharp eyes taking in the bucket at Caell's feet and Night Plume's bedraggled tail. "Well, dark quetzal? Is it true you've escaped Frazhin's clutches?"

Night Plume hooted. In the Memoryplace he saw this was the man who had rescued his ancestors after the Starmaker had chopped off their wings, many years ago. He could trust him.

"Prisoner Rialle say need help and tell me where to go, so I fly across sea. But my friend Sky Swooper in danger! Starmaker say he chop off her wings if I not get back safe with Starmaker's daughter, but she —" Too late, he realized his mistake.

Kherron cast a triumphant glance at Renn. "See? I *told* you it was hiding something! It knows something about Kyarra!" He pushed past the Karchlord and seized Night Plume's wrist. "What do you know about Frazhin's daughter, quetzal?" he hissed in his broken voice.

"Know nothing," Night Plume said, hoping Kherron wouldn't break his arm. "Not know where she go."

Which was true. Sort of.

Kherron scowled, his green eyes fixed on the shivering tips of his wings. "Truth," he grunted. "But not all of it! Speak, quetzal! Tell us what happened."

Night Plume eyed Singer Renn, who was gazing at him with the same intensity as Kherron. "If you saw her, Night Plume, we need to know where." There were Songs in his voice, commanding Songs. With an effort, Night Plume shook them out of his head.

Caell's eyes were wide, staring from one to the other. "Ky? *Frazhin's* daughter? No, it can't be true . . ."

"Talk, quetzal!" Kherron snapped, ignoring Caell and giving Night Plume another shake.

Renn put a hand on the old Singer's arm. "Let me try."

Again, his voice filled with Songs as he spoke softly to Night Plume. "Lord Azri and his men are in Silvertown to investigate the poisoning. Unfortunately, we can't tell what color flowers were used in the lake, but from what you've already told us it seems certain Frazhin, who you call Starmaker, is behind it. Lord Azri knows all about Frazhin and his methods — when he was still a boy in the Karchhold, Frazhin tried to poison him as well. Azri has sworn to finish the task he started thirty years ago when he chased Frazhin's priests out of his Karchhold. He was about to send an expedition up the River Plume, but it's slow going by boat and Karch warriors are trained to fight on horse-back. What we need you to do is guide us to Frazhin's strong-hold the quickest way for ponies. Can you do that, Night Plume? We'll have to trust you. We'll have to let you fly ahead to scan out the land. And we'll need to know exactly where you saw Kyarra, because it's important we find her before Frazhin does."

Night Plume held his breath. Singer Kherron was still muttering about not being able to trust him half a sunstep and finding a cage to put him in. Caell was obviously shocked about what he'd just discovered about his friend, but he slipped past the Singers and touched Night Plume's hand.

Please, Night Plume, he said in wild-speech. *Please tell us where you saw our girl, Ky. Is she all right?*

See girl in hills at edge of forest. Dangerous place. Need bow back if fly there.

Caell's face brightened. He eagerly passed the words on. But Singer Kherron shook his head. "Oh, no you don't, quetzal! Talk aloud so we can truth listen, or I'll get that cage sorted for you right now!"

Even Singer Renn was frowning now, rubbing his chin as he peered at Night Plume. He hummed low in his throat. Night Plume's head whirled.

They don't trust you, said Caell. *Tell us what happened, you have to. For Ky's sake. Please.*

Before he knew it, his beak opened and the words came out. "She run into powerful human weapon. She vanish into green light. Think she dead."

Caell paled and raised his hands to his mouth. Lord Azri frowned. Kherron's green eyes bored into him. Night Plume edged to the rail and lifted his wings. These Singers' Songs were more powerful than he'd thought. Now he didn't have any choice but to take his chances alone.

But as he was about to take off, Singer Renn stepped forward and laid a gentle hand on his arm. "Green light? Are you sure?" *Shh, calm,* he sang. *We won't hurt you.*

Night Plume nodded. "I sorry, I too late to save her. Wild quetzal attack and she run fast."

Unexpectedly, the gray-eyed Singer began to laugh. "Vanishing into green light . . . does that sound familiar to anyone?"

Caell and the Karchlord stared at him in confusion, but Kherron's scowl deepened. "Centaurs don't roam that far north," he said.

"It's Shaiala!" Renn said, still smiling. "I know it is! Caell, don't look so gloomy. I think Kyarra's fine. This is an excellent example of truth listening failing to give us all the facts. Night Plume believes he saw Kyarra die. But when I was your age, a girl was brought to the Isle for Song treatment. She told us she had been raised by centaurs. They're Half Creatures — half human, half pony — and they have green stones that can bend the light. From the outside, it looks as if people vanish. She'd be my age now, but we left her with a friendly Horselord tribe called the Kalerei, and they sometimes trade north of Rivermeet. Everything fits."

Kherron scowled again. "That doesn't mean Kyarra's safe. I doubt the Kalerei will be very friendly when they find out whose child she is."

Renn's smile died. "All the more reason to hurry. We'll head down the Trade Route, and Night Plume can tell us where he last saw her. We should be able to pick up the trail from there and follow it to wherever the Kalerei are camped."

The Karchlord frowned. "What about Frazhin?"

"I'm sorry, Lord Azri, but we have to find Kyarra first. Then we'll help you deal with Frazhin and rescue my mother. How long is the journey to Rivermeet from here?"

"At least five days," grunted one of the Karchlord's men. "And that's if you don't get attacked by highway robbers. Safest way is to join a big caravan. Fastest way is to ride hard with a small group."

"We'll ride," Renn said, glancing at Caell. "The boy has to learn how to stay on a horse sometime. We've our Songs and the pentad to protect us."

"And no one will dare attack you if you're with the Karchlord's army," Lord Azri put in. He smiled as everyone stared at him. "Didn't think I was going to sit around twiddling my braids in Silvertown while you have all the fun, did you? I could do with a few more bones in my hair. It's been a while since I killed anyone worthy of supplying me with a new death-braid."

The pentad glanced at one another. The fierce-looking men who wore bones in their hair grinned. Everyone seemed to have forgotten Night Plume. He looked at the stars coming out over the roofs of the town and tried not to think of Sky Swooper. At least when they found the place where he'd lost the human girl, he'd know the way back to the Temple.

Renn inclined his head. "The Echorium thanks you, Lord Azri," he said gravely. "Can you find a quiet pony for the boy? And I think we can trust Night Plume with his bow now, don't you? With Frazhin around, the more weapons we have on our side, the better."

Kherron's scowl deepened. "Half Creatures and ponies!" he grumbled. "Here we go again."

9
HORSELORDS

After Jilian vanished into the green light, everything took on the feel of a dream. Kyarra pinched herself, but it didn't help. The air on both sides of the trail *shimmered*, and suddenly they were surrounded by dancing horses with tasseled bridles, shaking green glimmers off their manes. Their riders wore flowing robes with wide green scarves wrapped around their heads. Jilian had been disarmed and put facedown across one of the horses. She was struggling furiously and yelling at the rider to let her go. Her crystal star hung down, glittering in the remnants of the strange green light. Kyarra stared at it, trying to make her befuddled brain understand.

Protection . . . these men might be armed, but they weren't protected from her Songs.

Kyarra drew a deep breath. But before she could hum a note, Jilian twisted her head to stare up the hill and muttered, "I don't believe it! It's a stupid centaur!"

The Song died in Kyarra's throat as a wild-looking woman came cantering down through the rocks on a silver mare, followed by two creatures that were half pony, half human. One of them was pale lilac with a woman's upper body where the pony's neck and head ought to be; the other was black all over with a young man's body and a thick mane of dark hair. All three wore glowing green stones hung from horsehair ropes around their necks. They stamped to a halt before Kyarra and looked down their noses at her.

A handsome young man on a gray horse, his scarf blowing loose to reveal the shadow of a mustache on his upper lip, pointed to Kyarra's dusty blue hair and said, "We seem to have caught ourselves a Singer, Shai!" He leaned forward in his saddle and asked, "Who's your friend, little Singer?"

"The girl's no one," one of Asil's men muttered with a warning glance at Kyarra. "Just a kid we picked up someplace."

Jilian stopped struggling and glared at him. "I'm not no one! I'm Jilian of the Hills! And my father's the famous pirate Asil," she added defiantly. "So you'd better let me go, or he'll kill you all!"

Asil's men groaned. But the man on the gray, who was obviously the leader of the horsemen, smiled. "Is that so? I hadn't heard the pirates had sunk to slave-trading, though it doesn't surprise me." He turned back to Kyarra. "Are you all right, Singer girl? You look a little faint."

"We're thirsty," she whispered.

The handsome young leader nodded. He signaled to one of his men, who brought across a water skin and passed it down to Kyarra. He watched in silence as she poured some down her mother's throat and told her to swallow before drinking herself. The water was warm, but right then she'd have drunk salt water straight from the sea. Jilian had been allowed to sit up, but with her hands still tied behind her. Her captor had taken off her star and was examining it curiously. Jilian's face was set hard, glaring at Kyarra as if she'd planned the whole thing.

"Jilian's thirsty, too," Kyarra said.

The leader waved his man across with the water, but Jilian

spat it out again, making him chuckle. "So the fiery little fighter is Jilian, the famous pirate's daughter. And you're . . .?"

"Kyarra," she said, still not sure whether to trust him.

"Ky-aahra," he repeated, giving it the same pronunciation as Jilian. "And this lady is . . .?" He frowned at the midnight-haired woman who, as usual, appeared totally unconcerned by what was going on around her.

"She doesn't have a name," Kyarra told him. "But she's supposed to be my mother. Singers gave her *Yehn,* which is why she looks like that."

The leader's eyes flashed to her face. His men muttered uncomfortably. The woman he'd called Shai kicked her silver mare closer and jumped down. She walked up to the blank-eyed captive and stared hard into her face. With a choked cry, she suddenly whirled and kicked the air beside the helpless woman's ear.

Kyarra ducked, dragging her mother down beside her. "Stop it!" she shouted. "What did you do that for? You nearly cracked her skull open!"

The wild woman turned away. She mumbled something that made no sense, remounted, and trotted off. The Half Creatures hesitated. Then the lilac centaur pointed to the chain linking the two captives and made a snorting sound in her throat. Before Kyarra could recover her breath, the centaur stallion struck out with a dark fore hoof. There was a *CRACK*, and sparks showered over her hand. She snatched it clear with a little scream and fell sideways. By the time she realized what they'd done, the centaurs were trotting after the woman on the silver mare, and the men were lifting Kyarra on to one horse and her mother on to another, the broken halves of the chain swinging from their wrists. Kyarra struggled, but the man riding behind her held her tightly, and once she realized they weren't going to hurt her mother she gave up the unequal struggle.

Her wounded arm burned. She ceased to care where they

were being taken and drifted into a strange dream in which they rode underwater with the merlee swimming around them. Only instead of fish tails, the merlee had hind legs like a centaur, which they used to kick her mother until blood filled the sea, while Kyarra screamed at them to stop. At least the wild woman stayed well away from them, having disappeared with her Half Creature friends into the hills, where the green light soon began to sparkle again.

They pressed on through the heat of the day at a tireless canter and far into the night, eating and drinking on horseback without slackening their pace. The only time they paused was so the horses could drink at a trickle of dusty water that wound out of the hills. Once their mounts were refreshed and the sun had gone down, they went even faster.

At one point, Kyarra jerked awake to discover they were trotting through a town made up of huts and stalls, where merchants slept rolled in blankets surrounded by dark piles of their goods. There was the smell of water and the silhouettes of ships and boats below. They were crossing a bridge. It was the thud of hooves on the wood that had woken her. They turned along the opposite bank of the river and the huts fell behind. She sank briefly back into her dream. Then they were stopping among low, dark tents, where the green glimmers that had surrounded them for their entire journey faded into the night.

Men came out of the tents with flaming torches and crowded around in a confusion of smoke and billowing robes. "It's the Prince!" they clamored. "Prince Erihan's back!" They unloaded the pony's bundles and carted them off. One of them poked Jilian's leg and laughed when she tried to kick him. Kyarra twisted her head to check on her mother, who was being carried toward one of the tents. The movement made her dizzy and she slipped off the horse into the arms of the man who had ridden behind her. She couldn't see the centaurs or the wild woman anywhere.

"I have to stay with my mother," she protested, making an

effort to clear her head. "You don't understand! She can't look after herself —"

The leader, the man they'd called Prince Erihan, took her by the wrist and pulled her toward the biggest tent. The ground seemed to be lifting up and down, the torches flaring around them. "The Lady Yashra will be well cared for," he said in a firm tone. "I know you're tired, Kyarra, but it's important you tell Father everything you know so he can decide what to do. Then we'll tend your wound and get that manacle off so you can sleep."

"What about Jilian?" Kyarra pulled back weakly, barely registering the name he'd given to her mother. The pirate girl was being taken to another tent, her hands still tied, shouting that Asil would come after them and then they'd be sorry. "You won't hurt her, will you?"

The Prince shook his head. "She's a valuable hostage. Come along, young Singer. My father never sleeps when we're out pirate-hunting. He'll be anxious to meet you."

Kyarra could fight no longer. She could hardly keep her eyes open. Her arm was sore, and she felt hot and dizzy. She didn't think she would ever feel normal again.

The Prince pushed back the flap of the tent and led her into a fog of sweet-smelling smoke. Layers of rugs softened the ground, and flames reflected off gold all around. In the smoke sat an erect old man with piercing black eyes and a scar that divided one wrinkled cheek in two. Across his knees lay a scimitar. At his feet were the bundles Asil's men had hauled up the cliff from the ship, sliced open now, with their contents spilled across the carpets.

Father and son spoke rapidly to each other. Kyarra didn't hear what they said. She was staring at the contents of the sacks. Every one of them was stuffed full of raw, unpolished bluestone cut from the Isle of Echoes. Enough bluestone to supply half the world with Trust-Gifts, which the Singers used to transmit Songs across the sea.

"Why did they steal our bluestone?" she whispered as the tent began to spin gently. Her legs gave way, and she found herself lying with her head on a sack. Though her brain assured her bluestone made a lumpy and uncomfortable pillow, it felt deliciously soft.

The old lord's eyes focused on her. "Erihan!" His words came from a long way off. "The girl's not going to tell us anything in that state. Her arm looks infected. Take her to the women and instruct them to look after her. Meanwhile, we'll gather the tribes. If what you've told me is true, they ought to be here. It's not every day someone comes back from the dead." His next words were soft and troubled, not meant for Kyarra's ears. "If the woman really is Lady Yashra of the Harai, I'm not sure what they're going to think about a girl of their blood being brought up as a Singer. Watch them both carefully, Erihan. If anything happens to the girl or her mother while they're in our camp, it could upset the delicate balance of peace between our tribes."

*

The four days it took the Karchlord's army to trek down the Great South Trade Route were the most frustrating of Night Plume's life. Even riding their shaggy ponies at the fastest pace allowed by the terrain, the humans were so *slow*. Flying, given good weather, Night Plume could have made the journey in less than two days. But every time he thought about leaving the humans behind, he'd imagine arriving back at the Temple with only a handful of arrows in his quiver, and fear of the Starmaker's anger would send him circling back to the dust cloud kicked up by the army, where he sought out the small figure clinging tightly to the mane of the pony the Karchholders had given him to ride. Poor Caell! The boy was obviously suffering, though he kept his mount up at the front with the other members of the Singer party. Singer Renn rode loosely and well, talking quietly with Lord Azri and glancing across from time to time to check Caell hadn't fallen off, while Kherron bullied his pony along beside the dark-skinned Lazim and snapped at everyone.

The green-eyed Singer grew grumpier the longer they rode, and Night Plume was amused to see he was just as stiff as Caell when they stopped to camp.

The nights were the worst, when the Karchholders lit fires and played rowdy games involving handfuls of their death-bones extracted from the ends of their braids. They seemed delighted at the prospect of a real fight and teased Night Plume and Caell, challenging them to guess where the small, bleached finger bones had come from.

"This one here's from my manhood braid!" a grizzled warrior said. "I got the bone off a quetzal carcass, back when the Karch used to trade in Half Creature meat." He laughed at their disgusted expressions and flicked a lock of Caell's blue hair. "Not got your manhood braid yet, boy? Soon will, if the Singers are right about old Frazhin still bein' alive. I'm savin' a place in my hair for his finger! All of us are."

Night Plume ruffled his plumage, uncomfortable among these rough men with their red swords across their knees. The Memoryplace said the Karchlord's men no longer ate quetzal, but he couldn't be sure if these were true memories or false ones left over from the Starmaker's enchantment.

"Frazhin's only got ten fingers," Caell pointed out stiffly. "You can't all have one."

The Karch warrior threw back his head and laughed. "Better make sure you're at the front of the line then, hadn't you, Singer boy? But I hear he hasn't even got ten anymore. Rumor has it those Half Creatures of his ate a few before he tamed 'em! What do you say, quetzal? How many fingers has the old Khiz-devil got left?"

Night Plume hooted. "Starmaker wear crystal gloves and mask, not show flesh."

More laughter. "That sounds like Frazhin, all right! Can't wait to see his face when Lord Azri turns up with the Singers in tow! Bet he's not countin' on *that*."

Night Plume hooted again. He tried to tell the Karchholders

about the Starmaker's quetzal who would protect the Temple with their lives because they were still enchanted, but the men were too busy laughing and gaming with their death-bones to listen.

Every time the army stopped, Singer Renn pulled out his bluestone and went off quietly by himself. Night Plume's head hummed when this happened. Not finding anything in the Memoryplace to explain this, he asked Caell what the Singer was doing.

Caell bit his lip. "He's trying to contact the Isle of Echoes, but the First Singer still isn't answering. Maybe when the ships get there with the physicians and clean water . . ." His expression gave him away. He blinked hard. "Oh, Night Plume! Why did the merlee betray us? They're supposed to be the Singers' friends."

It not merlee's fault, Night Plume said in wild-speech. *Starmaker enchant them.*

"I know," Caell said sadly. "Singer Renn thinks maybe we can free them with our Songs, like Singer Rialle freed you. But it'll take time to find all the corrupted ones, and we haven't got much of that just now." He frowned at Singer Renn, who was still humming to his bluestone. "Why does Frazhin hate us so much, Night Plume? What have we ever done to him?"

"Memoryplace say Starmaker do evil things because of black-stars," Night Plume said slowly, trying to make more sense of the smoky memories the prisoner's Songs had enabled him to see. "When Starmaker put blackstars in our heads with his spear, they hide true quetzal memories in our Memoryplace and replace them with false ones. And when prisoner sing her Songs to me, they restore true memories. So maybe Starmaker forget something from when he fledgling? Or remember something false that make him hate Singers?"

"Forget something?" Caell frowned at him. Suddenly, he froze. "That's it! You said when Frazhin was a boy he came from across the sea, didn't you? What if he was given a Song like Ky's mother? Only when he was younger? Oh, echoes . . . what if he was a *novice* who was turned into an orderly but ran away? That would explain everything! Why Ky has such a good voice, even though her mother's not a Singer, and why Frazhin hates us so much. A lot of boys don't want to be orderlies because it means they have to forget the Songs. Except . . ." His face fell. "Frazhin's supposed to be dark-skinned, and Singers have pale skins. And if he'd had the orderly-Songs, he'd not have run away and done such horrible things . . ." He sighed and shook his head. "Your Memoryplace must mean something else."

Night Plume thought of what the wild flock had said about knowing truths about the Starmaker that even the stone-singers didn't know, but said nothing. It would hardly change anything now, even if the Starmaker did turn out to have been a Singer himself.

To distract himself from thinking too much about what may have happened to Sky Swooper, Night Plume searched for sticks suitable for making arrows. While the Karchholders sharpened their swords and played their death-bone games, he trimmed the sticks and fitted them with flights plucked from his own plumage and flints gathered from the path. Not as good as the arrows Dawn Crest and the other quetzal mothers made back at the nest, maybe, but they'd be better than nothing.

On the third day out from Silvertown, hills began to rise on both sides of the Trade Route, and the Karchholders rode closer together with their hands resting on the hilts of their swords. Night Plume took the bow off his shoulder and fitted an arrow to the string. When he flew high enough, he could see the forest as a dark line on the eastern horizon. The sea was hidden under a gray mist to the west, growing farther away as the Trade Route turned inland and started to climb. The rocks took on a purple tint that deepened as the sun sank toward the western hills. Night Plume shivered with tension as the terrain became more familiar. He flew lower to search the hillside, his shadow rippling over the gullies.

Green light. Here.

He circled the area to be sure, and his plumage prickled.

Caell, he called in wild-speech. *Find place where girl vanish. Nobody here.*

The reply came at once, full of suppressed excitement. *Wait there, Night Plume! We come!*

Night Plume circled the area again. His wings were tired, but he didn't feel safe enough to land. The dust around the area where the girls had vanished was churned up as if many hooves had passed this way since.

Finally, with Caell guiding it to Night Plume's position, the army arrived. Lord Azri and some of his men broke away from the main party and cantered up the hill, warily eyeing the rocks. Most of the men had their swords out. Only the Singers and Caell were unarmed. Their ponies' hooves rattled on the rocks as they pulled up, and one of the Karchholders jumped down to examine the tracks. Kherron dismounted and bent to look as well.

"Horses, Lord," said the Karchholder, putting his finger in some dried dung and lifting it to his nose. "Perhaps nine or ten days old. And a large party of men, more recent. Also . . . He sifted through the dust and straightened with a scarlet feather in his hand. "Looks like a quetzal's to me."

"Let me see that!" Singer Kherron snatched the feather from the Karchholder and scowled at it. He passed his pony's reins to Renn and strode a short way up the slope, shading his eyes against the sun. A stillness came over him.

"Something's going on to the south," he called back down. "Renn, come with me. We need to farlisten." He struggled back into his pony's saddle and urged the animal up the slope. It shied at Night Plume's shadow and Kherron almost fell off. He cursed and shouted up into the sky, "Make yourself useful, quetzal! Fly south and tell us what you see."

Night Plume was still staring at the feather in Kherron's hand. Quetzal . . . yet none of the Starmaker's quetzal could leave the forest boundary. Could it be from a wild one? What if the wild flock had known about the trick with the centaur stones, doubled back and gone after the Starmaker's daughter, still seeking revenge for what the Starmaker had done to their fledglings?

He turned cold. The sun was sinking rapidly and darkness shrouded the hills. Lord Azri's men and Caell were hard to see in the shadows. At the crest of the hill, the two Singers sat their ponies side by side, robes billowing in the breeze and faces turned to the south, utterly still. Night Plume gripped his bow and flew higher. He could hear nothing, see nothing but the amazing colored sky and the shadows flowing through the hills like black water, except . . . was that a glow on the horizon?

See fires to south, he called to Caell in wild-speech, hoping they weren't too late. *Go investigate.*

10
Prophecy

On the south bank at Rivermeet, fires burned like stars where a sea of tents had sprung up since sunset. Banners streamed proudly in the wind, marking the territory of nearly a hundred tribes. In their picket lines, horses snorted and pawed the dust. Rival stallions squealed. Colts and fillies were galloped up and down to show off their paces, while men looked on with narrow eyes and women handed out sticks of spiced meat. A gathering of the Horselords was rare, and horse trading at such times went on far into the night.

But the most important business tonight was taking place in the center of the camp, where Kalerei tents were pitched around their distinctive green banner. Torches had been planted in a circle to illuminate the storytelling area. Within this ring of fire, the two leaders of the most powerful Horselord tribes — Lord Nahar of the Kalerei and Lord Zorahan of the Harai — sat drinking from the same pot of *fohl*. Nearby, the leaders of the other tribes sat warily with their families, watching to see if the peace treaty the Singers had negotiated eleven years ago would hold. The Kalerei Prince, Erihan, sat at the far side of the circle, guarding the bluestone he'd taken from Asil's men. Next to him crouched the wild woman who had been with him in the hills. These people called her Lady Shaiala, though she didn't act much like a lady.

Kyarra leaned against one of the torch posts, hugging her knees and picking at the scab on her arm. She'd spent the past few days feverishly tossing and turning inside a tent, living one nightmare after another, while the Kalerei women held her down, put foul-smelling paste into her wound, and wrapped it in one of their wide scarves that they called sharets. Now that the bandage had been removed, her arm itched like crazy. Flames streamed above her into the night, and every so often a freak draft would billow smoke into her face, making her splutter and cough. But she didn't move because she didn't want anyone to notice she was listening.

Earlier in the evening, Lord Nahar had made her sit in the middle of the circle and tell the Horselords everything that had happened to her since leaving the Isle of Echoes. It had been harder than she anticipated. Her voice kept breaking. She had resorted to Songs, using *Shi* to explain how she'd felt when she'd caught Blackbeard kissing her mother on the ship, and later when her mother's hand had been burned when they were manacled on the beach. *Shi makes you cry*. When she looked up, she'd been surprised to see tears rolling down the hard faces of every Horselord present. Afterward, she'd asked Lord Nahar if she could see Jilian, but the Kalerei Lord said they had important things to discuss first.

Kyarra thought about creeping off to find Jilian herself, but then she wouldn't be able to listen. Her mother sat where she'd been placed — behind Lord Zorahan, staring blankly into the night. Someone had removed her manacle and treated her burns, and the women had washed her hair and dressed her in the tribal style. She looked very beautiful in the torchlight. Kyarra's heart gave a funny little twist. *The Lady Yashra*. It was going to take some getting used to. She knew now that her mother had been born among these people, which made them partly her people as well. Many years ago, her mother had been the leader of the Harai tribe, but she'd done something bad. Something bad enough for *Yehn.* They were about to hear what.

Lord Nahar took another swallow of *fohl,* glanced at Lord Zorahan and climbed to his feet. He cleared his throat. "We've heard the young Singer's tale of how Lady Yashra of the Harai comes to be with us tonight. I myself no longer question her identity, but if anyone has any doubts let them speak now."

A few people muttered. After being prodded by several others, a middle-aged Lord stood up. "I remember Lady Yashra of the Harai! This woman —" He pointed to the silent figure sitting behind Lord Zorahan. "— looks exactly like her, that's true. But eleven years have passed since the Singers took Lady Yashra to their island. Surely she ought to look older by now? I know my favorite wife has a lot more wrinkles today than she had eleven years ago." He yelped as the woman sitting next to him slapped his knee. Several people chuckled.

Lord Nahar held up his hand for quiet. "It's true what our friend says. But Lord Zorahan and I have discussed this matter, and we believe the Song the Singers gave to the Lady Yashra has somehow kept her from aging. They sang her their Death Song. It sent her soul to the Great Sky Plain and left her body here with us. Without the soul, the body cannot age. I do not understand the magic that separates soul from body without killing it, but Singer magic is strong." He glanced in Kyarra's direction, and she ducked her head in alarm as everyone followed his gaze.

"Make the Singer girl give Lady Yashra her soul back!" someone shouted, spotting her blue hair in the smoke. And others called out, "It's not fair!" "Unnatural!" "The poor woman!"

Kyarra clenched her fists. Didn't they understand? She wanted to cure her mother more than anyone. If only she *could* sing Lady Yashra's soul back into her body.

Again, Lord Nahar held up his hand. "Not all of you are aware of what Lady Yashra did to deserve her punishment.

Some of you weren't present at the Dancing Canyons Festival eleven years ago, when Lord Zorahan and I swore beneath the eye of a Singer to keep the peace. I'll leave it to Lord Zorahan to tell this tale, because it concerns the Harai." He sat down again.

Lord Zorahan took his place, looking grave. "Lady Yashra deserved her punishment," he began slowly, sparking off whispers of surprise among the assembly. "She ordered us to enslave the centaurs, who are now our friends. She had hundreds of children snatched from the streets of Southport and Silvertown. They were brought to our palace of black crystal deep in the Mountains of Midnight, where their souls were enslaved by a powerful crystal called the Khiz. We were instructed to make the children wear these crystals at all times, but it wasn't hard. Once they'd spent a night with the Khiz, they were as malleable as Lady Yashra is now." He glanced down at the passive woman who sat at his feet. "We forced the centaurs to use their special kicks to mine more of this evil crystal. Lady Yashra and her lover — a crippled old man named Frazhin who rarely left the tunnels under his palace — used the crystal in secret experiments we knew nothing about. I was there. I carried out her orders. I am ashamed."

He looked around at his audience, as if daring them to contest this, and spread his hands. When he next spoke, his voice was stronger.

"But we know now that the Khiz affected us all, Harai as much as captives. We were surrounded by it. It muddled our thoughts until we were no longer sure what we were doing. I'm not saying Harai history has been admirable, and I know many of you believe it's in our blood to carry out such evil deeds. But Lady Yashra wore a mask of that same crystal, so who can say what evil it worked on her? For this reason, the Harai will take her back into our tribe and care for her as if she were a small child. It is our penance for carrying out her orders eleven years ago and ruining the lives of so many children and centaurs." His gaze picked out Lady Shaiala, whose dark glare had been fixed on him while he spoke, and something passed between them before the Lord of the Harai sat down.

In the silence that followed his words, Kyarra discovered blood on her palms where her nails had pierced the skin. She slowly unclenched her fists. *Black crystal.* Like the stars Jilian and Asil and his men had worn to protect them from her Songs. With a shiver, she glanced across the Kalerei camp at the tent where the girl was being kept.

As if reading her thoughts, Prince Erihan stood and held up the crystal star Jilian had been wearing when she was captured. Swinging from its frayed thong, it glittered darkly in the torchlight.

Lord Zorahan leaped to his feet again with a hiss. "Where did you get that?" he demanded.

The other Horselords stiffened. Several hands moved to their scimitars.

Lord Nahar raised his arms, empty-handed, dispelling some of the tension. "You all know of my son's pledge to put an end to the pirates who prey on the Great South Trade Route and the coastal shipping route between Southport and Silvertown," he said. "When Prince Erihan rescued the young Singer and Lady Yashra from the hills, he also managed to capture the daughter of Asil, the pirate leader. I have her safe in my camp. She was wearing the black star when we found her."

People jumped to their feet. "Are you crazy, Nahar?" an old Lord shouted from the back. "Asil will be furious! It won't take him long to work out who's taken her. You've effectively killed the next caravan that heads up the Great South Trade Route!"

Lord Nahar waited until the protests died away and said, "I've plans for the girl. When the time comes, we'll use her as bait in a trap to catch her father. But first, my son Prince Erihan has something else to tell you . . ."

His words were drowned out by more excited shouts as people who had lost goods and horses to the pirates speculated what they'd do to Asil when they got their hands on him. Several Horselords pledged men to the venture. Kyarra listened in growing horror. They didn't seem to care about what happened to Jilian.

But Lord Zorahan, who had been examining the dark crystal star, said, "We shouldn't be too hasty to send our warriors into those hills. This is the same crystal the centaurs mined in the Mountains of Midnight. We'd do better finding out *why* the girl was wearing it. Where is she, Nahar?"

Lord Nahar shook his head. "Safe. I've already questioned her. She knows nothing about the crystal."

"Are you sure?" Lord Zorahan's tone was dark.

"She says only that her father's men were given the stars by the Lord of the Forest to protect them from the Singers' magic when they went to the island to capture Lady Yashra and her daughter. It makes sense."

"The *Lord of the Forest*?" Zorahan said. "I don't like the sound of this at all. Bring the girl here, Nahar! This could be important. You weren't in the Mountains of Midnight as long as the Harai were. You don't know what filthy things Frazhin got up to in his tunnels."

"Neither do you," Lord Nahar reminded him. "Or so you keep telling us. Is it possible you know more than you're telling?"

The two Horselords glared at each other, hands hovering over their scimitars. Again, tension rippled through the assembly. The treaty flask of *fohl* lay forgotten at their feet with its two hollow reeds still sticking out of it. Not wanting to see the leader of her mother's people hurt, Kyarra hummed calming *Challa* under her breath.

With visible effort, Lord Zorahan moved his hand away from his weapon and said through gritted teeth, "I told you everything back when the Treaty was agreed between us. Singers have the gift of listening for truth. They would have known if I had lied."

"I'm not accusing you of lying, Zorahan," Nahar said sooth-ingly. "I'm just wondering if maybe you didn't remember every-thing clearly at the time. After all, you admit this khiz-crystal muddled your thoughts. If you know anything else, you should tell us now for the good of all the tribes."

Lord Zorahan inclined his head. "For the good of the tribes, I'm saying any sample of this crystal, however small, should be investigated. This isn't the time to go looking for a fight in the Hills. If Asil comes here looking for his daughter, fair enough, we'll fight. Otherwise, I say we should wait until we know more about this so-called *Lord of the Forest*." He sat down firmly.

There were a few mutters of agreement. Those who had pledged themselves to go with the Kalerei looked at Lord Nahar to see how he would answer this challenge.

Nahar smiled, his scar unfolding like a fan. "I said only that I've got plans, not when I intend to put them into action. I, too, think we should discover more about this Lord of the Forest and where he got the crystal from, before we set our trap for Asil. And now I think you ought to hear what my son has to say. Erihan?"

The young Prince rose softly to his feet and beckoned to someone standing in the shadows at the edge of the circle. A man walked into the torchlight, where he stopped and waited until everyone was quiet. He was naked except for a short skirt of plaited leaves and feathers, though he'd painted his glossy black skin with bright whorls and patterns that glowed in the torchlight. His head was shiny with no hair at all. He watched the assembly from large, brown eyes, so absolutely still that he might have been carved from rock. One by one, the gazes of the Horselords and their families settled on the newcomer. Women giggled. Men frowned. Whispers passed around the torchlit cir-cle. "Where did *he* come from?" "What's that stuff on his skin?" "Is he a demon?" "No, silly, he's from the forest. I've seen men like him in Rivermeet. They bring plants and potions to trade, miracle cures and such nonsense. Shh!"

Kyarra sat up straighter, her heart beating fast. *Miracle cures?*
Had the painted stranger brought something from the forest
that might help cure her mother?

Prince Erihan reached out a hand to draw the painted man
closer. "This is Speaks Many Tongues," he said. "His people
have lived beside the Red River in the Quetzal Forest for many
generations. He agreed to come here tonight because of something I saw after we found Lady Yashra and the two girls."

Kyarra leaned forward, hoping for more about the miracle
cures, but Erihan began by telling everyone what had happened
in the hills. Kyarra must have been the only person no longer
listening. She was too busy working out a way to get close
enough to ask the painted man if he had any potions that could
reverse the effects of a Song as powerful as *Yehn.*

Then Erihan extracted something from one of the sacks of
bluestone, and her attention jerked back. There were angry
mutters as people realized the Prince was holding a black-feathered arrow, and for a horrible moment Kyarra was back in the
forest with the quetzal whistling and diving at her, running
through the trees as their arrows thudded down . . .

"The pirate's men seized the chance to escape," Erihan went
on. "We let them go, thinking it wiser to get out of the hills
before Asil's entire band could attack us. Only the arrows
weren't coming from a human enemy as we'd thought, but from
the bird that had flown over us earlier. Except it wasn't a bird,
of course. It was a quetzal. A *black* quetzal with plumage as dark
as the flight on this arrow." He held the arrow aloft for all to see.
"We gave the quetzal the slip when we entered the centaurs'
bent light, which confused the poor creature no end."

There were a few chuckles. Erihan waited for them to die
down before he drew the painted stranger forward. "The forest
people have a prophecy about the dark quetzal, which I think
you should hear."

The painted man stood alone in front of a hundred staring
Horselords. The whorls on his skin glowed in the light of the

torches as he looked round at his audience, searching the faces. Kyarra thought she knew how he felt. But he wasn't nervous as she had been. He spoke in a high, rapid voice like a bird's.

"I am called Speaks Many Tongues! This is only one of the tongues I speak. In the forest, my people speak in other ways. The Prophecy of the Dark Quetzal comes from our interpretation of the quetzal Memoryplace. I repeat in your tongue what our holy man, the Xiancotl says when he chews the Yellow Flowers and enters the Memory Trance."

The painted man raised both hands to his skull with its spirals of red and ochre and clutched at his head. When he next spoke, his voice was deeper and he stared straight ahead.

"When the dark quetzal flies above the Forest and across the Misty Sea, then will come a time of reckoning. The sun will vanish behind clouds thick as night, the ground will flow like a river, and fires will burn in the green places. The air and water will become poison and all living things will choke upon it. Half Creature will fight against Half Creature, and Man against Man. Black stars will rule in the darkness, and the buried truth will be known. This I have seen in the Memory Trance. So it will be."

He removed his hands from his skull and continued his study of the openmouthed Horselords, his brown eyes roving slowly around the circle until they found Kyarra, where they rested a moment before moving on. She shivered. The painted man smiled to himself. Before anyone thought to stop him, he walked between the torches and set off across the camp, vanishing into the shadows as he rubbed the paint off his skin with a dark hand.

There was an uproar behind him as people jumped to their feet, demanding to know what he meant and what business he had to come into the Horselord camp and frighten their children with his crazy forest stories. Everyone was so busy arguing about the painted man and his prophecy, no one noticed when the first scarlet-and-gold arrow thudded out of the sky. Then more arrows rained out of the darkness, and people began to run in all directions. "They're attacking the camp!" they cried. "That stupid story of his must have been a Kalerei trick! Where'd he go? Get him back here!"

"No!" Prince Erihan shouted. "Those are quetzal arrows, not the forest people's! Get out of the light so they can't see you. KALEREI, TO ME!"

He and Lady Shaiala raced off toward the horselines, while behind them Lord Nahar bellowed for calm at the top of his voice. But the other Horselords weren't listening. More arguments broke out. Someone kicked over the treaty flask, and two hot-blooded young lords started a duel. Lord Zorahan was the only person who didn't seem surprised. He sent some of the Harai to escort Lady Yashra and the women and children back to the tents, and looked around at the fighting with a sigh. "Told you so, didn't I?" Kyarra heard him mutter to one of his tribe. "Wherever that black crystal turns up, you can be sure there's trouble close behind."

Kyarra edged away from the torchlight and the angry Horselords, who seemed as ready to fight one another as the threat from the sky. In all the confusion, it was easy to evade the Harai who had been sent to take her to safety. The painted man had passed so close to her, her neck hairs were still standing on end. She couldn't see where he had gone. But *listening* like a Singer and thinking of curing her mother, she followed the soft sound of his footfalls through the night.

Quetzal who fired arrows from the sky . . . dark crystal with the power to muddle thought . . . strange prophecies of doom . . . her mother's soul banished to the Great Sky Plain . . . her mother in the hands of the Harai who were her people and would care for her but who had done terrible deeds . . .

Everything spun in her head, twisting and tangling until she could barely think. But one thing blazed clear. Kyarra had to find the painted man and discover more about his miracle cures before he vanished back into the forest.

11

BATTLE

Night Plume hesitated as he approached the fires. They illuminated a large human camp beside a wide river with a town and a bridge nearby. The Singers and the Karchlord's army would take half the night to reach the bridge, even if they rode as fast as they could. By then, the quetzal he'd been following would be long gone. He gained height and set his wings in a glide, bow at the ready, every feather prickling.

As he neared the river, noises came to him on the night breeze — shouts, screams, hoof beats, and the clash of metal. Humans on horseback galloped along the bank with their dark robes billowing out behind them, shouting and brandishing scimitars. Other humans were scrambling out of the water to fight them, apparently having swam across the river in the dark. The bridge farther upstream was guarded by mounted men, though there was fighting in the town beyond and smoke coiled up from the roofs. Loose horses galloped in panic through the tents, shying at the fires. Night Plume thought he saw a centaur in the distance, its blue tail streaming across the plain as it fled.

Some of the quetzal followed it, but they were too far away for him to see if they carried weapons.

The centaur disappeared in a glimmer of green light. The pursuing quetzal whistled in frustration and circled the area before returning to the battle. Directly below Night Plume, a man with a crimson-and-black scarf blowing around his shoulders sliced his scimitar across the neck of a man wearing a green scarf. The victim thudded backward off his horse, which scented Night Plume and fled. The human with the crimson scarf warbled like a forest creature and whirled his scimitar above his head, sending fiery glitters through the night.

"Harai! Harai! Harai!"

His war cry cut off as the moon came out from behind a cloud. His eyes met Night Plume's and he froze. "Dark quetzal!" he yelled, pointing at the sky with his scimitar. "It's the dark quetzal!"

Heads turned. Horses splashed into the river and swam toward him, their riders staring upward, trying to pick out Night Plume in the dark. Heart beating fast, Night Plume wheeled away. Most of the quetzal were on the opposite side of the river above the human camp, their plumage glowing in the light of the flames as yet more tents caught fire and blazed into the night. But, alerted by the shouting, a small group detached themselves from the main flock and flew straight toward him.

He stiffened. There was no question of it now. They carried bows, and every feathered back bore a full quiver. As he hesitated, wondering if it would be safer after all to head back into the hills and wait for the Singers, the moon came out again, bathing the scarlet-and-gold quetzal in the lead.

Relief flooded through him. He changed direction and flew to meet his old patrol. "Sun Glimmer!" he whistled. "How you escape forest —?"

The arrow came swiftly and silently out of the night. The first Night Plume knew about it was a fierce pain in his left wing, just below his shoulder. He flapped desperately with his other wing. Then he was falling. Stars whirled. The dark hillside came rushing up to meet him.

The ground hit him like an enormous version of the Starmaker's spear, knocking all the breath out of his body. Pain shot up his left arm. He rolled down the slope and came to rest against a rock. Air would not come. The fighting continued across the river, faint and far away. He lay motionless, afraid to move. His bow was still in his fist, though most of his arrows had fallen out of his quiver when he'd crashed, and were scattered across the slope. He didn't seem able to use his left hand. There was a peculiar ringing in his ears.

The quetzal dropped out of the sky and landed around him in a circle, the overexcited youngsters beating their wings and whistling. Sun Glimmer hooted and two of them took off again. They headed back toward the river, where the fighting was fiercest. Sun Glimmer raised his bow and aimed a second scarlet arrow at Night Plume's heart.

Night Plume stared at his nestmate in pain and confusion. "Sun Glimmer?" he whispered. "It me, Night Plume!"

Maybe he hadn't recognized him in the dark? He might have thought he was one of the wild flock and shot him by mistake. The hope died as Sun Glimmer opened his beak and hooted, "I know it you, Night Plume! Starmaker say disable you and bring you back to Temple. Starmaker very, very angry. You stay here, not try escape. Men come soon, take you back."

"But —" Night Plume tried to fold his injured wing. It would not bend. The arrow protruded from it like a half-plucked feather, dripping blood. His left arm hung uselessly at his side. He looked at the ring of arrows aimed at him and turned cold. "What you do here, Sun Glimmer? Why fight humans? How leave forest?"

Sun Glimmer lowered his bow slightly. The rest of the flock watched in silence.

"Starmaker send us," Sun Glimmer said. "He put new

memories in our heads with enchantment spear, every quetzal and every naga and every merlee. He say go out of forest and find human fledgling girls. Find both fledgling girls, then kill men who take them. We fly with humans-from-hills to camp. Memoryplace not have blackstars anymore. See enemies, many enemies, more than leaves on trees. That why Starmaker not let us see beyond edge of forest before. We not ready at first, but we ready now. We strong, we good archers, we kill all Starmaker's enemies!" He lifted the bow again, seemed to struggle with something, then shook his head. "Can't fight enchantment," he whispered.

Night Plume stared at the scarlet-and-gold quetzal. He hardly dared ask. "Did you —? Did —? What happen to Sky Swooper?"

Sun Glimmer hooted, softer than before. "Sky Swooper fly no more. I try to help her, like you say, but Starmaker touch me with spear. Enchantment too strong." Another soft hoot. "I sorry. Starmaker say not to store in Memoryplace what he do to Sky Swooper."

Night Plume's beak opened, and out poured the sadness-song he'd heard the prisoner sing back in the Temple. He closed his eyes and imagined Sky Swooper's beautiful blue wings mutilated like Dawn Crest's. Never again would they ride the thermals together above the forest canopy, joyful and free. His fist tightened on his bow. He tried to lift his wounded wing and pain surged over him. "Hurts," he whispered. "Hurts, Sun Glimmer . . . not your enemy. Please."

One of the youngsters hooted a question. "Quiet," Sun Glimmer said. "Wait for men-from-hills to take Night Plume to Starmaker. Then you can go kill more enemies."

Night Plume started to shake. Sun Glimmer. His friend and nestmate — enchanted by blackstars. Sky Swooper — crippled for life.

Tears filled his eyes. He blinked them away. He gripped the arrow sticking out of his wing, shut his eyes and snapped off the shaft. Pain washed over him, making him feel sick. He huddled

as small as he could, unable to look at the quetzal who used to
be his friends.

Caell, he sent in wild-speech. *Need help. Hurry!*

*

Kyarra was listening so hard to the faint sounds of the painted
man creeping through the camp, she hardly registered where
she was going. The noise of the battle, the arrows that fell from
the sky, and the Horselords who galloped past her in the dark,
were like part of another world. When she tripped over a picket
stake driven into the ground beside one of the tents, it snatched
her back to reality with a disorientating jerk.

She rubbed her shin and scowled at the stake. A taut hobble-
rope ran from it, under the side of the tent, and emerged from
the other side, where it was secured to a second picket. With a
flicker of guilt, she recognized Jilian's prison. The Kalerei guard
at the entrance was staring across the camp at the circle of
torchlight where the Horselords could still be seen waving their
scimitars at the sky. Their shouts carried through the night,
along with the clash of blades.

She closed her eyes, trying for the footfalls again. But her concentration had been broken and the last traces of the painted
man had gone. In their place, she heard a muffled sniff from
inside the tent, like someone crying but trying to hide it. At
once, she felt bad. She'd forgotten how scared Jilian must be.

Pushing her mother's cure to the back of her mind, she
marched boldly up to the guard.

"I want to see the hostage!" She added an undercurrent of
Aushan to make him listen.

He whirled so fast, her heart had barely started to bang before
his scimitar was out of its sheath and glinting at her throat.

"You!" he said in relief, lowering his weapon. "You're supposed to be safe in the women's tent. What's going on? Who's
attacking us? Where's Prince Erihan?"

"He's busy," Kyarra said, fighting to keep her voice steady. "He
sent me to look after Jilian. I'm supposed to question her about

the crystal stars. He said you should go and help the others fight."

The guard's eyes narrowed. "And leave you alone with the pirate's daughter?" he said, looking doubtful.

Kyarra raised her chin. "Yes!"

The man frowned at her, then shook his head. "You don't fool me, little Singer! I've strict orders not to let you two be alone together. Go back to your tent, there's a good girl. Things can get nasty when there's fighting among the tribes, people get hurt —" He broke off as a large winged shadow whispered overhead, blotting out the stars. "What was *that*?"

Though her whole body broke out in goose bumps, Kyarra resisted an urge to duck. "Can I go in and see Jilian. Please? The Prince thinks she'll talk to me because we're friends . . . sort of."

The guard glanced across the camp again, unsure. "You're wasting your time. She won't tell you anything. The little wildcat's not stopped kicking and biting people since the Prince brought her in. Questions only make her worse. Sorry, Singer girl, it's more than my life's worth to let you in there. If either of you get hurt, Lord Nahar will feed my bones to his horse."

Kyarra hummed more *Aushan*. *Aushan makes you scream.* "Lord Nahar'll feed your bones to his horse if you *don't* let me in!" Still singing, she sidled toward the flap.

"Hey! Where do you think you're going?" The man made a grab for her, but she sang louder and ducked past him as he gripped his head in confusion.

Kyarra was wondering how she was going to get Jilian out of the tent and find the painted man again before the guard recovered and came after them, when another quetzal flew overhead and an arrow thudded into the dust not two paces away. Kyarra dived into the tent. The guard, already confused by her Song, let out a yell and took off across the camp, screaming "Demon! We're being attacked by demons!"

Kyarra let the *Aushan* stop mid-note. Crouched in the gloom, she called in a whisper, "Jilian?"

There was a little cry, and a dark shape flung itself at her. "Get out of here! I don't want to talk to you! I heard what you said to the guard about trickin' stuff out of me, and I'm tellin' you now, it won't work!"

Kyarra scrambled backward in alarm. "No one sent me, you idiot! I just told the guard that so he'd let me in here." She looked anxiously at the entrance. "I don't know how long he'll be gone, so we'd better move fast. And there are quetzal outside, so keep as quiet as you can."

As her eyes adjusted, she made out a tangle of hair, bare legs, and — around the girl's left ankle — one of the manacles the Kalerei had removed from their wrists. Probably Yashra's because mine wouldn't fit, said one part of her mind, as she realized what the pickets outside were for. A rope was twisted through the loop on the manacle and stretched across the tent so the girl couldn't reach the knots on either side. In the absence of anything sharper, she'd been chewing the rope in an attempt to free herself, but it was thick and her teeth hadn't made much impression on it. Kyarra remembered the crying.

"Jilian?" she whispered again. "Are you all right?"

"Do I look all right?" The girl tugged furiously at the rope. "They hobble me in here like one of their horses and take away my boots. Then they keep comin' in here with food and expectin' me to tell them where Father's cave is, like I'm some stupid baby ruled by my stomach! They can starve me all they like, I'm not goin' to tell them nothin'! And when I get my dagger back, they'd better watch out!"

"They're starving you?" Kyarra looked around the tent in horror. A jug of water lay within Jilian's reach, but a goblet and plate were upside down near the entrance. So was a bruised fruit.

Jilian saw her looking and colored. "I have to throw *somethin'* at them, don't I?" she said. "So, are you goin' to get me out, or what? You left it long enough to come in here."

"They wouldn't let me see you."

"Huh! Didn't hear you tryin' very hard."

"My arm got infected. I had a fever for days. Then they called this big meeting and they wanted me there. This is the first chance I've had to slip away. The camp's under attack. You can probably get away in the confusion, but watch out for the quetzal arrows — they must have followed us here from the forest." Kyarra pulled at one of the ropes. It wouldn't budge.

"Don't you think I've tried that?" Jilian said bitterly. "Go outside and bash the stakes loose, if you really mean to help."

"Don't talk so loud," Kyarra whispered, glancing anxiously at the tent flap as a shadow ran past outside. "Wait here." She snatched up the jug and ducked out.

Jilian's hard-edged laughter followed. "Where do you think I'm goin' to go?"

The battle seemed to have moved downstream of the camp, where horses were galloping up and down in the dark while their riders brandished scimitars. Everyone else was rushing that way to join in, leaving the area around Jilian's prison shadowy and deserted. There was no sign of the guard or the quetzal. Calming her breathing, Kyarra crouched by one of the stakes and gave it a hard clout with the jug. The jug acquired a dent and most of its water slopped out. The stake didn't move. She swore under her breath and hit it again, making another dent in the jug. As she hit it a third time, a hand descended on her shoulder.

Her heart missed a beat. She spun round, jug raised, expecting to see the guard, and found herself staring into the amused dark face of a smaller version of the forest man she'd been following. He was tying a little pouch of red pollen back around his waist. He pointed to a man lying on the ground nearby and mimed singing. With a start, Kyarra recognized the Kalerei guard. Red dust around his nose showed how the boy must have put him to sleep.

As her heart slowed and her brain caught up, the boy grinned at her, put a finger to his lips and showed her the mallet in his other hand. Not stopping to ask questions, she crouched beside the guard and hummed *Challa* into his ear to keep him asleep, while the boy worked on the stake. She didn't understand why he was helping to free Jilian, but she wasn't going to let him vanish as the painted man had done.

The boy gave the stake two blows with the mallet, wriggled it loose and pulled off the rope, then ran silently round to the other side and repeated the process. A moment later, Jilian emerged with a big grin on her face. She lifted an eyebrow when she saw the boy, but didn't stop to ask questions, either. The first thing she did was hurry to the sleeping guard and retrieve her blue-handled dagger. She was starting to unbuckle his scimitar when they heard shouts coming closer. The boy pulled Jilian away from the unconscious man and pointed to the river upstream of the battle. She looked as if she would argue. Then she cast a glance at the approaching Horselords, grinned, and stuck the dagger through her belt so she could run after the boy. Kyarra hurried after them, glancing anxiously over her shoulder. She couldn't tell which way the quetzal had gone. She hoped her mother was safe.

They followed the boy from shadow to shadow. It seemed to take forever to work their way around all the fires, crawling through the legs of surprised horses and freezing whenever an armed man raced past. But the boy seemed to have an uncanny sense of when it was safe to move on. The whole way across the camp no one noticed them, and not a single arrow fell near them. Kyarra began to hope that in all the confusion the Kalerei wouldn't discover Jilian had escaped. But as they neared the edge of the tents, they heard the shout they'd been dreading.

"The girl's gone! Find her!"

Jilian's hand dropped to her dagger. Kyarra's heart began to thud again. The Purple Plains lay to their right, wide and open under the stars, and somewhere above them in the dark were the quetzal and their lethal arrows. Their guide pointed to the river, where the water slid blackly under the bridge at Rivermeet. Horselords were already on the bridge, the hooves of their mounts thudding on the wood as they formed a blockade. Smoke rose from the roofs of the town, where knots of men were fighting in the streets.

Kyarra turned to Jilian and whispered, "They're not after me. I'll try to distract them. If you can get across the bridge, you might have a chance —"

The boy's hand went across her mouth. He shook his head and pointed again to the shadows below the bridge. With a glimmer of renewed hope, Kyarra recognized the painted man standing like a statue and staring straight at them. He smiled and beckoned to her. Silent as a snake, the boy slid on his belly into the reeds and held up his hand, watching the horses above him. He was so still that she doubted the riders would have seen him even if they'd looked straight at him. He waited like that for what seemed an interminable age. Then his hand descended sharply.

The two girls ran for the bank, bent double, backs prickling. The boy pulled them into the reeds beside him, and the next thing they knew they were sliding down the bank toward a dark square that floated on the water. Kyarra hit wood, which shifted under her. A raft. She found herself lying across a pair of black feet and looked up at the smudged, recently painted legs of Speaks Many Tongues.

"Please, you have to tell me!" she gasped. "Is it true you know miracle —?"

"Not here." He pushed her back down and lowered broad leaves over her and Jilian. Peeping between the leaves, Kyarra saw him motion to the other men on the raft. She made out four of them, kneeling at the corners, their unpainted skins blending into the night. They dug their paddles silently into the water, and the raft made its slow way upstream from the torchlit bridge while the noise of the battle faded behind them.

She wasn't sure how long they lay under the leaves, facedown, while their hearts slowed and their sweat dried. Whenever they tried to get up, Speaks Many Tongues pushed them down again with a whispered, "Not yet." At first, there was an open plain beside the river, with the occasional rider galloping past unseen in the night. But at some point, the river entered a dense line of trees, which grew darker and thicker with every stroke of the paddles. Soon there was no avoiding where they were.

The scar on Kyarra's arm throbbed in memory. She pressed her cheek to the rough wood and closed her eyes. She might have found the painted man, but her mother was back in the Harai camp and every paddle stroke was taking her farther away, deeper into the forest, the last place she wanted to be.

12
WOUNDS

When Night Plume next became aware of his surroundings, the eastern horizon was streaked with red and someone was singing.

He jerked awake, knocked his wounded wing against a rock, and hooted in pain and memory. Sun Glimmer and the others were airborne, fleeing along the first red rays of the sun. A sweaty black pony stood in front of Night Plume, its sides heaving, rolling its eyes at the sky. Astride the pony, singing as loudly as he could, was a small, dusty figure who wore a blue stone around his neck.

"Caell!" Night Plume whispered in relief.

The hillside was strewn with bodies — humans, horses, even a few centaurs. More bodies floated facedown in the river. Men in dark robes with colored scarves wrapped over their noses were fishing these out, while others kept a wary watch with drawn scimitars. The town by the bridge was a smoking ruin. Shivering, subdued people wandered up and down the streets or huddled together on the riverbank. A few of the tents on the other side of the river had escaped unscathed, but most were skeletons, their hide covering burned away. Tattered banners trailed from poles that had been knocked askew. Exhausted horses were being led back to the picket lines by equally weary humans.

The ground vibrated as a group of the Karchlord's men galloped up to the boy, death-braids bouncing on their backs and their red swords burning in the dawn. They pulled up and brandished their swords after the fleeing quetzal. "Get off with you!" they shouted. "That's it, Singer boy! Let 'em have it!"

At last, the terrible Song stopped. Night Plume's ears rang with the sudden silence. Caell dismounted and bent to examine Night Plume's injured arm and wing. "Hang on, Night Plume, we'll help you now," he said in a hoarse voice. "Singer Renn and Singer Kherron are down in the camp. They were too late to stop the fighting, but they managed to calm things down before the Horselords completely massacred one another. The Karchholders were pretty mad about missing the battle, I can tell you!"

Night Plume shut his eyes. *You find your girl?*

Caell's face closed. "No. Ky's not here. The Horselords did have her, apparently, and another girl they'd taken as hostage, but both of them disappeared during the fighting. No one knows where. The Kalerei and the Harai are at one another's throats, and none of the Horselords are ready to trust anyone else, least of all Lord Azri and his Karchholders. Apparently, the Karch attacked the Horselords once. It was years and years ago, but everyone around here has a memory longer than a quetzal's — no offense!" Caell glanced over his shoulder at the waiting Karchholders. "Don't worry, though," he added. "Singer Renn and Singer Kherron have called a meeting with all the leaders of the Horselord tribes, and Lord Azri's in there as well. They'll work it out, you'll see. You wouldn't believe some of the stories going around down there! Magic arrows, poisoned treaty flasks, a painted man who was supposed to have hypnotized the whole camp, quetzal so numerous they darkened the sky . . ."

Night Plume hooted sadly. *Quetzal enchanted by blackstars.*

"I know." Caell's face fell again. "They hurt you, didn't they?" *They not my friends anymore.*

"I'm your friend," Caell said firmly, taking hold of Night Plume's good hand. "We have to get you to the camp. I don't suppose you can ride?" He looked at the pony's rolling eyes. "No, maybe not a good idea, you don't look like you'd survive another fall, even a small one from Blackie's back."

Night Plume looked around for his bow. There. He bent, awkwardly because of his injured wing, and picked it up.

Caell frowned. "You won't need it, Night Plume. No one's going to hurt you. You'll be safe in the Horselord camp. Lord Azri's men will protect you, and so will Singer Renn and Singer Kherron when they've finished talking to the Horselord leaders."

Night Plume clamped his beak tight to stop the pain and reached over his shoulder for the last arrow in his quiver. The Karchholders stiffened.

"This for Starmaker," Night Plume said, showing them the arrow. He didn't need to look in the Memoryplace to feel Sky Swooper's pain. His words emerged hard-edged and rough, like the shattered place in his heart.

There was some consternation when they arrived in what was left of the Horselord camp. News of the forest people's prophecy about the dark quetzal had spread, and everyone seemed ready to blame Night Plume for the battle. They scowled at the arrow clenched in his black-feathered fist. Then they saw the way his left wing dragged in the dust and their expressions changed to pity. He was taken to a tent where Horselord women were tending the wounded. One of them put his arm in a sling and shook her head at the damage to his wing. She washed the wound and smeared it with ointment, making the feathers sticky.

"The arm will mend, but this one won't be flying again for a long time," the woman said to Caell. "Better get him away from here before someone decides to finish the job."

There were mutters of agreement from the wounded lying on mats at their feet. Caell rested his hand on Night Plume's shoulder and hummed gently. *No one's going to hurt you. Shh, calm, sleep.*

Night Plume pushed his way out of the tent. It was small and crowded and smelled of creatures in pain. As soon as he was in the open, his good wing lifted by instinct. He made himself fold it again. He'd have to get used to walking on the ground like a human.

"Not sing enchantment songs for me," he said. "I stay awake, kill Starmaker for what he do to Sky Swooper."

Caell smiled sadly and glanced at the tent where the two Singers were still in deep discussion with the Horselord leaders and Lord Azri. Near its entrance, Karchholders and members of the various Horselord tribes paced up and down, eyeing one another distrustfully. The pentad leader, Lazim, was inside the tent as well, though the other four Echorium bodyguards waited outside with their swords resting across their knees. They told Caell not to wander off, because Singer Kherron wanted to make a start for the forest as soon as possible.

Caell scowled. "They'll be ages yet," he said, yawning. "They've captured the pirate who took Ky, and they still have to interrogate him. Truth listening always takes forever to do properly, and I bet he won't talk. C'mon, Night Plume, let's go find something to eat. I'm starving after all that singing!"

They didn't have far to search for food. Fighting gave men an appetite, and once the wounded were safely in the hands of the women and the dead piled on pyres ready for burning, the men turned their attention to breakfast. Caell collected two beakers of warm mare's milk, some freshly baked bread and dried fruit from one of the fires, and brought the food across to Night Plume. They settled down to listen with the orderlies near the entrance of the Singers' tent.

It seemed the Kalerei Prince's wife, Lady Shaiala, had disappeared at the same time as Kyarra and Asil's daughter, together with the painted man who had predicted the trouble the dark quetzal would bring, and who had therefore been indirectly responsible for Night Plume's hostile reception. It wasn't certain where they had gone. Singer Kherron insisted that the missing girls had been taken into the forest against their will; Singer Renn said they might have escaped to the Purple Plains with the centaur herd; Prince Erihan said no one could make his wife go anywhere against her will, and anyway she'd never be separated from her centaur friends. A few of the people inside the tent still insisted Night Plume had been responsible for the battle, saying that the forest people's prophecy had obviously been invalidated when he'd been wounded. Most, however, took Singer Kherron's view — that prophecies were nonsense, and that if anyone had the power to shatter the peace treaty between the Kalerei and the Harai, it was Frazhin.

Eventually, the pirate leader Asil was escorted out between two Horselords, looking pale but walking with a proud step and glaring straight ahead. Finally, the two gray-robed Singers emerged from the tent with the leaders of the tribes and transferred themselves to the blackened story circle where the trouble had started. There, in the light of the new day and in an unprecedented act of cooperation, the Karchlord and the leaders of the Horselord tribes drank a treaty flask of *fohl* and swore in front of the Second Singer of the Echorium to fight on the same side until their common enemy Frazhin was dead.

The morning breeze ruffled Night Plume's feathers and he shivered as he recalled Sun Glimmer's words. *Many, many enemies.* His nestmate hadn't been exaggerating. All around him, men and horses covered the plain like the leaves of the forest.

But they did not ride to war immediately. Singer Kherron turned to Lord Zorahan of the Harai and said, "There's one more thing to take care of before we leave. We need to see the woman."

Uneasy mutters rippled through the assembly. Singer Renn put a hand on Kherron's arm and whispered something. Kherron shook him off, a stubborn glint in his green eyes.

Lord Zorahan nodded to one of his men, and a few moments later the crowd parted to allow him back into the circle gently leading a woman by the hand. Night Plume hooted in sympathy. She was unusually attractive for a human, with long midnight hair and smooth, pale skin. But her eyes stared like a dead creature's, and she did not react when Singer Kherron examined her as if she were a beast at market, lifting her arms and peering into her mouth.

"It's Ky's mother!" Caell breathed, sitting forward, his gaze fixed on the woman. "I saw her when the pirates were taking her and Ky to the ship. Now I know why they didn't have to knock her out like they did Ky. Look at her, she's like a little child."

"No child I've seen ever looked like that!" one of the Harai muttered darkly beside them. "I hope you're proud of what you did to her, Singer boy."

"Shh!" another man said. "It's not the boy's fault. He could not have sung to her, could he? He's too young."

Night Plume glanced at Caell. But the boy was far too engrossed in what was happening within the circle to worry about what the Harai thought. Night Plume looked at the woman, uncomfortable. The Memoryplace had nothing like this . . . except maybe there *was* something, very deep and faint, a memory previously hidden by the Starmaker's blackstars — a human with dark skin, who chewed Yellow Flowers . . .

"We'll take her with us," Kherron decided, before Night Plume could chase the elusive memory. "Frazhin obviously wants her with him, or he wouldn't have gone to all the trouble of having his pirate friends kidnap her from the Isle. We might be able to trade her for Singer Rialle."

"No!" Lord Zorahan was on his feet, glaring at the old Singer. "I forbid it! The Lady Yashra has suffered enough."

"Lady Yashra suffers nothing," Kherron said. "She's had *Yehn*, which takes away all feeling. I agree it's unusual for someone's body to live on for so long afterward, but in this case she has had unusually vigilant caretakers. Don't worry, we'll keep her alive until we meet Frazhin. What he does with her after that is up to him."

Singer Renn was whispering to Kherron again, using the soft words Night Plume could not overhear however hard he tried. Kherron's scowl deepened. Lord Zorahan's hand moved to his scimitar. Lord Azri touched his red sword. The Karchholders and Horselords stiffened, eyeing one another suspiciously.

Caell gripped Night Plume's good hand. "What does Singer Kherron think he's *doing*? They've only just negotiated another treaty!"

Just when it seemed the fighting would start all over again, the old Kalerei leader Lord Nahar, who had suffered a minor wound during the battle, scrambled to his feet and addressed everyone. "I agree with Lord Zorahan! Unless the Singers can restore her soul to her body, Lady Yashra of the Harai should be left in the care of her people. Since I'm wounded, this seems a good time to officially pass the leadership of the Kalerei on to my son, Prince Erihan. I'll stay here with a core of volunteers to guard the camp and make sure Frazhin's creatures don't get their hands on the bluestone or Lady Yashra. And now the Singers have made the pirate leader tell us where to find his hideout, we should send some men into Asil's Hills to flush it out. You'll need someone here to guard the spoils, and you won't want a stiff old man slowing you up when you go into the forest, any more than you'll want a young woman without a soul." The scar on his cheek opened like a fan as he smiled. "I'm assuming you can't bring back Lady Yashra's soul, Singer, even if you wanted to?"

Singer Kherron tightened his lips, but gave a stiff nod. "Lord Nahar is right. *Yehn* is irreversible, and it's true the woman would be a hindrance to us on the journey."

Singer Renn had been humming under his breath. His Song made Night Plume want to tuck one foot up into his belly plumage and roost. But now Renn stopped singing and addressed the assembly with a deeper, darker note. "We don't need to trade with Frazhin. We have the pirate to show us the path into the forest and Night Plume to lead us to his Temple. Our priorities are to rescue Singer Rialle and find our girl Kyarra. After that, you're free to deal with Frazhin and his creatures as you wish." He glanced at the Karchlord. "If you will, Lord Azri?"

The Karchlord sprang to his feet and raised his red sword to the sun. Lord Zorahan and Prince Erihan were quick to follow. Around them, spreading in ripples to the edge of the camp, swords and scimitars scraped free of their scabbards, glittering like blades of grass across the plain as a great shout went up from thousands of throats.

"Death to Frazhin! Death to the Lord of the Forest!"

Night Plume gripped his black-feathered arrow tighter as he mimicked the battle cry. "Death to Frazhin! Death to the Lord of the Forest! Death to Starmaker!"

13
XIANCOTL

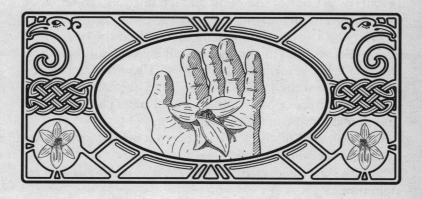

Dawn came slowly and noisily to the forest. As the mist gradually cleared to show color and shadow between the tall trunks on either side of the river, unseen animals and birds let out screeches that made Kyarra and Jilian jump. They crouched together at the center of the raft, nervous of the plops in the water, which was so murky they wouldn't have known if an entire shoal of merlee were swimming beneath them.

The dark-skinned forest dwellers were still paddling tirelessly up the center of the Red River and showed no sign of taking them to the bank so they could get off. As they paddled, the boy applied red and blue dye to everyone's skin from a pouch hanging beside the one containing sleeping-pollen among the feathers and leaves at his waist. But when he tried to daub some dye on Jilian's arm, she snatched out her dagger and pointed it at him. "Don't you dare!"

The boy sat back on his heels and grinned at her.

"Camouflage," Speaks Many Tongues grunted without looking around from where he crouched at the edge of the raft watching the trees as they slid past. "It will help you blend into the forest."

Jilian shook her head. "We don't need no camouflage." Then she seemed to remember that these men had helped them escape and made an effort to be polite. "We appreciate you helpin' us get out of the camp and all, but you can let us off now, thanks. We'll find our own way back."

Kyarra bit her lip as something flickered on the bank at the edge of her vision. The thought of walking back through those trees made her break into a fresh sweat. They wouldn't get lost if they followed the river, but what if the quetzal found them again? And Speaks Many Tongues still hadn't answered her question about the miracle cures.

"You will not find the way back on your own," Speaks Many Tongues said calmly.

"That's silly!" Jilian glared at him. "You let us off this here raft right now, or I'll —"

Kyarra put a hand on her arm. "Let me try," she whispered.

She did a quick breathing exercise, though the air was thick with strange scents that clogged her lungs. Putting as much skill into the Songs as she could, she said with an undercurrent of *Kashe,* "My friend is still upset about the Horselords taking her hostage." She added some *Aushan.* "We'd like to go back now, please. I want to make sure my mother's all right."

The boy kept grinning.

Speaks Many Tongues smiled. "No," he said, pleasantly enough.

"Are we your prisoners then?"

"In the Memory Trance that he enters to foretell the future, our holy man the Xiancotl says: *The Power Stones of the earth are three. One girl knows the black. One girl knows the green. One girl knows the blue. Bring the three together so the future may be clear.* That is why I came to take you to him. He needs to enter the Memory Trance with the three of you so he can decide what to do about the man who calls himself the Lord of the Forest. And your Songs do not work on us as they work on the quetzal, so stop wasting your breath."

Kyarra's heart gave an extra thud at the mention of quetzal. She looked uncertainly at the painted man. "So we *are* your prisoners."

His brown eyes regarded her in amusement. "What you call yourselves is up to you. But I thought you were looking for a way to help your mother? Our Xiancotl sees many things in the Memory Trance. Maybe he sees the answer you seek."

Was that a promise? Or was he just saying it so she would not try to escape?

Jilian snorted. "There are only two of us, not three, in case you hadn't noticed," she said. "The Horselords took my crystal, and Kyarra ain't got no stone at all, so you might as well take us back."

Kyarra thought of the sacks she'd seen back in the camp. "You mean Singer bluestone, don't you?" she said. "And Jilian's black crystal. They were talking about that back at the camp. They called it Khiz. And the green . . ." She frowned again, chasing a glimmer of memory. Then she had it. "The green stones the centaurs used to bend the light! I saw Lady Shaiala with one."

"Huh!" Jilian said. "She's a grown-up, not a girl. Any rate, she's not here, so you'll have to go back and get her, won't you?" She stared triumphantly at Speaks Many Tongues.

The painted man simply smiled and glanced again at the bank where Kyarra thought she'd seen the shadow move. "Camouflage takes many forms," he said. "And every woman was once a girl."

Jilian shook her head. While Kyarra had been trying her Songs on Speaks Many Tongues, she'd been working her way toward the edge of the raft. Now she jammed her dagger into her belt, pinched her nose, and jumped over the side.

"No!" Kyarra shouted, realizing too late what the girl meant to do. Even as she spoke, there was a froth of green bubbles and Jilian disappeared beneath the surface.

The men moved with the same swiftness the boy had demonstrated back at the camp. Two of them dived in after Jilian, hollow reeds appearing in their mouths. They blew sharply through the reeds, and there was a churning in the water. After a moment, a long, sinuous creature surfaced between them and floated as if dead. It was the size of a large child with midnight-blue scales, weedlike hair, human hands, and rows of tiny, sharp teeth. Two little feathered darts stuck out of its neck. Kyarra stared at the creature in horror, thinking: It's eaten her! It's eaten Jilian!

But the men dived again. They reappeared with the struggling girl and heaved her back on to the raft, where Jilian spluttered and coughed green water over Kyarra's boots. As the forest men pushed the unconscious creature away from the raft and climbed back on board themselves, another movement among the trees distracted Kyarra. She stared at the spot, but could make out nothing in the shadows. She shivered and pulled Jilian closer to the center of the raft, eyeing the water warily. The canopy met overhead here and vines hung down like beards, brushing the surface and casting deep shadows.

"Wh-what was *that*?" Jilian spluttered, her confidence shaken.

"Your people call them naga," Speaks Many Tongues said matter-of-factly, looking back at the floating creature. "They are half human, half water-snake. They search the waters for rare stones. We use a mild version of Purple Flower Poison on the darts. It knocks them out swiftly before they can send messages to the other naga for help. By the time it recovers, we'll be safely away, but I would not advise jumping in the water again."

Jilian stared into the murky water and gave a shudder. Kyarra reached for the girl's hand. "It's better than being back in the Horselord camp," she whispered, trying to convince herself as much as Jilian. "They were going to use you to trap your father."

Jilian stiffened, then sighed. "We're still prisoners," she said.

As the raft slipped deeper into the forest, Jilian lapsed into a sulky silence, staring at the water. Kyarra again tried questioning

Speaks Many Tongues about the potions they sold at Rivermeet. But, as before, Speaks Many Tongues merely smiled and said, "The forest has many secrets. It would take longer than our journey to tell them all. Wait until you meet the Xiancotl." The four men paddling didn't speak a word, and the boy had left the raft soon after the naga attack, disappearing up a vine into the canopy on some unknown quest. Kyarra sighed and hugged her knees. At least there didn't seem to be any quetzal in this part of the forest. She began to look out for the painted men's village, curious to see what kind of place they lived in.

But when the raft finally bumped against the bank, there was no sign of a village. Speaks Many Tongues stepped ashore and beckoned to them. Jilian stiffened and put a hand on her dagger, but seemed relieved they were leaving the water with its unseen monsters. They followed Speaks Many Tongues through the trees. He seemed to be looking for something, pausing at intervals to examine the ground and sniff the air.

Suddenly, he stopped, motioned Jilian and Kyarra to one side, and stared intently at a patch of lingering mist where the light seemed to dance. Kyarra blinked at the spot, feeling dizzy. She hoped she wasn't coming down with the fever again.

Then Speaks Many Tongues said, "The centaur cannot come to our Place, but you are welcome, Girl Who Knows the Green Stone." And the mist he was looking at exploded in a flurry of heels and hooves.

Jilian leaped back with a little scream and dropped into a crouch, her dagger raised. Kyarra opened her mouth to sing, but the shock of the attack had stolen her breath. Speaks Many Tongues stepped swiftly backward into a patch of leaf-shadow and put a tree trunk between him and the flying feet.

Kyarra stared, though she supposed she should have guessed. Before her stood the lilac centaur mare who had been with the Horselords in the hills. Next to her was the wild woman they called Lady Shaiala. They'd been using their green stones to bend the light, but now they abandoned hiding in favor of lashing out at the painted men — though they kept missing their targets as the forest dwellers shifted through the shadows.

"You fire arrows!" Shaiala shouted at them as she leaped into the air, twisted and kicked. Her heel knocked some bark off the trunk that sheltered Speaks Many Tongues. "You start Horselord fight! Tribes kill each other. Lord Nahar get wounded! You steal our hostage and take Yashra's daughter!"

Speaks Many Tongues shook his head. "We did not start it. And we stole no one. The girls wanted to come with us."

"You lie!" Shaiala made a flying leap through the shadows, both legs striking out at once with heels extended. Kyarra and Jilian ducked. There was a horrible *crack* and a muffled grunt from Speaks Many Tongues as he stumbled, clutching one of his arms.

Jilian whistled in admiration. "Wish I could kick like that!"

But Kyarra was staring at their guide's arm. She could see the bone protruding through the flesh. Her stomach turned. "You've broken it," she whispered.

At this, Shaiala seemed to remember why she'd come. She took a deep breath, put a hand on the centaur's arm and whispered, "Steady, Kamara Silvermane. First we must get the Two Hoof foals to safety."

Jilian raised her chin and kept her dagger between her and the wild woman. "Who are you callin' a foal? I'm not goin' nowhere with you! Think I want to be hobbled again?"

"Not be stupid!" Shaiala said, her speech losing its fluency as she became excited again. "I not come after you for argument! Get over here, both of you. You can take turns to ride Kamara Silvermane. She might look small, but she's strong."

Kyarra eyed the lilac centaur. She was smaller than the pony that had carried their packs from the coast. "Why did you hurt Speaks Many Tongues?" she said. "He was telling the truth about the arrows."

Shaiala pushed back her tangled hair and scowled. She

seemed ready to seize their arms and drag them out of the forest by force. But she shook her head and frowned at Kyarra. "How do you know? Can you use the Singer truth listening?"

"I saw the quetzal flying over the camp," Kyarra admitted. "They had bows and arrows like that dark one Prince Erihan and Speaks Many Tongues told us about. Only these were colored like the ones that attacked me and Jilian in the forest. That's why we ran."

In spite of his broken arm, Speaks Many Tongues laughed softly. "Girl Who Knows the Blue Stone speaks only half a truth."

Kyarra flushed. But his words had at least stopped Shaiala kicking while she thought about them.

"Has he hurt you?" she asked in the end, casting a glance at Jilian but looking mostly at Kyarra.

"No," Kyarra said. "His people saved Jilian's life when she jumped in the river. They knocked out a naga before it could eat her."

"I'd have dealt with the stupid naga myself if they'd given me half a chance!" Jilian added, still in a sulk.

"You hurt a naga?" Shaiala frowned at her, and the centaur made a snorting sound in her nose.

"The naga turned bad," Speaks Many Tongues said, clutching his broken arm to his chest. "Like the quetzal who fired arrows into your camp. We had to tranquilize it. Our Xiancotl told of this in the Memory Trance. Something powerful is corrupting the Half Creatures. They are changing."

The centaur shifted her delicate hooves uneasily in the leaf mold and made the snorting sound again.

Shaiala frowned again. "Has this anything to do with the Prophecy you told us?"

Speaks Many Tongues closed his eyes, as if in pain. "I do not go into the Memory Trance that connects with the quetzal Memoryplace. Only our Xiancotl can make that journey safely. Soon he will not go there, either. The corrupted quetzal who shoot arrows take all the Yellow Flowers from the forest canopy and leave none for us, and without the Yellow Flowers our Xiancotl cannot enter the Trance. I sent my son, Hunts Like a Spider, to find a fresh bloom so the Xiancotl can enter the Memory Trance with you."

Shaiala was still frowning. "Where is this Xiancotl of yours?" she demanded. "I need to speak with him at once! Then Kamara Silvermane and I will take the Two Hoof foals back to the centaur herd, where they'll be safe."

A smile spread across Speaks Many Tongues' painted face. He pointed upward with his good arm, indicating the vines that curled down from the green mist overhead. "We climb."

It looked impossible. But the painted men made seats of looped vines for their guests and swung them high into the forest canopy where a network of woven paths had been cleverly constructed in the branches so that they wouldn't show from below. Every so often, they passed a rounded structure of leaves and twigs with a small entrance hole lodged in the treetops like the nest of a large bird. Brightly colored feathers fluttered at the entrances of these nests. Curious faces peered out at them, laughing at their clumsiness on the vine swings and calling out to Speaks Many Tongues in whistles and trills. The nests smelled of fruit and flowers overlaid with a faintly familiar musky odor that made Kyarra uneasy.

Shaiala, too, was staring around with a worried expression. Her bare feet twitched as she swung in her vine harness, as if they longed to kick something. She kept fingering her green stone, and giving Kyarra sideways glances when she thought she wasn't looking. Remembering the way she'd broken Speaks Many Tongues' arm, Kyarra kept well away from her.

At last, they came to a much larger nest in the branches of a tree that had dark green leaves shaped like human hands. This nest had been decorated entirely with yellow feathers, not only across the entrance, but woven into its curved walls until it glowed like a captured sun. The musky smell was stronger here.

The boy who had been with them on the raft was waiting for them on the broad branch outside the entrance, a waxy Yellow Flower clutched in one dark hand. He held up his prize with a grin.

Speaks Many Tongues squeezed his shoulder. "Well done, Hunts Like a Spider." He nodded toward the nest and said, "Welcome to our Xiancotl's nest."

"Is this the — er — Memoryplace?" Jilian asked hesitantly, trying to see into the dark interior.

But Speaks Many Tongues shook his head. "No. Only the Xiancotl can go to the Memoryplace. You have to be in the Trance to get there. It is not a place your body can travel to, only your thoughts. Go inside. Hunts Like a Spider will mediate for you. I have to mend my arm." He hooked a leg over a waiting vine and swung expertly down through the tree, holding his cracked arm in place against his chest.

"Wait!" Shaiala called, but he'd already vanished among the leaves. She frowned after him, then turned to Jilian and Kyarra. "You two wait here. I'll go in and check this Xiancotl isn't going to hurt you."

Jilian clutched her dagger. "If he tries anythin', I'll stab him!"

Kyarra drew a deep breath and eyed the entrance. "Let me go first," she said. "I can sing to him if he tries to hurt us — maybe my Songs will have enough power to send him to sleep."

The boy, who had been grinning at them as they discussed the matter, held up his flower. "Our Xiancotl does not hurt anyone. He already asleep. You will see." He beckoned to them and ducked through the feathered curtain.

As they followed him inside, Shaiala took hold of both their hands as if they were little girls, but neither Kyarra nor Jilian pulled away. The sickly smell turned Kyarra's stomach. It was darker than she'd thought. A rustle came from somewhere ahead. She stood very still. When her eyes adjusted, she made out the shape of a man, sitting very still and cross-legged in the center of the nest. His black skin was wrinkled and painted with mottles of gold that exactly matched the pattern of light falling through the woven walls. All around him were bowls containing what looked like dark honeycake, some dry and shriveled, others fresh and sticky. Flies buzzed around them.

The man didn't move. His eyes were open, but they stared straight through his visitors as if he couldn't see them. Kyarra wondered if he might be blind. But the motionlessness and the passive, vacant stare reminded her more of her mother. A little shiver went through her.

The boy touched his forehead to the floor in front of the Xiancotl. The Xiancotl opened his mouth and stuck out a glowing golden tongue. The boy carefully placed his Yellow Flower onto the tongue and drew back, watching expectantly.

Slowly, as if he had to remember how to do it, the Xiancotl began to chew.

The boy scurried back to them. "Sometimes it takes him a long time to travel to the Memoryplace," he whispered. "What do you want to know?"

"Ask him what corrupts the Half Creatures," Shaiala said at once. "Why did the quetzal attack our camp? Can centaurs be corrupted, too?"

Jilian scowled at her. "Ask him somethin' useful! Ask him what happened to my father. Last we saw of him, he was bein' attacked by quetzal in this stupid forest."

The boy nodded and turned to Kyarra. "You have question to ask, Girl Who Knows the Blue Stone?"

Kyarra licked her lips. She glanced at the Horselord woman and the pirate girl. Jilian was carving patterns in the branch with her dagger, acting as if she didn't care whether the Xiancotl answered her question or not.

"Ask him . . . ask him if he knows how to cure my mother," she whispered.

As the boy scurried back to the slowly-chewing Xiancotl, the other two stared at her. Kyarra's cheeks went hot.

Jilian grinned and said, "I knew you was soft on her, Kyarra!"

But Lady Shaiala shook her head. "You heard what your mother did, Singer girl, and how she was punished. She doesn't deserve to be cured."

"I heard only that she was under the spell of a mask of dark crystal!" Kyarra said, the woman's attitude making her angry. "Sounds to me as if my mother took the punishment for that Frazhin you were all talking about back at the camp. Did the Singers give her *Yehn* before she had me, or after? But I don't suppose you'd tell me even if you knew, would you? It's all such a big secret, isn't it? Not only back on the Isle, but also everyone here on the mainland seems to know more about me and my parents than I do!"

Shaiala pressed her lips together and looked away.

"And Frazhin . . ." Kyarra went on, not noticing her expression in the gloom. "I suppose if he was Yashra's lover, that makes him my father. I'm not sorry he's dying. He's worse than the lot of you! Some father, to have me and my mother kidnapped and dragged halfway across the world by savage pirates who don't even know how to protect their captives from Half Creatures!"

"Oy!" Jilian looked up. "Who are you calling a savage? I helped you when the quetzal attacked us, remember?"

"And I helped get you out of the Horselord camp," Kyarra said. "So now we're even."

"Fine," Jilian said, stabbing her dagger violently into the branch. "Soon as we're out of this stinky hut, I'm goin' to look for *my* father, and then I'm goin' home. You and your wild Horselord friends can do what you like."

"Just because they're related to my mother doesn't mean they're my friends," Kyarra said. She glanced uncertainly at Lady Shaiala, who was staring at her in the strangest fashion. "Why *did* you come after us?" she asked. "Was it to take Jilian back so you could use her as bait in your trap? Why did you come alone? I mean, with just one centaur like you did?"

Shaiala's eyes flashed in the shadows. "I have my reasons," she said.

There was an embarrassed silence. Jilian resumed carving the bark, but not as energetically as before. Kyarra sighed. Everyone else seemed to believe her mother had deserved her punishment, yet the more she heard, the more it seemed Yashra was innocent. But it was obvious that if she was going to cure her, she would have to do it secretly. She wished now that she had waited to ask her question.

The Xiancotl eventually stopped chewing and spat into the bowl the boy was holding patiently near his lips. He didn't speak, only stared at them with burning eyes that were no longer vacant of expression. The boy quickly brought the bowl across and offered them each a lump of the well-chewed petals of the Yellow Flower, which was now a dark mush like that in the other bowls. The flies buzzed across to sample it.

"Yuck!" Jilian scrambled backward in disgust.

"Want to know answers, need to share Yellow Flower," the boy said. "Not worry, Xiancotl make it safe for you."

Jilian was still shaking her head. But Shaiala glanced at Kyarra and lifted a lump of the mush onto her own tongue.

"Swallow it," instructed the boy.

Shaiala swallowed. Her face screwed up and she gagged. Then she jerked upright and stared at the Xiancotl with wide eyes. "It's almost like centaur speech," she whispered. "Oh! I understand now! The centaurs don't hatch from eggs, so they can't be corrupted. That's how Frazhin did it — he corrupted the other Half Creatures before they were even born!" She stared at the Xiancotl a moment longer, then broke into a smile. "It's all right, Singer girl," she said. "It's not poison. But —"

Kyarra had already swallowed her lump. It burned her throat slightly, but didn't taste much worse than Song Potion.

What happened next was strange. The walls and her companions were sucked away until they seemed to be a very long way off. Her ears buzzed as if she were underwater. Something shifted in her head, like a door opening. On the other side of it sat the Xiancotl, staring at her, surrounded by the swirling presence of many, faint dreams.

We are in the Memory Trance. I have traveled as far as I am permitted to go. I see the Dark One and he has black stars in his head. I see a ship that carries the Singers' shame. I see your mother but she is not cured. Change destroys good as well as evil. Remember this, Girl Who Knows the Blue Stone.

The door in her head began to close. The Xiancotl vanished in a cloud of yellow feathers and the walls whirled toward her again.

"No, wait!" Kyarra said. "What do you mean? I don't understand! Come back, you have to come back!"

She squeezed her nails into her palms, willing the door in her head to stay open. The walls were getting closer, the roaring in her ears louder. She hummed desperately, trying to stop it. *Challa* — no good. *Kashe* — no, don't be silly. *Shi.* The Xiancotl blurred, half in her head, half sitting in the pattern of light that so perfectly matched the paint on his skin. For a moment, she thought she saw wings on his back like a quetzal's. But he was going. The door was closing, and she didn't understand the answer.

"Wait!" she cried, giving him a burst of *Aushan* and *Yehn* mixed together the way the First Singer did when she was very displeased with a novice.

There was a horrible snap in her head as the Xiancotl gave a cry of warning and fell sideways. The walls rushed back toward her. Only now they were made of black crystal, and there was terrible fear. A face — pale and sunken-cheeked, dirty silver hair knotted with shells, wide gray eyes — stared at her without recognition, then started with surprise and sudden hope. The bruised mouth opened and faint words came out: . . . *stop him, tell Renn he must stop Frazhin* . . . But before Kyarra could hear any more, a mask loomed between them. A mask of black crystal surrounded by quetzal plumes and shadows, through which eyes stared at her, as cold and dark as the voice that invaded her head.

So you want to cure your mother, do you? Forget the Xiancotl. He's a fool, too afraid to change anything. Come to me, Daughter, and I'll show you how to change the history of the world. It's the only way to help your mother now.

The mask loomed closer. It filled her head with feathers and beating wings. She panicked, vaguely aware of hands, shouts, and Jilian calling to her from a long way off. "Kyarra! Hold on, Kyarra!" She was being swung back through the branches, not always gently, but she didn't care.

The Xiancotl's Trance had answered her, after all.

Come to me, Daughter, and I'll show you how to change the world.

14
ALLIANCE

The forest was eerily silent. No small animals scurried through the undergrowth, no birds called. The entrance to the robber's path was like the mouth of a sleeping monster: the trunks its enormous teeth; the darkness beyond, its unknown belly. Night Plume's feathers prickled. Everything looked so different from ground level. The forest was his home, yet he understood only too well the fear the humans were feeling.

The army had reined in to check they had the correct place. A long line of battle-scarred men faced the trees, tense and silent as every eye searched the shadows for concealed enemies. Their equally nervous horses and ponies swished their tails and stamped their feet. Night Plume was the only one not mounted, since no pony could be persuaded to carry him. The pirate leader Asil sat stiffly on one of the Karch ponies, his hands bound behind his back. A blue Singer stone like the one Caell wore had been secured around his neck. Caell had explained the stone was a Trust-Gift, and that if the pirate tried to escape Singer Renn would be able to control him with Songs. Night Plume thought of the priests' crystals and shuddered.

Caell persuaded his black pony closer. "What's wrong?" he whispered. "Are the quetzal coming?"

Night Plume shook his head, unable to explain why the Starmaker's flock wasn't there to challenge them. The men had spent the night making weapons to defend themselves against another attack from the skies. Some had made crude bows and arrows and practiced shooting at sacks stuffed with grass. They were terrible shots. Even with his sprained arm, Night Plume could have done better. Others had made leather slings with which they could throw stones high into the air. He didn't know what he'd do if Sun Glimmer and the others did come to fight.

Stay away, Sun Glimmer, he sent in wild-speech, though of course there was no chance his nestmate would hear.

The Singers seemed satisfied at last that Asil was leading them the correct way, and motioned the army toward the forest. The Kalerei went first, the men hacking at the undergrowth with their scimitars while their mounts reared and lashed out with their hooves, snapping branches and breaking trunks. Trees fell in their wake, leaving a swathe through the forest wide enough for the army to ride along six abreast.

"They learned those kicks from the centaurs, apparently," Caell said, his eyes shining with excitement. "It was a pity we were too late to see the fighting at the camp — a centaur in a battle must be quite a sight!"

The Karchholders weren't so impressed. "They're making enough noise to wake the dead!" Lord Azri shouted to Singer Kherron, whose gaze was fixed on the falling trees. "He'll hear us coming leagues away!"

"Good," Kherron said. "Let him hear." He raised his broken voice and called, "FRAZHIN! Can you hear me? We're coming for you! You've nowhere in the world left to hide. This time you'll not escape!" He kicked his pony into a trot, had a brief struggle with it at the entrance to the path, and disappeared into the shadows.

Singer Renn sighed. "Losing his voice was a terrible blow for

Singer Kherron," he said to the Karchlord. "I don't know what he's going to do when he meets Frazhin again."

"I don't know what Singer Renn's going to do when he finds Frazhin, either," Caell whispered as they followed the leaders along the path. "He told me he was just a novice when they last met. Frazhin put his crystal mask on him to make him scream. I bet he's scared. I know I am."

Night Plume hooted in sympathy and touched the black arrow he was saving for the Starmaker. "I scared, too. But Starmaker die soon."

Caell bit his lip and watched the trees with worried eyes. "I only hope Ky hasn't found out Frazhin's supposed to be her father. It'd be just like her to rush in there and confront him. After all, he's responsible for what happened to her mother —" He broke off. "Do *you* think Lady Yashra's guilty, Night Plume?"

Night Plume thought of the empty-eyed woman they'd seen back in the camp. There wasn't much in the Memoryplace about what she'd done, not as much as there was about the Starmaker. "She not as guilty as Starmaker," he said in the end. "I hope your girl keep away from Temple. It bad place."

"Ky'll be all right," Caell said, as if trying to convince himself. "She's almost a Singer, you know!" He grinned, though it seemed forced.

As the trees closed around them, familiar scents surrounded Night Plume, bringing memories. He saw the clearing off to the right, where his flock had found one of the pirates with his heart torn out. The blackened remains of the humans' fire were still there, but the body had gone. He pulled his injured wing closer to his body and eyed the shadows. *Something wrong,* he told Caell in wild-speech. *Feel strange.*

Caell hunched into himself. "I know," he whispered back. "I can feel it, too."

The army beat its way deeper into the forest, stopping more and more often to check the direction with their prisoner. The pirate leader grew more stubborn each time, defying even the

Singers' skills. Singer Renn quietly asked Night Plume if he
knew this path. Night Plume shook his head. "Quetzal usually
fly. Forest look different from above." Renn sighed and told him
to let them know the moment he recognized where he was, and
returned to his interrogation of the pirate. But the prisoner set
his jaw, refusing to make the little movements that would aid
Singer truth listening.

Night Plume returned his attention to the surrounding shadows. Although it must only have been early afternoon, it was
already dark under the trees. The army had lit their torches,
which glimmered back along the path like the scales of some
monstrous snake. The ground had been rising steadily since
midday. They had to be getting close. If only he could fly — "I
climb tree!" he said, wondering why he hadn't thought of it
before. "Get head above canopy, look around."

Caell frowned. "You've only got one good arm! What if you
fall?"

"Not fall. Quetzal know how to perch in trees, not need
hands."

Singer Renn considered this. "It's a good idea, actually. Looks
like it's still light up there. If we can confirm the direction,
maybe we can press on through the night. Are you sure you can
climb with your injuries, Night Plume?"

Night Plume was already looking for a suitable tree. The
thought of being up above the canopy again in the light and air
was a lot stronger than his fear of falling. He selected a tall trunk
with lots of branches, and squirmed his way up one-handed.
Caell's anxious face, the Singers, and the army's torches were
soon out of sight below the leaves. He swung on up. The tree
swayed beneath him as he burst through the canopy and hung
there, panting, one arm hooked in a loop of vine and his good
wing spread for balance.

The sun was sinking into the mist behind him, turning the
canopy golden under a darkening sky. Ahead, so close it made
Night Plume's heart miss a beat, the Starmaker's Temple thrust

through the leafy sea, blowing its rings of smoke and spitting sparks into the sky. A bad smell drifted toward him, making his stomach turn.

Caell, he sent in wild-speech. *We close! But Temple spits fire —*

He never finished his warning. A whistle pierced his head, dislodging him from his perch. Twigs and small branches snapped as he crashed down through them, grabbing desperately at leaves. There were wings all around and a storm of colored feathers. Something broke his fall. He clung to a swaying branch, his heart hammering, and found himself surrounded by wild quetzal.

-dark-quetzaalll-not-understand-
-mountain-spits-fire-because-blackstarhuman-prepare-to-enter-
  Memoryplace-with-traitor-flock-
-if-blackstarhuman-destroy-Memoryplace-
-he-change-world-

Night Plume hardly registered what they were saying. He needed all his concentration to hold on. The wild flock flapped agitatedly from branch to branch, shaking the tree. He'd left his bow and arrow below in Caell's care. He dared not let go of his perch to fight, anyway. His injured wing was useless and his left arm had gone numb again. He closed his eyes, wondering if it would hurt more to fall or have his heart torn out.

But the wild quetzal didn't try to hurt him. They spread their glorious wings, burst through the canopy, and whirled away into the setting sun.

-painted-humans-come-with-yellow-flower-dreamer-
-you-must-stop-blackstarhuman-
-stop-him-
-stop-

They were gone as quickly as they had come, leaving Night Plume trembling so violently that for a moment he couldn't move. The faint shouts of the men below and their badly aimed arrows and stones crashing into the leaves around him jolted him from his stupor. They didn't hit any of the wild flock, but they were in serious danger of knocking Night Plume out of his tree.

"Not fight!" he called. "They gone."

Night Plume! What's happening up there? Caell's wild-speech was anxious.

Wild quetzal speak to me, he sent back. *Coming down.*

Somehow he made it back into the gloom of the forest floor, where the Karchholders rushed to enclose him in a protective ring of red swords. There was now no question of pressing on through the night. Horselords trotted through the trunks with burning torches, lighting piles of wood the army had gathered while Night Plume had been aloft. Soon the forest as far as they could see in all directions was ablaze with camp fires and the men relaxed a little. The army had swelled in Night Plume's absence. The firelight picked out more humans standing among the trunks with spears in their hands, their dark bodies painted with golden whorls. A short way off the path, Singer Renn and Singer Kherron were talking to a group of these newcomers, who carried with them a withered human male sleeping on a litter of woven vines, whom they introduced as their Xiancotl.

"Where they come from?" Night Plume asked.

Caell shook his head. "They just appeared from nowhere, swung down out of the trees. Seems they want to join the army. The men thought they were quetzal at first — good job they're such bad shots with those arrows!"

"Wild quetzal say painted men come with Yellow Flower dreamer . . ." Night Plume said slowly. "Memoryplace very strange. I think wild quetzal know about painted men, but Starmaker hide the memory from us with blackstars, so we not see what Yellow Flower dreamer do." He shivered.

"Maybe we'll learn something now." Caell handed back Night Plume's bow and arrow with a grim expression. "That old man they're carrying must be your 'Yellow Flower dreamer.' Singer Kherron's furious about the way they crept up on us. And would you believe, the pirate escaped? Got his bluestone off in all the confusion and slunk off into the trees. Singer Renn is worried he's gone to warn Frazhin, but I think he's gone to look for his daughter Jilian. If he's got any sense, he'll get her out of this forest as quickly as he can."

*

While the army made camp, their leaders pooled information and made plans for the attack on Frazhin's Temple. It turned out that the painted people's interpreter — a man called Speaks Many Tongues — was the same one who had told the Prophecy of the Dark Quetzal back at the Horselord camp. It took a Song from Renn to persuade the Horselord leaders to sit down peacefully and listen to what he had to say. Night Plume was asked to tell them exactly what the wild flock had said, and repeat various memories of his time with the Starmaker, which he retrieved from the Memoryplace and mimicked word-for-word in quetzal fashion while the men listened with frowns on their faces. They shook their heads when he described the crater and the underground tunnels. The Karchlord, especially, looked grim.

Speaks Many Tongues apologized for the trouble he'd caused in the Horselord camp. He claimed he'd only meant to cause a distraction so he could get the girls away to the forest, and it was unfortunate that the corrupted quetzal and the pirate's men had chosen that moment to attack. He went on to explain how the Lord of the Forest had been harvesting Yellow Flowers in great quantities and upsetting the equilibrium of the forest. Their holy man, the Xiancotl, believed that if he could enter the Memory Trance with Frazhin's daughter and the other two girls who knew how to use the Power Stones of the earth, he might see the best way to restore things to their natural balance. Only something had gone wrong in the Trance when Frazhin's daughter had tried using her Songs, and he'd been unable to finish his analysis of the memories. During the confusion afterward, the girls had disappeared.

They put Ky in danger! Caell clenched his fists and glared at the painted man.

Night Plume hooted sadly. *Now your girl lost again.*

We'll find her soon — she can't be far. I'm glad she escaped from that weird old man.

Speaks Many Tongues also explained the process of the Memory Trance — how the Yellow Flowers opened doors in the head and dissolved the barriers between present and past. "Quetzal are very important to the Trance," he told them, glancing at Night Plume. "Each flock has long memories, ancestor-memories reaching back to the beginning of time, which they call their Memoryplace. By tapping into this Memoryplace, we can mimic the exact conditions at any point in history, and this lets the Xiancotl see clearly how everything fits together. In the Memory Trance, the Xiancotl travels mentally back in time, then forward again. He makes use of the quetzal memories to foresee all the possible futures from the present time, and foretells the most likely of these. He can see consequences, but cannot change things, because the Memoryplace is fixed — or so we always believed. But now we're not so sure. After our Xiancotl entered the Memory Trance with your girl, he saw the man who calls himself the Lord of the Forest preparing to start his own Trance with the corrupted quetzal flock. They have different memories, false memories implanted by the Lord of the Forest. He is trying to use these invented memories to change the history of the world. We have to stop him."

There was an uneasy silence. "False memories?" Singer Renn looked thoughtfully at Night Plume. "The dark quetzal was corrupted by Frazhin before Singer Rialle freed him with her Songs — do you remember what any of these false memories were, Night Plume?"

"See true memories in Memoryplace now, also still see some old ones," Night Plume said. "It confusing, not sure which are which."

Lord Zorahan scowled. "The quetzal's no help! It's all nonsense, anyway. No one can change the past."

But Singer Renn let out a hum that silenced the Harai Lord.

"Night Plume, please try. What did your false, uh, Memoryplace memories say about the Singers? Do you remember that?"

Night Plume started to shake his head. Then he remembered how the Starmaker's blackstars had hidden information about the Singers, and fluffed his plumage uncomfortably. "In old Memoryplace, Singers not exist."

Renn went pale. He and Singer Kherron exchanged a glance. "I still can't contact the Isle," Renn whispered. "You don't think Frazhin might have already changed history?"

"The Xiancotl does not think it very likely that all Singers will disappear from the world," said Speaks Many Tongues. "That is only one possible outcome."

"So you can't actually tell the future at all?" Singer Kherron said, leaning forward, his green eyes fixed on the painted man. "I wondered about that."

"We were talking about the past, not the future," Renn said, then went quiet as if he'd only just realized how much one depended upon the other.

"But what about the Prophecy?" Lord Zorahan said, jumping to his feet. "What about all that doom and destruction you said would follow the flight of the dark quetzal? Man against Man, you said, and Half Creature against Half Creature! How did you know *that* would come true?"

Speaks Many Tongues smiled. "We didn't know. I simply told you one possible future the Xiancotl said might follow the flight of the dark quetzal." He shrugged. "Prophecies come true if enough people believe in them. You make them come true yourselves." He looked again at Night Plume. "But maybe you change things, anyway, by wounding the dark quetzal so he cannot fly."

"It wasn't us who wounded him," Prince Erihan said in his quiet voice. "His own flock did that — though I think both the Kalerei and the Harai were ready to kill him at one stage, poor thing. That Prophecy of yours was a cruel trick to play on Night Plume. I don't blame Shai for breaking your arm."

"Mmm," the Karchlord said, shifting his position. "And that's another thing! It seems you forest people have been changing history a bit yourselves. Where I come from, bones take a lot longer than a day to heal. I say Speaks Many Tongues is lying."

There were uneasy mutters around the fire.

But Singer Renn, who had been truth listening, shook his head. "He's telling the truth. The arm *was* broken, and now it's healed."

More mutters broke out as Singer Kherron shifted farther forward and said in his croaky voice, "How did your arm heal so quickly? Did you really change the past?"

Speaks Many Tongues looked amused. "Hardly. I treated it with a simple mixture of Numbing Moss and Orange Flower Lotion."

Kherron became very still. "And can this moss of yours heal other things?" He spoke so quietly, not many people heard.

"Kher, we've other things to think about just now." The dark-skinned orderly, Lazim, rested a hand on Singer Kherron's arm and indicated the leaders, who were arguing about who should lead the charge on Frazhin's stronghold.

Prince Erihan said Kalerei horses knew the centaur kicks, so of course they should do it. Lord Zorahan said the Kalerei were obviously exhausted from beating a path through the forest, whereas the Harai were fresh and ready to fight so they should lead. The Karchlord interrupted them, saying his men should be first because Frazhin had originally come from the Karch and they knew his tricks; he was unlikely to fight fair. At which Lord Zorahan jumped to his feet and shouted that the Karchholders knew nothing about fighting fair, as had been proved when they'd ridden down the Great South Trade Route and attacked his tribe in their tents at night, slaughtering men in their bedrolls.

In the middle of all this, Kherron shrugged off the orderly, scrambled stiffly to his feet and seized Speaks Many Tongues' arm. "I *said* can your moss heal other things?"

His voice, rough and broken as it was, silenced the arguments. The leaders' heads turned and they seemed to remember the treaty flask they'd drunk back in the camp. Lord Zorahan and Lord Azri sat down again, looking ashamed. Prince Erihan flushed.

Speaks Many Tongues smiled. "Such as your voice, Singer?" he said simply. "Yes, I think it can."

Kherron dropped the painted man's arm as if it had burned him. "Truth," he whispered.

Singer Renn warned softly, "Just because he believes it doesn't necessarily mean it's true, remember."

But Kherron wasn't listening. "Where do I find this . . . Numbing Moss and . . . Orange Flower?" His voice sounded even more cracked than usual.

"We haven't time for this now, Kher," Lazim whispered again. "I know how much you want to sing again, and echoes know it would be useful right now! But a cure's sure to take time, even if the moss works as well as you hope. Maybe later —"

Kherron still wasn't listening. He had hold of Speaks Many Tongues' arm again and was whispering urgently to him.

Finally, Speaks Many Tongues motioned to two of the painted men, who melted into the forest. "They go to harvest," he said, settling himself back on the ground. "Meanwhile, let us speak of our plans. The Xiancotl says the Lord of the Forest is feeding Yellow Flowers to his corrupted flock to make it easier for him to access their corrupted Memoryplace. This will help us. If the wild quetzal can collect the flowers they have chewed and bring them to the Xiancotl, then he should be able to enter the same Memory Trance and stop the Lord of the Forest from changing history." He glanced at the withered holy man, who lay on his litter staring at the fire with vacant eyes. "But this cannot be too soon. The Xiancotl is exhausted after his last Trance. The Lord of the Forest's daughter asked a difficult question which took him by surprise. That is part of the reason he lost control of the Trance."

"Good for Ky!" Caell said, but not loudly enough for anyone to hear.

Lord Zorahan grunted. "We'll have to leave the flowers and trance-stuff to your people and the quetzal," he said. "But we'll take care of any threat from the ground, never fear. The Kalerei and the Harai will ride side by side. That way, Kalerei horses who know the centaur kicks can help Harai scimitars, and Harai scimitars can shield Kalerei horses. Agreed?" He looked at Prince Erihan, who pursed his lips and nodded.

"While you're dealing with the defenders, my men will get inside the Temple and rout out Frazhin's priests," the Karchlord said. "We know their tricks from when they lived in the tunnels of the Karch — and as my Harai friend has pointed out, Karch-holders are good at fighting dirty." He grinned to show it was a joke, and Lord Zorahan laughed and slapped him on the back.

"That just leaves Frazhin himself," Prince Erihan said quietly.

Everyone turned to look at the two Singers. Singer Renn nodded. "Our first priority is to get Singer Rialle and any other prisoners out of there. Then we'll deal with Frazhin. This time, he's made a mistake. From Night Plume's description of his Temple, we've enough men to surround the crater and block all the exits. He'll be trapped in his own lair. He won't escape us this time."

People got to their feet, still discussing tactics. Night Plume stretched his good wing thankfully. He was stiff after his fall through the tree, and his head still hurt from the wild flock's urgent wild-speech.

Caell tugged Singer Renn's sleeve. "What about Ky?" he whispered. "What if Frazhin's got her in his Temple, too?"

Renn turned with a weary smile. "He hasn't, Caell. Didn't you hear Speaks Many Tongues? Kyarra and the pirate's daughter ran off with Lady Shaiala and at least one centaur. She'll be fine, don't worry. I know Shaiala and how well she can kick. No one could ask for a better bodyguard. And it sounds as if Frazhin's preoccupied with this Memory Trance business — that might be a blessing. With luck, we'll catch him while he's still under the influence of the flowers."

"But what if he change history?" Night Plume asked, little shivers making his feathers stand on end.

The Second Singer patted him on the arm. "Don't worry too much about that. Lord Zorahan's right. Remember what Speaks Many Tongues told us about the Prophecy of the Dark Quetzal? I expect all these forest superstitions have alternative explanations if you look deep enough. I'm more worried about what Frazhin might do to Singer Rialle when he realizes we're attacking his Temple. Go and get some sleep, you two. I'm going to try to contact the Echorium again." Renn twirled his bluestone confidently, but they both saw the worry in his eyes as he turned away.

Night Plume whistled. Caell was still muttering about Ky. Singer Kherron was off with the painted men, having a foul mixture of moss and boiled petals pushed down his throat with a stick. Singer Renn paused to look at a sketch of the Starmaker's Temple that the Karchlord and the Horselord leaders had scratched in the earth, then walked off alone into the trees, his gray robe swirling around his ankles. Thousands of fires glowed between the dark trunks, where men sharpened their swords and talked in low voices about the coming battle. They looked up uneasily as Renn's hum vibrated through the night.

Night Plume looked in the Memoryplace, sensed the Starmaker's faint presence, and felt very scared.

"It starting," he whispered. "Starmaker start Memory Trance."

15
BAIT

Kyarra woke from the nightmare to find a hand over her mouth.

"Shh, Kyarra, don't make a sound."

She was lying on her back in moist grass beside a waterfall that sparkled with green light. Hoots and whistles filled the air. A yellow feather floated down and kissed her cheek, bringing back everything that had happened in the Xiancotl's nest. She started up, sweating all over. "Quetzal!" she gasped.

"It's all right, they can't see us. Just stay still a moment." The hand lifted, and Jilian's face swam into focus. Her bright hair was stuck to her cheeks and there was concern in her eyes. But when Kyarra blinked at her, she sat back on her heels and grinned. "You had us worried!" she whispered. "Have you any idea how long you've been asleep?"

Kyarra frowned. "I wasn't asleep! I was with the Xiancotl in the Memory Trance. I saw —"

"Shh! Not so loud." Jilian slammed her hand back over Kyarra's mouth and twisted her head to watch the quetzal. "All right," she said finally as the last bright feather disappeared into the trees. "I think they've gone for now."

Kyarra sat up and looked around in confusion. "Where are we?" Her voice trailed off as the green light around the waterfall sparkled. The lilac centaur they'd had to leave behind when they'd swung into the trees stepped out of the mist, followed by the tall, dark male she'd seen in Asil's Hills. A third centaur appeared, this one stocky and stormy purple in color. Then a fourth. And then a fifth, and — "How many of them are there?" she breathed, staggering to her feet and shrugging off Jilian's hand. "There was only one before."

"You think I would venture into the Quetzal Forest with only Kamara Silvermane to help me kick?" said an amused voice behind her. "The dark one is Rafiz Longshadow and the purple one is Marell Stormtemper. The others are from the same herd. They all remember Frazhin before he called himself Lord of the Forest. He made slaves of them when they were foals. He overpowered them then, but they're bigger and stronger now, and they have their herdstones that give them the power to bend light."

Kyarra whirled. She blinked at Lady Shaiala, who smiled. "Rafiz Longshadow carried you here from the Xiancotl's nest, actually, so you have him to thank for your escape."

Kyarra stared at the tall, dark centaur and tried to imagine being on his back. She was glad she hadn't been awake at the time. "But what happened? I remember the Xiancotl answered my question, and then something went wrong. I saw my father . . . at least, I think I did . . ."

"I saw him, too," Shaiala said gravely. "When you sang to the Xiancotl, your Songs affected the Trance somehow. The Xiancotl collapsed as well."

"That's how we got away," Jilian said. "The painted men were so worried about him, they forgot to keep a proper eye on us. Lady Shaiala used her green stone to hide us, and we got you down out of the trees and back to where the centaurs were waiting. The wild quetzal followed us, of course — that sneaky

Xiancotl must've been working with them all the time — but the
centaurs kept us hid."

Kyarra wiped sweat off her brow. She didn't feel at all well.
The nightmares might have gone, but her head still hurt and her
legs were trembling.

"The quetzal tried to kill us when we were here before," she
said.

"It doesn't surprise me," Lady Shaiala said. "As Frazhin's
daughter, you're the most wanted person in the world right now.
We must get you out of this forest as soon as possible. We've
been following the river upstream because the Xiancotl's people are sure to expect us to go downstream. Another river enters
the forest at Silvertown. Rafiz Longshadow thinks if we go far
enough, we'll come to the place where the two rivers meet, then
we can follow the River Plume all the way out. The quetzal and
the painted men are probably searching for us, but if we use our
herdstones and stay quiet, we should make it."

"No." Kyarra set her jaw. "We have to find Frazhin."

They all stared at her, centaurs as well as humans.

"What *is* it with you, Kyarra?" Jilian said. "First, we have to
drag you into this stupid forest in chains. Then you persuade me
to come back into it with you after some weird painted man who
almost got you killed in his Memory Trance. And now you're
rescued and have a chance to get out, you want to go in even
deeper and find Frazhin! You're not making any sense."

Kyarra shivered. It didn't make much sense to her, either,
when Jilian put it like that. But she had to know if her father was
telling the truth about the cure. She couldn't admit this, though,
or Lady Shaiala and her centaurs would try to stop her. They
still thought Lady Yashra deserved her punishment, so she
needed to give them another reason.

She took a deep breath and put all the subtle Songs she could
manage into her words. "When I was in the Memory Trance, just
before Frazhin interrupted us, I connected with Singer Rialle."

Seeing their blank looks, she explained: "That's the Crazy Singer Jilian's father picked up from the merlee and took to the forest Temple before he came to the Isle to get me. She was in a horrible cell of black crystal and she looked really ill, but I heard her clear as I can hear you now. She said we have to stop Frazhin. I don't know what he's doing exactly, because she didn't get a chance to tell me, but she said we had to hurry. She wanted me to tell Singer Renn, but it'll take too long to get out of the forest and send a message back to the Echorium. Frazhin's my father. He wants me with him. Maybe I can get close enough to stop him in time."

No one spoke. The waterfall roared beside them, enclosing them in its mist. The centaurs' manes and tails dripped. Lady Shaiala's hair was smeared untidily across her eyes, and Jilian's tunic was stuck to her back. Kyarra no longer knew if she was sweating or simply wet.

"So you see, we have to find him," she added, before they could say it was too dangerous. "And quickly."

Jilian started to shake her head. But Lady Shaiala surprised them both.

"I agree!" she said. "Frazhin has already corrupted far too many of the Half Creatures. Whatever he's up to is bound to be bad. We'll come with you. The centaurs can kick a way into his stronghold." She flashed Kyarra a girlish grin and flexed her feet. "I can still kick good, too."

Jilian scowled. "It's the stupidest idea I ever heard! That Memory Trance, or whatever it's called, has twisted both your brains! We've no idea where we are, anyway. How are we goin' to find the Lord of the Forest's stronghold in *this*?" She indicated the trees that grew thickly on both sides of the river.

Kyarra's heart sank slightly. "I don't suppose you can find the robber's path you were going to take me along?"

Jilian gave her a withering look. "Not without going all the way back to Asil's Hills and starting again! It wasn't a proper path, anyway. Father was the only one who knew the way through. And in case you've forgotten, we've got a whole tribe of painted men and a flock of wild quetzal between us and Rivermeet."

But Lady Shaiala was eyeing the river thoughtfully. "Maybe we don't have to find him. The centaurs say this water is full of his corrupted naga."

Jilian frowned, then shook her head violently. "Oh no! Bad idea! Bait usually gets swallowed alive, you know."

Kyarra was the last one to realize what they were suggesting. She turned cold, thinking of the naga that had attacked the raft. But Lady Shaiala — and she was starting to wonder if the Horselord woman might be even crazier than she'd thought — was already making plans.

She said Jilian should ride Rafiz Longshadow, while she herself would ride Marell Stormtemper, who was the strongest stallion. They'd use their herdstones to stay hidden, while Kamara Silvermane would try her best to keep up with the naga when they took Kyarra, and guide the rest of the herd to her. "It's all right, Kyarra," she said with the same girlish grin as before. "Erihan and I once used a similar naga route under the Mountains of Midnight, and we survived."

That left the question of a weapon for Kyarra. It was certain she would be searched upon arrival, so Jilian's dagger — that the girl immediately insisted she should take — wasn't practical. Lady Shaiala mentioned trying to get hold of one of the painted men's blow tubes, but Kyarra protested that there wasn't time to practice aiming with it, and the thought of swallowing a poison dart by accident made her cringe. Besides, Shaiala would have to use her herdstone and creep back to the forest people's nests to get hold of one, and that would waste time, too. Jilian suggested Kyarra should at least take one of the centaurs' green stones with her so she could hide herself if she needed to, but Shaiala shook her head.

"Only centaurs have the skill to use the herdstones," she told them. "I was able to learn how, because I lived with them when I was little, but no other human has ever managed to bend the light."

Kyarra was slightly relieved, because the centaurs' vanishing trick still sent shivers down her spine. "I don't need a weapon," she reminded them. "I'm nearly a Singer."

Shaiala shook her head impatiently. "Even trained Singers need five voices on a Pentangle to work their Songs. Renn told me that."

Jilian grinned. "Kyarra doesn't! She sang old Blackbeard to sleep after he attacked her mother, no trouble at all."

"You can't kill Frazhin with your voice, don't be silly," Shaiala said. "We need to kill him properly, not leave his body alive so he can come back again like Lady Yashra."

Kyarra's stomach twisted. She turned away from the Horselord woman and stared at the waterfall, its rush and roar filling her head. Shaiala was still discussing the weapon problem with her centaur friends, but Jilian came over and put a tentative arm around her.

"She didn't mean it like that, Kyarra."

She shrugged the girl off. "I'm all right. I just wish my mother —" She shook her head again. "I'm fine."

She turned to face Lady Shaiala and took a deep breath. "I obviously can't take a weapon with me. When I get close to him, maybe I can Sing him to sleep like I did to Blackbeard and find a weapon . . . if I need to."

Missing her hesitation, Shaiala grinned and slapped her on the back. "Good idea! But don't take any risks, do you hear? Sing him straight to sleep and let us in." She turned to examine the river. "I think it'll be best if we go above the fall where the water is quieter. You can sit on the edge there and maybe sing something to call the naga? Renn told me that's what he did when he wanted to talk to them."

As they climbed above the waterfall, Kyarra started to sweat again. Her head still felt strange, as if the contents were too big for her skull. The centaurs used their herdstones to bend the light and walked as silently as possible, avoiding twigs that would crack underfoot. Jilian slipped a hand into hers and gave her a quick smile.

"I think you're very brave," she whispered. "If we ever get out of here and find Father again, I'll make him give you half our treasure to make up for everythin' we did to you."

Kyarra shook her head. "I don't want your treasure."

"Whatever you want, then."

"You can't give me what I want."

They had come to a pool where the water was deep and green. Shaiala motioned the centaurs back and looked at Kyarra. Unexpectedly, she hugged her. "Don't worry, Princess Kyarra!" she said fiercely. "We'll be right behind you. We won't let Frazhin hurt you."

Kyarra looked speculatively at the strange, wild woman. "You never did say why you came after us. If it wasn't to take Jilian back, then why?"

Jilian turned her attention from the pool, curious.

The Horselord woman sighed. "I nearly killed Kyarra before she was born," she said very softly. "I kicked her mother when she was pregnant. It was a long time ago, before we smashed the Khiz that was brainwashing all the children Frazhin and Yashra had kidnapped and imprisoned in their Khizalace in the Mountains of Midnight. Yashra captured me, too, and tried to put her crystal mask on me. I panicked and kicked her in the stomach. I used a centaur kick, like when I broke Speaks Many Tongues' arm. I thought she was just fat. Then later Erihan said she was pregnant. I didn't know at the time, but that's no excuse. I've felt bad about it ever since. So when you needed help, I came." She looked embarrassed. "I feel responsible for you."

Kyarra blinked, trying to imagine the horror of that kick. "You knew my mother before she had *Yehn*? What was she like?"

Shaiala set her jaw. "She was evil. You weren't born then. You didn't see what she did. Lord Zorahan thinks the mask of khiz-crystal made her evil, but she didn't wear it all the time. Think about it."

*

Kyarra had plenty of time to think about what Lady Shaiala had told her, sitting on a rock at the edge of the pool above the waterfall. She'd donated her boots to Jilian and dipped her bare toes in the water, which was pleasantly warm. Trees brushed its surface with their leaves, and feathery purple flowers reflected in its depths. The water moved lazily around her blisters, soothing them, and dappled sunlight fell across her back. In different circumstances, she'd have enjoyed the chance to rest. But every bubble in the river and every rustle in the undergrowth made her stiffen. Although she knew her friends and the centaurs were hiding nearby, ready to rush out and camouflage her with their herdstones if the wild quetzal or the painted men should show up again, the knowledge did nothing to calm her.

"I *have* to see him," she whispered to the river. "I have to find out."

What if Frazhin had been lying about the cure? Worse still, what if the cure worked but her mother really was as evil as Lady Shaiala claimed? What would she do then?

She shook the worry away and blinked at the pool. The light was turning golden-brown as the sun slipped lower. The only things plopping in the river were fish. This wasn't going to work. A feeling of relief washed over her, followed by anger at her own cowardice.

She closed her eyes and filled her lungs. "FATHER!" she shouted, sending a cloud of small birds whirling up from the canopy. "Fa-ther! I'm here! Come and get me-e-e!"

Silence followed her shout. The forest seemed to be listening for more. Shadows breathed across the back of her neck. She heard a twig snap behind her and whirled in alarm.

Hunts Like a Spider stood there, his small body painted with gold and green whorls, a half-length spear pointed at her. He grinned. "I knew you came upriver! Centaurs careful, but have too many hooves to hide. Where are your friends?"

Kyarra froze. She glanced over her shoulder at the pool.

The boy's teeth flashed white in the shadows. "Come away from the water — dangerous, remember? Our Xiancotl sees a bad future for you if you go to the Lord of the Forest. He says to remember your Songs do not work properly on the dark ones."

Kyarra looked behind the boy, where green glimmers showed between the trees. Suddenly, a foot flew out of the green light and kicked the spear from his hand. Hunts Like a Spider dropped to one knee with a surprised yelp, cradling his wrist. A hand appeared from the air, seized his arm and dragged him upward, still kicking and yelling.

Kyarra jumped to her feet. "What do you mean, our Songs don't work on the dark ones? What does your Xiancotl know about it? Lady Shaiala, wait! He said —"

She didn't have time to finish. A long, snakelike tail whipped out of the pool and fastened around her waist. She screamed, struggling against it. "No, not now! Wait!" The tail tightened and pulled with alarming strength. Green-scaled hands closed about her ankles and jerked. She lost her balance and her knees cracked painfully on the rock. The next thing she knew, she was in the river fighting for breath.

More scaled hands tightened on her arms and legs. Tails thrashed everywhere. She was tangled in weed — no, it was hair, slimy green hair. A scaled face pushed up close to hers and smiled, revealing two rows of tiny, sharp teeth.

She started to scream again, to tell Shaiala and Jilian she'd changed her mind, but the naga had already dragged her under-water into the main flow of the river. She kicked desperately as the light disappeared in a muddy swirl of bubbles. She couldn't breathe, no longer knew which way was up or down. She sucked in river water, began to drown . . . Scaled lips pressed against hers, and suddenly her mouth was full of air. She gasped and struggled again. The naga who had given her air withdrew and wriggled back through the gloom to the surface, while others held Kyarra in the depths.

Fast. They were going so fast through the water, it roared in her ears, blinded her, filled her.

Another mouthful of air from another naga — or maybe the same one. Some of the panic left her. They were keeping her alive, after all. But down here in the depths, she was completely in their power, dependent upon the mouthfuls of air they gave her every time she thought her lungs would burst. The time between the mouthfuls was longer when she struggled. She gave up and let them pull her along, every limb slack. Maybe if they thought she was dying, they would give her more air?

She wasn't sure how long that terrifying underwater journey lasted. But at some point, the river darkened and grew noticeably warmer. She became aware of splashing all around her . . . a distant rumble . . . more air blown into her mouth . . . then a hot draft against her skin. The scaled bodies left her, slithering back into the water with echoing plops. And she was coughing and coughing as if she would never stop, crouched on her hands and knees on rough rock while the dark water streamed from her.

Kyarra thought she'd never be able to breathe properly again. But, eventually, the last of the water choked out of her lungs and she raised her head, able to think again about more than where her next breath was coming from.

She was in a huge, black-rock cavern filled with smoke. Behind her was the underground lake from which she'd emerged, slightly luminous, casting green ripples around the walls. The hot drafts indicated tunnels, though she couldn't see them in the shadows. And in the center of the cavern, still as a statue on his crystal throne, sat the man she'd seen in the Memory Trance watching her through the holes in his mask.

"So, my naga have brought me a jewel worth something, at last," he rasped in a voice that sent prickles along Kyarra's spine. "I must say I thought you would be bigger. Such a small, fragile thing to give everyone so much trouble. Well then, Daughter, get up and greet your father properly. Let's see what damage the Singers have done."

16
FANE

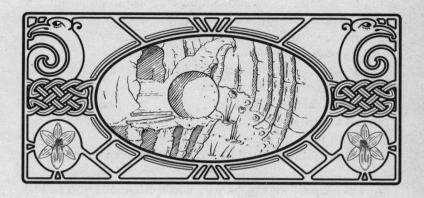

At dawn, the army broke camp and fought its way through the last of the dense forest of tree trunks to the Starmaker's Temple. After studying the plans they'd drawn from Night Plume's descriptions, the leaders had dispatched men to surround the crater and concentrated their main attack on the tunnel above the lakes and breeding ground, hoping to take Frazhin by surprise. It hadn't worked. The entrance to the tunnel was sealed by huge rocks, and the priests were waiting for them — a silent circle of men on the rim of the crater, their black robes whipped by the wind and the mountain spitting sparks behind them. Thunderclouds massed overhead, turning the morning darker than the night the army had just spent in the forest. The dark crystal stars around the priests' necks glittered ominously as the earth trembled.

The leaders hesitated. Their horses snorted in fear. Night Plume's legs turned weak. Forgetting he couldn't fly, he spread his wings, startling Caell's pony.

"Shh, Blackie, it's all right," the boy whispered, but his voice was too tense to calm the pony. "What are they waiting for?" he said, staring up at those silent defenders. "Why don't they attack?"

Night Plume refolded his wings. With the tunnel blocked, it would be difficult for a land-bound creature to get inside the Temple. The earth shook again, and a large boulder came bouncing down and crashed into the trees nearby.

"Back!" shouted the Karchlord. "Take cover!"

There was a moment of panic as men turned their horses and pushed back between the trunks.

"It's the same trick the Harai used in the Pass of Silence," muttered Singer Kherron, breaking off from the practice Songs he'd been humming constantly under his breath as they rode. "We've got to find out what they're using to make the mountain shake."

Speaks Many Tongues glanced at the Xiancotl, who still lay as if dead upon his litter. "They are not making it shake. It is the Lord of the Forest's Memory Trance, changing the world."

"Don't be stupid!" Although miraculously strengthened by the treatment he'd undergone the previous night, Singer Kherron's voice was still not quite under control. "Those priests are throwing boulders at us! Someone's got to get up there and stop them so the Kalerei horses can work on that blockage." He scowled up at the crater.

Even as he spoke, there was a *CRACK* deep under their feet, and the entire north side of the mountain split open. A great cloud of smoke and fiery ash poured down through the trees, obscuring the priests from view. Lord Zorahan was already winding his sharet around his mouth and nose. He drew his scimitar and glanced at Prince Erihan, who lifted his own sharet and nodded grimly. The Harai vanished into the ash with a faint rattle of hooves on rock. There was a pause, then Lord Zorahan burst from the cloud with a yell, whirling his scimitar around his head. The priests on the rim of the crater shouted in alarm. Some ran down toward the attacking Harai, while others toppled more boulders from the rim, which bounced among the

Harai mounts, knocking their legs from under them and sending screaming men and horses sliding back down the steep
scree. Night Plume was horrified to see a horse swept into the
burning ash, unable to escape with its broken leg. Others fled
into the forest, while their riders raced back up the slope on
foot, yelling their fury. But the ruse had served its purpose.
Under cover of the Harai distraction, Prince Erihan led a group
of his Kalerei to the blocked entrance, where their mounts
began to work on the rocks, lashing out with terrible blows that
resounded down the mountainside.

Night Plume looked anxiously across the lake, but there was
no sign of Sky Swooper or the other quetzal. So much noise and
ash, so many falling rocks, so many men, so much smoke and
confusion . . . he couldn't see if the duty mothers and the fledglings were all right. *Quetzal nest on other side!* he said to Caell. *Got
to rescue eggs and fledglings!*

The boy kicked his pony closer to the two Singers and relayed
this. Singer Kherron scowled at him, but Singer Renn called,
"Someone check around the other side! There might be young
quetzal in trouble. But keep an eye on the crater — I don't trust
those priests."

Some of the Kalerei who had been waiting their turn at the
tunnel drew their scimitars and trotted around the lake shore
into the smoke. Night Plume stared after them uneasily. He
scanned the sky. *Something wrong,* he said to Caell. *Too quiet over
there.*

The Karchlord had maneuvered his men into position on the
opposite side of the crater. The Karchholders could be seen urging their ponies around glowing boulders and broken trees,
forcing them up the slope where ash and smoke still obscured
the struggle going on above.

"There goes Azri!" Lazim muttered. He turned to Speaks
Many Tongues, who had been coordinating the painted men's
efforts to identify all exits from the volcano, and the two spoke
quietly a moment. Lazim came back to the Singers, smiling.

"Speaks Many Tongues believes his men have found another way in along an underground river. Frazhin's naga are guarding the way, but with luck we should be able to get past them. The Xiancotl's people are watching all the other possible exits, down to every tiny crack, so no one will get out without us knowing about it. Frazhin won't escape by the back door this time, don't worry."

Singer Kherron's eyes glittered. His fist clenched on his dagger as he hummed another practice Song that made Night Plume's feathers stand on end. Singer Renn smiled grimly and turned to Caell and Night Plume. "You two stay here with the Xiancotl. When we've found out what's going on inside, I'll send someone to collect you — or take you to safety, whichever's best."

Night Plume was still trying to see what was happening over at the nest, but Caell set his jaw. "I'm not a child! I can help."

Singer Kherron turned on him with a scowl and said in his new, powerful voice, "You'll do what you're told, boy! Stay here with the Half Creature. We're going in there after Rialle and Frazhin. We can't be looking out for you at every turn."

"I can help get you past the naga," Caell whispered, standing his ground. "I can sing to Half Creatures, remember?"

Kherron's face darkened, but Renn laid a hand on his arm. "Caell, I know you can. But all the Half Creatures in there are Frazhin's. You heard what Night Plume told us. They're corrupted. They won't listen to you. You're more use to us out here." He touched the bluestone that hung about the boy's neck. "Contact me using this if you see or hear anything we should know about. All right?"

Caell didn't look happy about it, but he nodded. He and Night Plume watched as the two Singers and the pentad made their way off through the forest, following their painted guide.

Night Plume pulled his injured wing closer to his body and touched Caell's ankle. *We go*, he said in wild-speech, pointing to the path around the lake.

Caell eyed the Xiancotl, whose litter had been laid at the roots of an old, gnarled tree a short way back into the trees. Speaks Many Tongues and a group of the painted men were standing around it, looking expectantly at the branches. No one was paying the two youngsters any attention. "Singer Renn said to stay here," Caell said doubtfully.

Something wrong. Humans not come back. We find quetzal mother Dawn Crest and others, find out what happen and where Sky Swooper is. You tell Singers using bluestone.

The boy needed no further urging. With much kicking and Night Plume pulling on the reins, they persuaded the unwilling Blackie through the cloud of drifting ash. A fiery river lay across their path. The heat and smell almost choked Night Plume, but they found a bridge of debris and Caell pulled him astride the pony to cross. Even so, Night Plume's tail got singed. They descended into the trees, eyes watering, blind. Then they were out of the ash and the Lake of Stars was spread before them, reflecting the fire from the mountain.

Night Plume's gaze immediately flew to the nest, seeking the mothers who would guard the eggs with their lives. What he saw made his head whirl in anguish. His beak opened and he let out a cry that rivaled the voice of the mountain. Caell's arms tightened about his waist. "Don't look, Night Plume."

One of the Kalerei, who had been picking his way around the edge of the nest, spotted them and urged his mount across the crystal to wave them back. But there was no way of hiding what had been done to the quetzal nest. Fear and pain lingered in the air. The tree where the wild fledglings had been hung as an example to others of their flock had gained several new bodies. The quetzal mothers who had cared for the nest dangled there upside down by their talons, wings drooping lifelessly. Among them was Dawn Crest with her mutilated flight pinions — and at the end of the line hung a smaller, younger female with blue and green plumage, her wings sliced off and nailed to the trunk.

Night Plume was off the pony before he realized he'd moved.

He half-flew, half-stumbled around the shore of the lake. Inside, he was one huge cry of pain. Even after what Sun Glimmer had told him, he hadn't quite believed the Starmaker would hurt one of his own creatures. There was always the hope his friend had been lying under enchantment, that the Starmaker had told him to lie to break Night Plume's spirit. But this was worse than Sky Swooper having her wings clipped, far worse, no hope of her flying, ever again . . .

"Sky Swooper!" he choked.

He stood beneath the tree, staring upward. Her beautiful blue tail curled down past her amputated wings to brush the forest floor. He stroked it tenderly.

Caell had dismounted and was holding the reins of his pony, staring about him numbly. The Kalerei were poking through the nest, scattering the crystal and fragments of rainbow eggshell. They shook their heads. Every egg had been smashed.

"I'm so sorry, Night Plume." Caell's voice startled him out of his misery.

"My fault," he whispered, still stroking Sky Swooper's beautiful tail. "All my fault."

"No. Frazhin did it." Caell's voice had a hard edge to it. He raised his eyes to the crater and clenched the bluestone in his fist. "Now I know he's evil. Anyone who can kill helpless Half Creatures like that deserves to die. Why did he do it, Night Plume? I thought he wanted to use them in his Memory Trance."

"Mothers no use to him," Night Plume said sadly. "They old quetzal, not enchanted by blackstars in eggs like we were. Unborn fledglings no use, either. And Sky Swooper . . . he punish Sky Swooper to hurt me."

Anger overcame his sorrow as he remembered his last arrow. He clamped his beak against the pain of his wounded shoulder and reached for his bow. Awkwardly, he fitted the black arrow to the string and flexed his injured wing. "I go over top, get inside, kill Starmaker." He started up the slope toward the rim of the crater, his vision blurred, misery and anger blinding him to the danger.

He didn't see the boulder come out of the smoke. The first warning he had was when Caell caught him around the waist with a cry. The boulder bounced high into the air as the two youngsters — human and quetzal — threw themselves flat to the ground. It ricocheted off a trunk and splashed into the Lake of Stars. Steam hissed skyward.

The Kalerei leader shook his head, looking down at where Night Plume and Caell lay trembling after their narrow escape. "There's nothing we can do here. I think we should —"

He never finished. The air around them shimmered green, and a whole herd of centaurs appeared from nowhere, the leading two ridden by a wild-looking, red-headed girl and an equally wild-looking woman with tangled black hair and bare feet. As she became visible, a small painted boy wriggled out of her grasp and ran off through the trees.

Caell gasped and tightened his grip on Night Plume. Some of the Kalerei had drawn their scimitars when the centaurs appeared, but their alarm turned to smiles of welcome as they recognized the woman. There was a shout behind them, and Prince Erihan came galloping around the lake, his sharet flapping loose, his eyes brighter than the fire in the sky.

"SHAI!" He dragged his horse to a halt and stared at the woman, drinking her in with his gaze. "Where have you *been*? You're just in time! We need the centaurs to kick us a way in. Our horses are trying their best but they're tired, and I think Frazhin must have enchanted the rocks because they're not cracking like they should. Have you got the Singer girl with you? She might be able to help —"

"Would we be here if we had?" interrupted the red-haired girl. "Them devil-nagas dragged her into the mountain through an underground water tunnel, or at least that's what Kamara Silvermane says. So now we've got to get in there, too." She poked her centaur mount in the back of his human torso. "What are you waitin' for, Rafiz Longshadow? Make us invisible again so we can get past them priests. They can't chuck boulders at what they can't see!"

The dark centaur twisted his head and scowled at the girl. His tail swished and he gave a strong buck, sending her sailing over his shoulder. She landed with a thud next to Caell and Night Plume. There were chuckles among the Kalerei as she jumped to her feet, dagger in hand, scowling.

Prince Erihan and Lady Shaiala barely noticed. They were too busy catching up on all that had happened while they'd been apart. Night Plume finally had a chance to observe at close quarters how he'd been tricked in the hills when he'd lost the girls. The centaurs shifted and blurred in and out of the green light, one moment visible; the next moment, apparently not there.

Caell grabbed the red-headed girl's arm. "Where is she?" he demanded, the undercurrents in his voice making Night Plume's feathers stand on end. *"What have you done with Ky?"*

"Oy, steady on!" The girl shrugged him off and looked him up and down. "I already told you. She's in there, ain't she?" She pointed to the crater. "I said it was a bad idea all along, but would anyone listen to me? Maybe this'll teach you all to take Jilian of the Hills more seriously in the future!" She gave his blue hair another stare. "You're one of them Singers, aren't you? What's your name? What's the funny-colored quetzal doing here? Is it friendly?"

Caell didn't hang around to answer. He ran to Blackie, dragged the reins back over his ears and leaped on the pony's back with all the skill of a Horselord. Kicking and yelling, he forced the pony into a gallop up toward the crater. Night Plume hurried after him, his injured wing dragging on the ground. There was a rattle of hooves behind as someone gave chase. A lilac centaur mare, her pale coat shining in the gloom, drew up and trotted alongside him, doing something with the stone around her neck. Green light glimmered through the ash cloud. There was a rumble — Night Plume couldn't tell if it came from the Temple or the sky — and suddenly he was being overtaken by a solid wave of centaurs and horses at full gallop.

The other Horselords, who had been waiting out of sight in the trees for the signal to attack, saw Prince Erihan and the Kalerei charge. A great yell emerged from thousands of throats as they burst from cover and galloped up the slope toward the crater, their scimitars glittering in the firelight. The priests rolled more boulders down, but there were so many horses that even the many who were swept away or injured before they reached the final scree left hundreds of others to surge on upward into the smoke. When the crater grew too steep to ride up, the Horselords put their scimitars in their teeth, flung themselves off their mounts and swarmed over the rim of the crater like ants. With terrible cries, they cut down the priests.

Unmounted, Night Plume soon got left behind and lost sight of Caell in all the confusion. But the red-headed girl, Jilian, was running beside him. She grinned at him through the smoke and brandished her dagger. "Hurry up, dark quetzal!" she called. "Or we'll miss the fight!"

With the lilac centaur shielding them both with her green stone that bent light, they made it to the rim, where the centaur had to fall back while they scrambled over. They paused for breath at the top and stared down into the crater. Bodies were scattered everywhere — priests, Horselords, a few Karchholders, centaurs and horses who had scrambled over, only to find spikes of rock and crystal waiting for them below. Night Plume looked anxiously for Caell, but there was no sign of the Singer boy. Half the rim had crumbled away under the force of the fiery lava. Amidst the smoke and sparks below, men struggled and yelled and blades clashed. It was unrecognizable as the place where Night Plume had reported the silver-haired prisoner's words to the Starmaker and spent his final night with Sky Swooper.

"C'mon, dark quetzal!" Jilian shouted, giving his tail a tug. "Kyarra's down there someplace, an' I promised not to abandon her. If we stick together, me and my dagger, and you and your bow, maybe we can make it out of here alive. How many arrows have you got?"

"Only one."

Night Plume searched the shadows at the edge of the crater, trying to get his bearings in the altered landscape. He half-scrambled, half-flew around the ridge, relying on his dark plumage to hide him in the smoke, until he was above the tunnel the Starmaker used to descend into his Temple. He peered down through the smoke.

After what they'd found at the lake, he was afraid of what he'd see. But these quetzal were alive; packed together in a corner of the crater, each and every one of them crouched down with trembling wings spread as if they supported a rock the size of the volcano on their flattened crests. He recognized Sun Glimmer, some of the others from his patrol, and the young fledglings from the nest who couldn't fly very well yet. The older quetzal still had their bows, and every beak was stained bright gold. Littered around them were yellow petals and the black mushy mounds of the flowers they'd already chewed.

Jilian scowled down at them. "Let's get into that tunnel and find Kyarra before those quetzal start shooting at us!"

Night Plume shook his head. "Help nestmates first."

He began to lower himself clumsily down the cliff, but Sun Glimmer whistled and sprang across the crater, talons extended and beak wide. An arrow rattled against the rock, parting Night Plume's tail. He hastily scrambled back up. "It me, Sun Glimmer!" he called through the smoke. "Not eat Yellow Flowers! They help Starmaker destroy Memoryplace! Get out of here. Fly! Temple on fire! Everyone die!"

The quetzal didn't hear him. While Sun Glimmer and his nestmates kept Night Plume at bay with their arrows, the others picked up more petals and chewed them. There was a strange hum in the crater, vibrating around the walls and invading Night Plume's head. Jilian tugged his tail.

"Forget it!" she said. "They obviously don't want to be helped."

Night Plume gripped his bow tighter and stared at his nest-mate, feeling helpless. "Wish I fly," he said. "Get down there easy."

Jilian grunted. "I wish I could fly, too! But this ain't helpin' Kyarra, and I don't trust those quetzal — the last thing they did was try to kill us."

"Not true! We rescue you from wild flock . . ." Remembering what Speaks Many Tongues had said about the Xiancotl needing the chewed flowers so he could enter the Starmaker's Trance and stop him from changing the Memoryplace, Night Plume raised his face to the circle of black sky. *Where you go, wild flock? Come get Yellow Flowers if you want them!*

He didn't think they'd heard. Then a familiar whistle pierced his head as the wild quetzal spiraled out of the smoke, sending Jilian staggering backward with a little scream.

-we-already-try-

-you-need-to-explain-to-stupid-blackstar-quetzal-

-we-not-enemy-

They not listen to me! Night Plume sent back, impatient. *They enchanted!*

-they-listen-if-you-use-wild-speech-

-all-creatures-hear-everything-

-in-memory-trance-

Night Plume looked doubtfully at Sun Glimmer. But it was worth a try.

So sorry, Sun Glimmer, sorry I traitor. But you must let wild flock take your chewed Yellow Flowers. You must stop chewing them. You must not do what Starmaker says. Not help in Starmaker's Trance. He evil, try to destroy our Memoryplace. Trust me. I leader!

The scarlet-and-gold quetzal jerked as if he'd been punished by the Starmaker's spear. Just for a moment, his eyes focused properly on Night Plume and the human girl crouched beside him with her dagger out.

Night Plume . . . ?

Yes! It me! Let wild flock take flowers, Sun Glimmer. They not enemy. They quetzal like us.

Slowly, Sun Glimmer lowered his bow. The others did the same.

-good!-

-we-take-chewed-flowers-to-yellow-flower-dreamer-

-so-he-stop-blackstarhuman-from-changing-Memoryplace-

They swept down in a flurry of bright wings, pecked up the black chewed mush, and flew off. The whole operation was over in a few heartbeats. The enchanted quetzal still crouched, crooning in the smoke, but now there was a new sound deep within the mountain. The rocks around them rippled like water and splinters of crystal exploded into the air, showering the quetzal with glittering black rain. The crater rim swayed as if it were made of leaves, and the section Night Plume and Jilian were clinging to began to slide downward.

Night Plume spread his wings in alarm and tried to scramble back up. But Jilian grabbed his tail with a wild laugh. "I wondered how we were goin' to get down there!" she shouted. "Quick, dark quetzal, before that tunnel collapses! We've got to find Kyarra!"

Night Plume let himself slide, using his good wing to slow their fall so they would get to the bottom in one piece. Sun Glimmer and the others watched, blank-eyed again. But they'd be free soon.

"Find Starmaker," he agreed, pushing his fear of the dark Temple aside and gripping the black arrow he'd saved for so long.

*

Deep within the mountain where Kyarra crouched, the tremor rippled the surface of the underground lake and shook stones down from the roof. She heard them splash into the water behind her, but her gaze remained fixed on the dark figure seated on the crystal throne in the center of the cavern, wisps of smoke coiling around him.

She climbed shakily to her feet. Now she was standing, their eyes were almost level. "Is it true?" Her voice emerged as a squeak. She took a deep breath and tried again. "Do you really know how to cure my mother?"

"Yes, Daughter, I do."

She watched her father very closely but it was impossible to see if he was telling the truth. The dark mask hid his expression, and he sat so still that not one of the crystal lozenges sewn into his robe glittered.

There was a cough in the shadows behind the throne. With a start, Kyarra realized they weren't alone. Four black-robed, shaven-headed men waited near the cavern walls. The tremor had showered one of them in dust. But after that single cough he stood motionless, not even raising a hand to wipe away the blood where a stone had grazed his temple.

"Why do you wear that mask?" Kyarra said, overcoming some of her fear.

"Would you like me to take it off?"

"I . . . yes!"

The figure on the throne stirred. Very slowly, one crystal glove raised to the mask, unfastened the hooks, and slid it from his face. "Take a good look, Daughter." His laugh was like fingernails scraping over rock. "See how beautifully the quetzal rearranged my face for me before I tamed them."

Every nerve screamed at her to run. But she made herself stand still and meet her father's gaze. With an effort, Kyarra held her stomach in check.

His face was so scarred and twisted, it no longer looked human. Except for the eyes. Those black, burning eyes that stared at her as if they could see inside her soul. Looks don't matter, she reminded herself, thinking of the Echorium's lessons in truth listening. It's what is inside that matters.

She swallowed the bile. "Everyone says you're evil," she whispered. "Are you?"

The mass of scar-tissue twisted. A dry chuckle emerged from

what might once have been a mouth. "The Singers are bound to say that, aren't they? Who says the Singers aren't evil? You're here because of what they did to your mother, aren't you? If I cure her, will that make me good?"

His words were like an arrow, straight to the heart. Kyarra's breath tightened. "They gave her *Yehn*. They say she enslaved the centaurs and captured children, that you made her do it. But she's so helpless . . . what they did to her is horrible, cruel."

The eyes studied her with interest. "Maybe they haven't quite brainwashed you with their Songs, after all. You're brave enough, I grant you that. Not many people would stand there with the mountain shaking all around them and look upon my face as coolly as you are now." He let the mask drop to the floor, where it landed with a rattle, its crystal beak pointing at the roof. "Soon I won't need this anymore, so I hope you'll forgive me if I don't wear it. It makes my scars itch."

Everything inside Kyarra was trembling like a novice sent to the Pentangle stool for their first Song. "They told me you were dying," she whispered.

The scars twisted. "We're all dying, Daughter. Some quicker than others, that's all. But I don't have to die, any more than your mother has to stay a zombie."

Kyarra did a quick breathing exercise and hummed some *Challa,* more to calm herself than anything else.

Frazhin lifted the crystal spear that lay across his knees and touched her lightly on the forehead. "No Songs, Daughter, I'm sorry. They don't work very well down here, anyway. I've lined this place with khiz-crystal to protect my faithful creatures and myself from the Singers. I'm sure you don't blame me, after you've seen the way they hate me."

Kyarra's heart thudded. She let the *Challa* fade. "Why did you have me kidnapped?" she demanded, moving her head away from the spear.

His face contracted again, squeezing the scars. It was her

father's version of a smile, she realized. "Would you have left the Echorium and come here of your own free will?"

"I . . . no, novices aren't allowed out on their own."

"There you are, then."

Another tremor shook the walls of the cavern, and the lake erupted with a sudden hiss of steam. As Kyarra ducked the hot spray, her father waved his spear. The priests ran forward, grasped the poles attached to the corners of the throne, and lifted it with its occupant onto their shoulders.

"I might have come once I was a Singer. You could have waited . . ."

"Waited until you were a Singer? I don't think that would have been very wise, do you? I've waited quite long enough." Her father's scars twisted. "Time to go to my Fane. We'll be safe there."

Kyarra darted a glance at the tunnels. More debris fell from their roofs. In some, a flickering glow warned of fire. He hadn't denied anything. So he must have been responsible for her mother's punishment. But Singers had actually carried out the *Yehn,* not Frazhin. And he said he knew a cure . . . It was so hard to think. The inside of her head sparkled with dark stars.

Her father looked back. "Coming, Daughter?"

She shook her head.

The scars did the smile-thing again. "There's no other way out of here, unless you fancy trying the underwater route again. I wouldn't recommend it. Things are getting warm down there, so my naga tell me. They can survive in boiling water, but they've got scales to protect them and you haven't. Your mother's cure is this way," he added, as if it were an afterthought.

Kyarra swallowed her fear and hurried after the throne as the priests carried it and its crippled occupant into one of the tunnels, where a fifth priest was waiting for them with a flaming torch. The tunnel sloped downward into the smoke. As they descended, the mountain continued to shudder. Every so often there was a groan, followed by a rattle of dust and rubble and a whoosh of bad air as the roof behind them collapsed. She was afraid they'd be buried alive. But an orange glow was visible ahead, like the sun rising over the sea. She pushed past the throne — and stopped with a gasp as the tunnel emerged on a narrow ledge partway up the wall of an enormous cavern. The priests lowered the throne and rubbed their shoulders. Dizzy, Kyarra crept forward.

Below — very far below — boiled a lake of molten fire, spitting out red-hot boulders the size of houses. Their ledge was out of range of all but the smallest sparks, but it was sweat-pouringly hot, and the air left ash on the tongue. Equally far above was a tiny ring of sky with an enormous plug of black crystal blocking the opening. Every so often, the crystal would lift a little in its bed and a twisting column of smoke and sparks would be sucked up the cavern, past the ledge where Kyarra crouched, to escape through the sky-ring. Even if they could fly like quetzal, they'd never survive that way.

"How . . . how are we going to get out?" she whispered.

"Ah, Daughter, don't you understand yet? We're not trying to get out. My Fane is right here. We're going to seal ourselves in. Then my priests will roll us into the heart of the mountain where everything is still unformed, and when we get there, we're going to change the world."

Her father reached out and touched what she'd taken to be another oversized boulder, covered in ash, balanced on the very edge of the ledge. As his glove scratched the ash from the surface, it revealed a pane of dark, semitransparent crystal. The Fane was hollow, with various straps and webbing visible inside. Nestled in a little dish amidst the webbing were two perfect yellow blooms of the same flower Hunts Like a Spider had found for the Xiancotl to chew. Lying nearby were two stout poles.

While his priests scurried around the Fane, brushing off the rest of the ash and inserting the poles under the side opposite the drop, Frazhin explained. "It took me many experiments, but I've at last discovered the secret of the quetzal Memoryplace. Who'd have thought their little party trick that the Singers brought to my attention back when I was humble Khizpriest of the Karch would prove to have such great potential? But I should have guessed. After all, merlee can control the wind and waves. Naga control the rivers and the deep places. Centaurs control the earth and the light. Quetzal had to have *some* power over their environment. At first, I thought the Yellow Flowers merely lowered resistance to questioning. How wrong I was! They dissolve barriers in the head, Daughter. They enable us to connect with the quetzal Memoryplace, where the history of the whole world is kept, past, present, and future. This forest has been hiding the greatest secret of all time!"

Dissolve barriers. Kyarra forgot her fear and stared through the dark crystal at the yellow blooms. "They're the cure, aren't they?" she breathed. "They'll open the doors in my mother's head just like they roused the Xiancotl so he could enter his Trance . . . oh, why didn't I see it before?"

Frazhin laughed. "Yes, they're part of the cure — but not all of it. Don't be deceived, Daughter. Giving Lady Yashra the flowers to chew would only be temporary. I can make her cure permanent. We're going to use the Yellow Flowers to connect with the quetzal Memoryplace and travel back to the time before the Singers existed. My faithful quetzal remember the world not as it is, but as it should have been. When we've changed history, my injuries will be healed and you'll no longer be a Singer, because Singers will not exist in my new world. I'd hoped to destroy the Isle of Echoes as well by taking some bluestone into the Fane with me, but unfortunately, in addition to losing you, that idiot pirate managed to lose the bluestone I sent him to collect from the Isle for me. He'll pay for his clumsiness in due course. But first, we have work to do."

He reached out with his spear, whispered under his breath,

and touched the Fane. There was a *click*, and one side sprang open to form a small, five-sided door.

"After you, Daughter," Frazhin said, waving at the interior. "I made it for two."

Kyarra knew the truth now. He wasn't merely evil. He was utterly crazy.

She began to move back along the tunnel. Maybe she could find a way around the collapsed sections, and —

"Where are you going, Daughter?" The question rasped across the back of her neck.

Kyarra retreated another step, watching the priests warily. "You don't really mean to cure my mother at all, do you? It was a trick all along to get me here. I'm not going in that thing with you — I'm not that stupid! If it doesn't seal up properly, we'll be burned to a cinder once we fall in that fire! And if it does seal, how are you planning to breathe in there?"

"We won't need much air. The Memory Trance shouldn't take long. My quetzal are already waiting for us to join them, and the Yellow Flowers I sent to the Isle of Echoes and Silver-town and a few other strategic places should have opened enough people's heads by now for the effects of my Trance to reach the whole world. We'll change things at the end so the mountain is cool. I've come back from the dead twice already. A third time will be no problem. All we have to do is chew the flowers and —"

Tears in her eyes, Kyarra turned and ran.

She expected him to send his priests after her, and readied her breath for *Aushan*. Even if the Song didn't have much effect down here, it might delay them long enough for her to give them the slip, find Jilian, perhaps get some of the Yellow Flowers to her mother so she could at least be cured temporarily . . . But what came after her was far worse.

Raspy words, almost too quiet to hear: "*If you come with me when I change history, Daughter, your mother will be healed. Otherwise, she won't have any reason to exist."*

Kyarra stopped.

Her legs must have carried her back to the ledge of their own accord, because before she knew it, the spear was touching her forehead. Her head filled with dark stars, taking away the fear. "Do you really know how to change the past?"

Her father smiled. "I promise I do, Daughter. When we go back in time and get rid of the Singers, they won't be able to sing your mother their Death Song because it won't even have been invented. Lady Yashra will be your real, living mother, not a Singer-made zombie. But it has to be your choice. I'm not going to force you to do anything you don't want to. Are you brave enough to enter the Fane with me and help change the world? Or will you run back to your Singer friends and wait to expire with them?"

A brief vision blurred before her eyes. A boy with blue hair, creeping out of the Echorium in search of merlee . . . She shook her head. Caell was already dead. Even changing history wouldn't change that — or would it?

"I don't believe it'll work," she whispered.

The spear lifted. Her father sighed. "Yes you do, Daughter. You know the Singer truth listening, so you know I believe it will work. As to whether I'm right, can you afford not to take that chance? For eleven years, I've worked closely with my Half Creatures and experimented with the secrets of this forest. I know everything the forest people know, and more. I'm not lying to you. You know I'm not."

She couldn't think straight. The heat and fumes from the fire were making her light-headed. But if there was a chance . . . any chance . . .

"Why do you want to destroy the Singers?" she asked.

Her father sighed. "You want the truth, Daughter, so I'll tell you. When I was your age, I wanted nothing more than to be a

Singer myself. But they told me my voice wasn't good enough. They made a mistake, but they sent me away rather than admit it. I've never forgiven them for that."

"You were a novice?" Kyarra whispered, her senses reeling.

"No — because they wouldn't have me."

"But —"

Frazhin touched her forehead with the spear again. "Time's running out, Daughter. I've been honest with you. It's time for you to choose. Will you come with me?"

What choice did she have? "All right," she whispered.

The priests moved fast. When one of them placed a Yellow Flower on her tongue, she didn't resist. Her father was busily chewing the other bloom. She chewed, too. The raw flower tasted foul — much, much worse than the Xiancotl's chewed petals — but before she could spit it out her limbs grew heavy and her vision blurred. The priests carried her inside the Fane and secured her in the webbing, drawing it tightly about her body like a cocoon until she was suspended in the center of the smoky crystal, surprisingly comfortable. They lifted her father off his throne and strapped him in beside her. They kept his crystal spear outside. There was a pause while another priest ran out of the tunnel, shouting something she couldn't hear and pointing back the way he'd come. Kyarra turned her head — oh so slowly — and blinked at the five-sided door.

The priest holding the spear quickly touched the mechanism with it. The panel sealed with a sigh, enclosing Kyarra in soft dark smoke. The other priests flung themselves on the levers. There was a moment of claustrophobia, then the crystal walls drifted away. The door in her head was already opening. On the other side of it sat the Xiancotl, his skin painted in gold like flames. He was speaking, but she couldn't quite hear.

. . . in the Memory Trance. I see the Dark One and he has blackstars in his head . . .

"NO, KY! WAKE UP! YOU'VE GOT TO WAKE UP!"

She blinked. Was someone calling her name? As the Fane

began to rock on the edge of the chasm, the Xiancotl swirled away. On the other side of the smoky panels, robed figures were struggling, indistinct and dark. Then two pale hands pressed against the crystal and a face she knew peered in at her. Blue hair. Boy. Singing.

"Caell . . .?" she whispered, and closed her eyes in sudden joy. If they'd brought Caell back to life, the Trance must be working.

*

Night Plume had barely entered the tunnel with Jilian when Caell's excited wild-speech burst in his head.

Quick, Night Plume! I found Ky, but she's in trouble. Bring men, any-one. Find the Singers! I used the bluestone and told them to wait for you. Bring them HERE . . . Tunnels flashed through Night Plume's head, as if the Starmaker were giving directions with his spear. *Starmaker with her,* Caell added. *Bring your black arrow. Hurry!*

We come, Night Plume sent back, taking Jilian's hand and dragging her deeper into the volcano. The tunnels were choked with smoke and struggling bodies, but he knew where he was. He'd been down here before.

At first, the Horselords they found fighting the Starmaker's priests in the tunnels were reluctant to follow Night Plume. But Jilian yelled at them, promising he knew where Frazhin was hid-ing, so they pulled their sharets tighter across their noses and hurried after him. They collected more of the army as they went deeper — Horselords, Karchholders, and the occasional centaur, all anxious to be the first to seize Frazhin. Some of the tunnels were blocked by falling debris, but the centaurs kicked a way through. It grew hotter as they descended. Night Plume gripped his bow and single arrow, filled with a great excitement. With so many men and centaurs following him, it was like leading his old flock. He hardly felt the pain of his injured wing.

They met the Singers at a fork of the tunnels where an under-ground stream steamed across their way. Night Plume quickly told them what Caell had said, and Singer Kherron paled. Singer Renn was supporting the silver-haired prisoner on his shoulder.

She was filthy, wet, singed and terribly thin, but her gray eyes sought out Night Plume's and she smiled. "Thank you, dark quetzal," she whispered. "I'm sorry I can't use the inside-speech to talk to you anymore, but it's been a while since I've eaten the Yellow Flowers — though if I'd known what Frazhin was keeping them for, I'd have pretended I had more to tell him."

Night Plume whistled. "Glad you find friends."

"No time for reunions!" Singer Kherron shouted in a voice so powerful, it brought more rubble down from the roof. "If we don't find Frazhin fast, we're going to lose both him and the girl! Which way, quetzal?" Night Plume pointed, and Singer Kherron leaped the stream and raced down the final tunnel, tattered robes flapping.

Lazim breathed a curse. "Kher never changes, does he? Never stops to consider if it might be a trap." He jumped the stream as well, and the Horselords, Karchholders and centaurs surged past Night Plume and pounded after the orderly.

Singer Renn exchanged a look with the rescued Singer. The remaining four members of the pentad closed protectively around them as sounds of a brief struggle carried back along the tunnel. There were a few yells that faded as if men had fallen from a high place, followed by silence.

Renn gave Night Plume and Jilian a worried look. "Give me a bit of room, you two. I don't like that silence. Stay here with Singer Rialle and the orderlies until I say it's safe."

He passed the silver-haired Singer into the care of one of the pentad. Surrounded by swirling steam and wisps of smoke, silhouetted against the fire-glow at the end of the tunnel, the Second Singer of the Echorium drew three quick breaths to clear his lungs and let out a hum that raised Night Plume's feathers and made Jilian clutch her dagger more tightly. Still singing, he stepped gracefully over the stream and disappeared after the others.

Jilian looked as if she longed to rush after him, but couldn't make up her mind if she'd been told to stay for her own protection or to help the orderlies protect the rescued prisoner. "Well?" she demanded, apparently deciding on the latter. "Contact that Singer friend of yours again, quetzal! What's goin' *on*?"

Singer Rialle pushed herself upright. "Yes," she said. "What's Frazhin done to Kyarra? Renn thinks I'm still too weak, but I can sing if I have to."

Caell? Night Plume sent in wild-speech. *What happen?*

The boy didn't reply at first, and they all feared the worst. Then Caell's wild-speech came back, shaky and subdued.

Oh, Night Plume! Frazhin's got Ky with him in a horrible crystal cell. We stopped the priests pushing it over the edge, but I think we're too late to save her.

17

YEHN

It took the Horselords and Singers the rest of the day to maneuver the Starmaker's crystal Fane and its unconscious occupants out of the mountain. They had to use an underground river for the final part of the journey, trusting the khiz-crystal to protect its prisoners against the heat. Now the Fane floated in the cooling water of the lake amidst reflected stars, tethered to the bank with a net of vines braided by the forest people. It looked eerily beautiful, glittering in the dark water. Inside, the Starmaker and the Singer girl lay side by side, their eyes closed. The girl's blue hair trailed against the lower panes, and the Starmaker's heavy robe draped one of her arms. Her lips were curved into a little smile.

The Singers had called a meeting on the lake shore to discuss what to do. Around them, in the wisps of cooling smoke, men were busy clearing bodies, tending the injured, digging through the rubble, and gradually setting up camp. The volcano had settled down after the Fane was extracted, and only the occasional faint tremor reminded them of its power. Most of the ash had blown away along with the storm clouds, and the surface of the water was still.

"I can't stand this!" Caell said, leaping to his feet, fists clenched. "They've got to decide what to do soon, or Ky will suffocate in there! What's the problem? Why don't they just *open* it?"

Night Plume kept silent. They'd all seen the Singers' attempts to open the Fane. A captive priest, dragged from the ledge inside the mountain before he could fling himself into the chasm after his comrades, had laughed in the Second Singer's face and told them only the Starmaker himself could open it. They'd thrown his Khiz-spear into the fire, and without it the panels would remain sealed because of the enchantment he'd put on them. "But when he changes history, he'll bring his spear back — then you'll be sorry, Singer!" The priest spat curses at them until Singer Kherron grew impatient and sang to him with his newly healed voice, whereupon the priest gave a sudden jerk, his eyes rolled up in his head and he fell down dead at their feet, poisoned by the Purple Flower bloom they found under his tongue.

The Horselords had tried to work out the mechanism, but couldn't even agree which panel was meant to open. The Karchholders had tried to force a way in. The centaurs had kicked it. Lady Shaiala had kicked it while Singer Renn sang at the same time, which apparently was the method they'd used to crack the Khiz eleven years ago in the Mountains of Midnight. Nothing worked.

"They're tryin' their best," Jilian said, putting a hand on Caell's arm. "Don't worry, she's still breathing in there. Look, she's even smiling! Havin' a far better time in her dreams than we're having stuck out here in this burned forest, I bet!"

Caell shrugged the girl off. "You keep out of this! If you and your stupid father hadn't taken Ky from the Isle in the first place, she wouldn't be in that . . . that foul crystal cell . . . at all!"

Jilian's face closed. Night Plume whistled. *She worry about her father*, he reminded the boy.

"I don't care!" Caell glared at the girl. "I hope the pirate's dead! He deserves to be." It was clear Asil hadn't run to warn Frazhin of the attack, but that didn't change what he'd done.

Jilian whipped out her dagger and put it to Caell's throat. "You take that back, or I swear I'll cut the tongue out of your head, Singer boy!"

Caell paled, but managed a soothing hum.

Jilian's blade lowered slightly. "It was your fault for takin' him prisoner in the first place and bringing him here. Now he's lost in this creepy forest."

"What did you expect us to do? Say thank you very much for kidnapping Rialle and Ky?"

Night Plume whistled again. "Not fight," he said. "You like wild quetzal against Starmaker's quetzal. Stupid. Enchanted."

They both looked at him in surprise. Jilian put her dagger away with a short laugh. "Listen to the Half Creature! He'll be trainin' as a Singer soon!"

Caell rubbed his throat, stayed angry for a moment, then gave a rueful smile. "Night Plume's right. This is getting us nowhere. We should be thinking how to help Ky, not fighting amongst ourselves." He gave Jilian a shy look. "Don't worry, your father was fine when I last saw him. I expect he's gone back to his hills." Then he must have remembered Lord Nahar's men were going to clean out the robbers' cave, because he bit his lip.

"Quetzal look for human-named-Asil later," Night Plume promised. "When flock recovered from Memory Trance."

Sun Glimmer and the others were still up on the reporting ground, trapped in the Trance. The Xiancotl sat cross-legged at the edge of the forest on the other side of the lake, also in the Memory Trance. The wild flock perched in the branches above him, their crooning drifting eerily across the camp. Night Plume felt left out. He'd offered to help, but the wild flock had said he would only confuse things since he could still see both sets of memories in the Memoryplace.

Jilian shot him a grateful glance. "Thanks, dark quetzal. But

I'll go look for him myself in the morning. They're bound to have got that thing open by then."

Caell clutched his bluestone harder. "They'd better. If they let Ky die in there, I'll . . . I'll —"

"Look!" Night Plume said. "They do something now." He picked up his bow and reached for his arrow. He carefully unwrapped the moss he'd tied around the end. Beneath it, the flint arrowhead was dark with Purple Flower Poison. He was careful not to touch it. He hoped it would still work now that it had dried — opening the Fane was taking a lot longer than he'd anticipated.

Caell sprang to his feet again and Jilian scrambled up beside him, startling the horses in a nearby picket. The Singers had organized some of the Karchlord's men to pull the Fane out of the water. The burly Karchholders grunted with effort as they rolled the crystal sphere and its precious contents across to where Singer Renn and Singer Kherron were pacing the remains of the quetzal nest. The two Singers used sharpened sticks to draw lines in the mixture of soft gray ash and crystal dust. They measured each line carefully and took frequent sights across the nest. Prince Erihan's men had cleared the area earlier and taken down the quetzal bodies, but a few fragments of rainbow egg still glimmered here and there in the ash. The Karchholders hauled their burden into the center of the nest and carefully adjusted its position according to the Singers' instructions. Then they removed the net and hurried back to the shore.

Night Plume gripped his bow harder and hooted uneasily. "What they do to nest?"

Caell and Jilian looked at each other in equal confusion. Then Caell grinned and clapped his hands in delight. "They're drawing a Pentangle! They're going to sing to it!"

Jilian frowned. "I thought they already tried that?"

"Only Singer Renn on his own, as Lady Shaiala kicked it." Caell's face was flushed with excitement. "Back in the Echorium when we give patients Songs, they sit in the center of a Pentangle in a special chamber, only it's made of bluestone instead of crystal. There are five Singers, one on each of the points, and they all sing together. The patient drinks Song Potion to relax them — a bit like chewing your Yellow Flowers! The Pentangle's very powerful, and Singer Kherron says we've used the khiz-crystal to transmit our Songs before, back when Frazhin first attacked the Isle. It'll work, I know it will! Except . . ." Some of his excitement died as he looked around, counting. "There's only three of us who can sing properly. Ky could have, if she weren't inside. And Singer Kherron's voice is —"

"Cured," Night Plume said. "You hear him sing to captured priest after battle — Xiancotl's people heal him."

Caell's face lit up. "You're right! His *Aushan* was perfect. That makes four Singers — counting me. Oh, I hope it's enough!"

He was already running around the shore of the lake, dodging the smoldering patches. Night Plume flexed his injured wing and half-flew, half-hopped after him. Although the forest people had treated his injuries with the same mixture of Healing Moss and Orange Flower they'd used on Singer Kherron's throat, he couldn't quite manage takeoff yet. His arm, however, felt as good as new. When the Fane opened, his aim would be true.

"Hey, wait for me!" Jilian called, racing after them. "Kyarra's my friend as well, you know."

By the time they arrived at the nest, Singer Kherron and Singer Rialle were already in position on two of the points. Singer Rialle still looked pale after her ordeal, but she stood unaided, and every line of her body showed her determination. The shadows in her gray eyes made Night Plume shiver. Singer Renn wore the same expression.

But Caell was backing away, shaking his head.

Don't do it, Night Plume!

What wrong? Night Plume used wild-speech as well. *I thought you want to sing?*

"They —" Caell jabbed an accusing finger at Singer Renn and glared at Singer Kherron. "They want me to sing *Yehn!* It'll kill Ky as well as Frazhin!" He swung back to the Second Singer. "I won't help you! If the First Singer knew what you were doing, she'd stop you. Without me, you can't do the Song. Even if Night Plume sings, you haven't enough quetzal. The others are all in the Memory Trance." Coldly, he turned away and gripped his bluestone.

"Caell, come back here."

Renn hummed softly under his breath. Night Plume shuddered even though the Song wasn't aimed at him. Jilian took an involuntary step backward.

The boy returned to stand stiffly before the Second Singer, jaw set, bluestone raised like a weapon.

"In spite of what you seem to think, I've already tried to contact the Isle about this," Renn said. "The First Singer is still not answering, so it's my decision. Singer Kherron and Singer Rialle agree with me. It's the only way to help Kyarra."

Caell's eyes filled. "You're not going to help her! You're going to kill her!"

Singer Renn sighed. "We've thought and thought about this, believe me. If there was any other way . . ." He glanced at Singer Kherron. "But there isn't. The air in the Fane is running out. We hope that by giving Frazhin *Yehn,* we'll break the spell on the lock so we can get Kyarra out of there. It should also help the Xiancotl to stop Frazhin from changing history."

"But Ky —"

"*Yehn* doesn't kill the body, you know that."

"But she'll be a zombie like her mother!" Caell was close to tears. Night Plume whistled in sympathy.

Jilian came and squeezed his hand. "I think it's a horrible idea! I saw what your Songs did to her mother. I won't let you do that to Kyarra!"

"It's either that, or let her suffocate," Singer Renn insisted, his face set. Again, he glanced at Singer Kherron. He lowered his voice to the level Caell had told Night Plume was called a pallet-whisper. Holding himself absolutely still, Renn spoke so only the three of them heard. "Mother . . . I mean, Singer Rialle . . . has a theory about *Yehn*. We use it so rarely, and normally the patient dies soon afterward because once the soul is gone it takes a lot of effort and care to keep the body alive. But it's just possible the effects of *Yehn* might wear off with time. Naturally, we'd do everything we could for Kyarra in the hope that one day she might recover. We can try some of the forest people's potions, sing her *Challa* and *Kashe* . . . I don't know how long it'll take, and I can't promise she'll recover before her body dies a natural death. But if you don't help us sing, she has no chance at all."

Caell's face twisted. Jilian glanced at Night Plume.

"But Ky might be a zombie for years!" Caell protested. "Lady Yashra hasn't recovered yet — or is that because you haven't tried to cure her?"

"Hush, not so loud. It's not a thing for public knowledge. If people knew our Songs might wear off eventually, they would not fear them so much."

Still Caell hesitated. His gaze flew to the Fane with its indistinct occupants, passed over the two Singers waiting on their points — Rialle very pale and determined, Kherron warming up his voice for its greatest test yet — fled across the starlit lake to where the Xiancotl sat chewing the quetzals' prechewed Yellow Flowers, rose to the crater where the Starmaker's quetzal were still locked in their Trance, and finally returned to the Second Singer. "If we sing, it'll break the spell on the lock and open that thing? You're sure?"

"It's the only way we can think of, Caell."

The boy took a deep breath and let his bluestone fall to his breast. "I've never sung *Yehn* before." His voice was small and worried.

Renn smiled and rested a hand on the boy's shoulder. "You'll do fine. Just work with us. Your bluestone will help give your

voice power. Night Plume, we need you to echo our Song —
you take the point between Singer Kherron and Singer Rialle.
Caell, you go between me and Singer Rialle. That way, we'll
spread our experience effectively."

Thinking of Sky Swooper and the quetzal mothers hanging
from the tree, Night Plume followed Caell on to the nest. Neither of them spoke.

"You won't need your bow," Renn said as he passed. "Not for
a Song."

Night Plume gripped his weapon tighter. "Always carry bow!"

"It'll be safe enough until we're finished. Give it to Jilian if you
don't trust the men."

They were interrupted by a *ping* from the Fane, as if the crystal were cooling. The figures strapped inside shifted in their
webbing, and their mouths opened and closed like fish out of
water.

"Hurry up, Renn!" shouted Singer Kherron, having completed his practice hums. "What's the problem? If we don't get
them out of there soon, it won't matter what Song we sing!
Show the quetzal where to stand and let's get on with it."

Seeing the stubborn expression in Night Plume's eye, Renn
sighed. "Oh, never mind, take the bow with you if you want." He
gathered his robes about him and crossed to his own point, his
sandals scrunching.

Night Plume perched where instructed, at the intersection of
two lines. It was strange being in the nest with no eggs. He'd
been born here, maybe on this very spot. The crystal was warm
under its coating of ash, good for hatching. The Fane nestled in
the center like an oversized egg. He hoped for the human girl's
sake that it would hatch.

They had collected an audience — the leaders of the army,
uneasy centaurs swishing their tails, Lady Shaiala, a few of the
painted people, some of the Horselords and Karchholders. They
all stood with Jilian at a wary distance and watched in silence as
the Singers did their breathing exercises in readiness for the

Song. Very slowly, in the shadow of his wings, Night Plume moved the black arrow to his bowstring and closed his hand around it. Caell gripped his bluestone and stared at the Fane as if he could crack it with his will alone. Singer Kherron glared at the crystal equally intently, his green eyes glittering. Across the Pentangle, Singer Renn raised his arms to the sky and let out the first terrible note of *Yehn*.

Night Plume's beak opened. Before he knew it, he was echoing that note. It was taken up by Singer Kherron, Singer Rialle, and finally Caell in his high-pitched boy's voice, then bounced back to Singer Renn, who sang another note. Night Plume forgot the audience. The nest softened under his talons. The Fane glinted in the starlight, so clear and sharp, it hurt his eyes. This was no soft lavender dream-song, nor even the swirling turquoise pain-song Rialle had sung inside the Temple. As the *Yehn* took him over, his grip slackened and his arrow dropped into the ash at his talons.

Death of deepest midnight shade.

*

Kyarra's head felt large enough to contain the entire world. The Xiancotl was still there, drifting in and out of focus, closer and farther away. Caell's face had gone. But he was alive. That made a difference. Somewhere at the edges of her consciousness were quetzal with their bright plumage. And naga, mere glimmers in the deep places. And, far off, merlee singing in the waves. And farther off still, a place that was blue and beautiful and peaceful where her mother ran along a beach, laughing in the sunlight . . .

If only she could reach there. But something was closing the doors in her head. The blue place and her mother vanished. The naga and merlee disappeared. The quetzal were gone. She could still see the Xiancotl, but he was fading fast, and soon she would be left with nothing. She began to struggle. But something held her fast. She could not move.

SLAM!

Another door shut.

SLAM! SLAM!

Each closing echoed in the space left inside her head, louder as that space became smaller, making her want to curl up and press her hands over her ears. Only she couldn't curl up, because she was held fast in the webbing. She saw her father as a small, blue-haired boy sitting on the Pentangle stool, and knew what had been bothering her.

"You can't have auditioned to be a Singer," she whispered. "Singers don't take children who aren't born in the Echorium."

SLAM!

The Xiancotl disappeared behind one of the doors, his sad gaze fixed upon her through the narrowing crack until it closed. *Remember Songs do not work on the Dark Ones. Remember the Singers' shame.*

Now there was only the darkness. And in that darkness, she saw her father's churning thoughts as clearly as if they were her own. He was looking at that same image of himself as a blue-haired boy on the Pentangle stool, and she felt his fury as he finally realized the truth about his past. How he'd been born in the Echorium, the son of a dark-skinned mother and a Singer father, trained as a novice, then given a Song to make him forget and sent away across the sea with the other dark ones.

"I can't do it!" he raged, still staring in disbelief at the image of the boy. "The Singers have played their meanest trick yet! We can't change history, or we'll destroy ourselves . . ."

The darkness whirled faster. Fear tightened about Kyarra like a chain.

"No!" she screamed. "You promised you'd cure my mother. We have to change it, we have to!"

SLAM!

Now even her father was leaving her. She fought the darkness with all her strength, fought to keep the final door from closing, but the pressure was too great and her father had abandoned her.

Death . . . death of deepest midnight shade.

*

The Fane exploded in a spray of crystal that fountained into the sky and rained down like dark ice. Men ducked as it pierced the rubble all around them and hissed into the lake. The centaurs shook their manes and people brushed shards out of their hair. The trees on the slopes of the mountain glimmered as fragments of crystal coated their leaves.

Night Plume closed his beak. It ached from singing. The three Singers and Caell slumped on their points. But in the sky above the crater, the Starmaker's quetzal were flying, their plumage glowing in the first rays of the rising sun. Fledglings flapped wildly among their older brothers and sisters, kept airborne by strong, feathered hands. As Night Plume spread his own wings, eager to join them, a groan from the center of the nest reminded him of what he owed Sky Swooper.

He snatched up his bow, fumbled in the ash for his arrow, and took aim at the larger of the two humans lying in the wreckage of straps and crystal. The blue-haired girl was still asleep. But the Starmaker was moving very slowly. Night Plume sprang across the nest and raised his bow.

The Starmaker blinked up at him. His scars twisted. "Didn't work . . ." He looked at the prone girl and the exhausted Singers and chuckled. "Your Songs don't work properly on me, do they? They never have!"

With a swiftness that alarmed Night Plume, he scrambled across the nest, grabbed the Singer girl by the hair and dragged her against his chest, where she flopped as if dead. "Back off, dark quetzal!"

Night Plume carefully stretched his bowstring. The Starmaker was holding the Singer girl in front of him like a shield, but she was small and his scarred throat showed above her hair. He could still get a clear shot. . . .

No, Night Plume! Caell cried in his head. *You'll hit Ky!*

The wild-speech distracted him long enough for the Star-maker to drag his unresisting hostage to the edge of the nest. The men and centaurs let out a collective hiss and started toward him, but stopped as the Starmaker put an arm around the girl's neck and pressed his crystal glove against her cheek.

"Anyone move, anyone sing, anyone even *breathe*, and I'll break her neck!" he threatened. "I underestimated you. I never thought you'd sing your Death Song to one of your own. But of course you've done it before, haven't you? Except I didn't remember until my daughter and the Xiancotl showed me the truth in the Memory Trance just now. It's easier to wreck a boy's life and send him away than admit your Songs don't work on him, isn't it? So easy for Singers to cover up their shame. And I wasn't the only one, was I? Soon the whole world will know. The truth will destroy you more surely than any change I could ever make. Stand back. I want a clear path to the lake."

Singer Kherron's eyes were terrifying. Singer Renn seemed rooted to the spot. Singer Rialle wore a horrified expression. Caell had stopped halfway across the nest, fists clenched. Night Plume tracked the Starmaker with his arrow. Out of the corner of his eye, he saw Sun Glimmer and the others swoop down the rays of the sun, bows raised. In a moment, the light would touch the lake and wake the enchanted naga. The Starmaker crept painfully backward, dragging the unconscious girl with him. Her eyes were open, but they were glazed and blank.

Another lifetime of crawling, and scales glimmered across the surface of the water. The Starmaker smiled. He, too, had seen the naga and the quetzal with their bows. "You made a mistake trying to use your Songs here," he rasped. "You might have twisted my dark quetzal to your purposes, but I'm still a god to the rest, as you'll find out. I'm going to take my daughter with me underwater, so don't try to follow us. Maybe I'll let her go later, maybe not. She's the most powerful Singer you've ever trained, isn't she? But she'll never be completely yours.

I haven't quite decided how to reward her for what she's made me see."

The quetzal glided lower. Night Plume kept the Starmaker in his sights. *Sun Glimmer*, he sent in wild-speech, unsure if his nestmate could still hear now he was out of the Trance. *Fire arrows in lake. Make Starmaker turn. I give order! I leader!*

The quetzal flock banked and came in low across the lake, arrows nocked. The assembled men and centaurs squinted into the sun and raised their weapons in alarm.

"Yes!" the Starmaker shouted, seeing the army's unease. "Show them who rules the new world, my beauties!"

Sun Glimmer loosed a scarlet-flighted arrow that pierced the Starmaker's robe. His scars twisted in shock as he scraped around, dragging the girl with him. "You can't hurt me, you stupid things! You're mine. I'm the Starmaker —"

Night Plume's poisoned arrow arced high over the heads of the Singers and buried itself in the back of the Starmaker's neck, a fraction below his skull. He stiffened. The girl fell out of his arms and rolled to the edge of the water. Everyone held their breath. But the Starmaker roused himself again and began to crawl toward his hostage, his crystal gloves scraping through the ash. The army watched, frozen to immobility.

Caell rushed forward. "Ky! Wake up! Get away from him, or he'll —"

Before he could reach the unconscious girl, a small, red-haired figure darted out of the crowd, shut her eyes, and plunged her dagger into the Starmaker's back. The blade skidded off a sheet of crystal in a shower of sparks, but her action broke the spell on the army. Karchholders and Horselords rushed forward with drawn swords and hacked their hated enemy to pieces. The naga and a few merlee surfaced and watched the execution with their luminous eyes. The quetzal passed over in a rush of wings and spiraled into a high turn.

You leader, Night Plume! came Sun Glimmer's joyful wild-speech as he brandished his bow. *Starmaker dead! We FREE!*

Jilian dropped her dagger and sank to her knees with a shudder. Caell knelt beside her and gathered the small, limp form of the Singer girl into his arms, sobbing uncontrollably. "Wake up, Ky, please wake up, I'm so sorry . . . I shouldn't have listened to them . . . I should never have agreed to sing *Yehn*. Please wake up, please!"

The army and the Singers were silent. A breeze ruffled the surface of the lake, teasing a hum out of the black feather protruding from the Starmaker's neck. A final echo of the Song of death.

18
CURE

Five Years Later

Waking was like crawling out of a small, dark room. Kyarra forced open eyes gritty with sleep. A reddish glow surrounded her. She was lying on her side, wrapped in a scratchy blanket that smelled strongly of horse. The cheek pressed against the ground had gone numb. A warm draft brought the smell of smoke . . .

The Fane!

She fought off the blanket and sat up, staring around wildly. But she wasn't imprisoned in crystal underground. She was inside a tent, its contours vaguely familiar. She yawned and rubbed her eyes. A brazier burned in the center, scenting the air with a fragrance that couldn't quite compete with the horsy smell. In a second blanket on the other side of the brazier huddled another sleeper. Long, black hair spilled over a sunburned arm.

"Mother?" Kyarra scrambled across and lifted the hair off the sleeper's eyes. She gazed down into that slack, beautiful face,

and let out a sob — half relief, half sorrow. "Oh, Mother, I tried!
I tried so hard to find a cure for you, but even the Xiancotl
didn't know one, so I went into the Fane with Father. But he lied
to me! He never really meant to help us. He only wanted to help
himself. He said the Memory Trance would cure you, but I don't
think he really knew if it would, and he didn't help me anyway . . ." Her memories of the Trance were fading fast, like the
memories of a dream, and she couldn't remember how she'd
come to be back in the Horselord camp with Lady Yashra. But
the important thing was that they were together again. "I'm
sorry, Mother," she whispered. "But at least you're safe, and I'm
here now. I'll look after you, I promise. I won't leave you again.
I'll stay here with the Harai and look after you until you don't
need me anymore." She sniffed again, stroking the beautiful
hair. She refused to think about what would happen when she
grew old yet her mother was still as young as she was now —
though, strangely, she did look a little older in this light.

The woman stirred and mumbled something.

Kyarra snatched her hand back as the sleeper sat up of her
own accord. She watched in disbelief as Lady Yashra rubbed her
eyes, exactly as she herself had done earlier. Had she made a
mistake? Could this be another Horselord woman?

But now Yashra was staring back, her expression mirroring
Kyarra's own. Disbelief changed slowly to hope. The joy in her
eyes shone brighter than the sun. "You're awake . . . oh, this is
all so strange. How do you feel?"

How did *she* feel?

Kyarra wanted to touch the hair again but didn't dare.
"Moth —" Her voice dried. She swallowed and tried again.
"Lady Yashra? Don't you recognize me?" Then she realized how
stupid that sounded. "I mean, do you know that you're . . . that
I'm . . . that we're . . ." She glanced at the tent flap, which had
been tied shut against the breeze. "I don't understand. How
come you're awake? The Singers gave you *Yehn!* What

happened? Did we do it? Did we change history? Where are the others? What happened to —" she shuddered "— to my father?"

Yashra smiled. "So many questions! You sound just like me, but I suppose that's not surprising. You'll learn everything in good time, Kyarra. For now, take it slowly. I know how much of a shock it can be, waking up after a long sleep."

One hand clutched at her throat. With a start, Kyarra saw she wore a bluestone on a knotted thong. Obviously she'd been unconscious longer than she thought, and in the meantime her mother must have woken from her death-sleep. She bit her lip, upset to have missed it, yet filled with happiness. Her mother was cured! Then she remembered what Lady Shaiala had said about her being evil.

"Do you hate the Singers for what they did to you?" she asked hesitantly.

Yashra gave her a sharp look. "For taking my baby away and singing me their Death Song, you mean? Yes, I hated them. Strapped on that stool in their Pentangle, I hated them almost as much as Frazhin did. But I've been asleep a long time. The world has changed. The Harai and Kalerei are at peace — would you believe that? And I have an eleven-year-old daughter with blue hair, almost a Singer herself." The pride in her eyes surprised Kyarra. "When they brought you to me in the Harai camp with your face so pale and your eyes so blank, and told me everything that had happened while I'd been asleep, what could I do? The little Singer boy I'd captured for Frazhin in the Mountains of Midnight all those years ago was grown up, in charge of everyone. He told me you'd been taken to the Isle for Songs, but the forest people had found a potion that worked on me so they'd brought you back to have the same treatment. He and his friends had as much reason to hate me as I had to hate Singers, but he offered me a Trust-Gift and put your hand into mine. The agreement was that I should look after you while the forest people treated you, even as they tell me you looked after me on our journey here from the Isle of Echoes. But I never really believed you'd wake up like I did. I thought the Singers had arranged your condition to keep me from making trouble again. I thought they sang you *Yehn* because you were Frazhin's daughter and they couldn't let you grow up to oppose them. Seems I was wrong."

Kyarra hardly knew what to say. As her mother spoke, she'd been drinking in every little frown, every movement of her mother's sunburned hands, and every touch of her lips with the soft tongue. Lady Yashra was looking at her in much the same way.

"I . . . it was horrible of them," Kyarra said. "But you're better now . . ." She glanced again at the flap. Was this the camp at Rivermeet? Lady Yashra had said something about the Singers bringing her here. She took a deep breath. There were so many things she needed to know. "Are the others here? Can I see them?"

Her mother reached for her hand. She stared at her without blinking for so long that Kyarra was afraid she'd fallen into the death-sleep again. She fingered the ends of Kyarra's hair with a little smile. "It's natural you want to see your Singer friends. I've hardly been the best mother to you, have I? At least not until recently, and then you didn't know a thing about it." She gave a little laugh. "I suppose we've been spared a lot of shouting matches. How about a ride?"

This was so unexpected, Kyarra almost laughed as well. A great lump rose in her throat. She swallowed what felt like a bucketful of tears and managed a smile in return. "I don't know how," she admitted. "I think I rode a centaur once, but I was asleep at the time. Except for that, I've only sat on a horse with one of the Kalerei — I was asleep mostly then, too," she added, recalling the long ride through Asil's Hills to Rivermeet.

"We're going to have to put that right. Can't have a Harai princess unable to ride a horse, can we? Come on."

"Now?"

"You want to see your friends, don't you?"

Kyarra gave her a cautious look, but it didn't seem to be a trick. She nodded.

They dressed quickly. The embroidered tunic, breeches, and soft boots waiting beside Kyarra's blanket fitted perfectly, though they were dusty as if they'd been worn by someone quite recently. Her heart banged as she pulled them on and let her mother adjust the crimson-striped sharet around her head. She wondered who the clothes could have belonged to.

She hesitated at the flap, fearing a trick. But this was definitely a Horselord camp. She recognized the purple dust of the plain and the picket lines. Except — where was the town and the river? Only a handful of tents remained where she remembered an entire sea of them, and there was no sign of the torchlit story-telling area where the painted man had told them the Prophecy of the Dark Quetzal. A haze on the western horizon hinted at clouds, but the sky above the tents was clear and blue. Two Harai boys were breaking in a colt. The hot Plains sun beat down on them, turning the colt's neck dark with sweat. They paused to wipe their foreheads and grinned at Kyarra.

Yashra had already untethered two horses from the nearest picket and was leading them across — a lively chestnut gelding and a smaller, silver-gray mare. Kyarra looked around carefully for centaurs. Remembering their skill with the green stones, she looked out of the corners of her eyes, but there was no telltale glimmer in the air. And although some of the Harai nodded to Yashra as she passed through the camp, they were all strangers to Kyarra.

"I don't think we should just ride off without telling anyone," Kyarra said doubtfully. "What if my fa — I mean, what if Frazhin sends his creatures after us again?"

Yashra had been straightening the mare's blanket. At the mention of Frazhin's name, her face closed a little. "You needn't worry about that."

A shiver went through Kyarra. "Why? Where is he?"

"Let me give you a leg up, and we'll talk about it as we ride."

There didn't seem any way of getting out of it. If she stayed in the camp and let her mother ride off, she might never see her again. So she let Yashra boost her up on to the mare's back and gathered the reins in the way her mother showed her, then sat nervously while Yashra sprang aboard the chestnut. Kyarra was alarmed to find even the effort of getting dressed and onto the mare's back had made her short of breath.

"Don't worry, that'll wear off," Yashra said with a smile. "I know what you feel like. Sleeping might be good for the complexion, but all my muscles were gone when I woke. Just let her follow. Keep the reins loose to start with, get your balance, feel her stride. We'll go slowly to begin with. Don't be afraid to hold on to the mane, that's much better than jabbing her mouth. It's not too long a ride — we're camped quite close to the sea and we've ridden to the beach many times, so your body should remember. Just relax and don't try to fight it."

Kyarra had been trying to concentrate on all the things Yashra was telling her and getting them hopelessly mixed up. But at the mention of the sea, she forgot she didn't know how to ride and urged the mare forward. "Beach? Which beach?"

"Where your friends come to meet us, of course," Yashra said, smiling. "The pirate had a cave there, where he used to store his ill-gotten gains before he accepted the Singers' Trust-Gift and put his ships at their disposal — not that he had much choice after Lord Nahar cleaned out his hideout in the hills and his daughter started on at him about how he had to make up for all the dreadful things he'd done to you, the poor man! The cave's warm and dry with access to the sea. Singer Rialle has transformed it. You wouldn't believe the treasure they found there! Horselord carpets, jewels the naga mined from the deep places, Karch gold. The Karchlord Azri took most of that back with him, of course, but he left enough to make the Kalerei rich. Good job I managed to persuade Lord Zorahan to demand a share as a peace incentive, or the Harai would have been the poorest tribe on the Purple Plains by now! Of course, your

Singers don't approve of all this treasure hoarding. They say it causes wars and makes their job harder, but then they would, wouldn't they?" Her eyes flashed in amusement as she turned her head. "That's it, Kyarra, give her a little more rein . . . now you're riding like a true Horselord princess!"

Kyarra looked down at her hands. She hadn't even thought about how she was riding the mare. Her head was spinning far too much with everything Yashra was telling her. *Many times.* Her mother had said she'd brought her here *many times*, and she'd somehow learned to ride a horse. The dust on her clothes now made a chilling kind of sense.

"Singer Rialle's there?" she whispered, remembering that Frazhin had imprisoned her as well. "Is she all right?"

"She's fine. She made her home in Asil's old hideout so she could remain near you while you were in the death-sleep. Said one cave was as good as another, and she could swim with the merlee just as easily from here as over on the Singer island. She sang to you every day, you know. Her voice is still very beautiful, though she's got this phobia about walls and doors dating back to what Frazhin did to her when she was your age — and I don't suppose her recent experiences helped." She gave a wry laugh. "Horselords can never understand why people should want to build themselves walls and lock themselves in, anyway. Rialle and I have come to know each other quite well. For a Singer, she's quite openminded."

"Is there —?" Kyarra swallowed and unconsciously clenched her fists, making the silver mare toss her head. "Is there a boy with her? About the same age as me?"

Yashra gave her a steady look. "Caell, you mean?"

"Yes! Is he there, too?" The sea was visible at last, a blue line glimpsed through the dunes. The breeze dried her sweat. There was a pirate ship at anchor in the bay. The sight of its masts sent a shiver down her spine. But the beach with its lilac sand was deserted.

Yashra reined in her gelding and glanced up at the sky. "Kyarra, there's something I ought to tell you."

A winged shadow passed over them, raising goose bumps on Kyarra's arms. She followed her mother's gaze and her breath stopped in her throat. *Quetzal.* It was a trick, after all! She kicked the mare into a gallop along the beach, heading for the only shelter she could see — the shell-hung mouth of the pirate's cave.

"Kyarra!" Her mother gave chase. "It's all right! Night Plume won't hurt you. The dark quetzal's friendly! All the Half Creatures are free of Frazhin's corruption now. Come back, I have to talk to you before you go in there —"

Kyarra's head whirled. She couldn't take in what her mother was saying. All she could see was the quetzal silhouetted against the sky, black as the night with an irregular patch of white on his shoulder. She flung herself from the mare in mid-gallop, landed in a spray of sand outside the cave, fought her way through the strings of shells — and stopped, face-to-face with a young man who had curly blue hair and kind brown eyes.

Her first thought was: He's even more handsome than Singer Renn! Followed by an ice-cold lump in her stomach as his eyes widened and met hers.

He caught her in his arms and whispered, "Ky . . . oh, Ky!"

She stared up at him in dismay. The old silver-haired Singer Rialle had climbed to her feet and was staring at Kyarra with an equal measure of joy and sadness. Another person had scrambled to her feet when she ran in — a young woman with red hair who seemed strangely familiar, except Kyarra couldn't think why. Behind her, the cave mouth was darkened by Lady Yashra and one other. She fought free of Caell's arms and swung around. The dark quetzal stood beside her mother, its black wings folded and its head on one side.

"Girl wake," it said with a soft hoot of pleasure.

Caell — the strange, grown-up Caell — smiled and took her hand. "Come and meet Night Plume, Ky," he said calmly. "He helped us sing open the Fane."

"And it was Night Plume's arrow that killed Frazhin!" the red-haired woman said, making Kyarra swing around again. "He stole some of the forest people's poison to put on the point, the little devil."

"Borrowed," the dark quetzal said with another hoot.

"But even the poison wasn't enough," Caell put in. "Jilian had to stab him with her dagger to stop him from taking you hostage again, and then the Horselords and Karchholders finished him off. It turned out Frazhin's body was half crystal, which was why the poison didn't work. We stripped off all his crystal and threw it back into the volcano. Then we burned his remains. Don't worry, Ky, he'll not hurt you again. He'll never hurt anyone again."

Kyarra looked closer at the red-haired woman, who had gone uncharacteristically quiet. "You killed my father?" she breathed.

"We did it between us," Jilian mumbled, with an embarrassed glance at Lady Yashra. "We had to. He was goin' to take you away again. But my dagger slipped off, so I still haven't stabbed anyone, not really."

"As good as," Caell said. "If it hadn't been for you, he'd have got away with his naga again, like he did back in the Mountains of Midnight. I reckon the Memory Trance helped, too. The old Xiancotl must have had something to do with it as well — but he died in the Trance, so we don't know how much he did. What do you think, Ky? You were in that Trance. What was it like? Was it very frightening?"

Kyarra felt faintly sick as her memory stirred. She'd been so close to her father at the end, yet she still didn't understand why he'd suddenly changed his mind and refused to help her. The sickness passed. She looked up shyly at Caell. "I thought *you* were dead," she whispered. "Jilian's father told me you'd drowned."

He gave his old boyish grin. "You don't get rid of me that easily! A wild merlee shoal saved me from Frazhin's corrupted lot — but all the merlee are back together again now, free of his enchantments. And after the Starmaker's death, Singer Renn finally managed to contact the Isle. Frazhin tried to poison the Echorium's water supply," he explained, seeing her blank look. "Remember those sacks we saw the pirates unloading before they kidnapped you? Don't worry, everyone's fine. First Singer Graia was very weak when we got back, but with a mixture of Songs and the forest people's potions she made a full recovery. Singer Renn and Singer Kherron have been busy sailing back and forth between the Isle and Silvertown, helping the sick people over there and looking for the remaining Half Creatures Frazhin corrupted. Jilian and her father helped, and I was allowed to sail with them to communicate with the merlee. But when the First Singer sent you back over here, we insisted on coming, too, so we'd be here when you woke up. Which reminds me, everyone will want to know you've recovered. I must contact Lianne." He twirled his bluestone and gave her a quick look. "She's a Singer now, too, you know. She volunteered to be the contact for our reports. I think it's her way of saying sorry for being such a twit when you were novices."

Kyarra could barely keep up with what Caell was telling her, but it seemed the Singers were still there, somewhere across the sea.

"Then . . . we didn't change it, after all?"

"Change what?"

"History. The world."

Caell exchanged a glance with Singer Rialle. Jilian looked at her feet.

The dark quetzal fluffed its feathers and hooted softly. "Starmaker gone. Enchantment gone. Everyone free. What you think?"

Kyarra looked at Lady Yashra, whose face was unreadable as she said, "This proves no one can change the past. Believe me, if Frazhin could have done it in that Memory Trance of his, he would have."

Kyarra pulled free of Caell. "That's not true! He *could* have, but he didn't. Something stopped him — something about the Dark Ones."

Silence. The two Singers exchanged glances again. "We couldn't allow it, Kyarra," Rialle said gently. "I'm sure you understand that."

She stared at them. "What's the Singers' shame?" she demanded.

There was another silence, longer than before.

Caell said, "It's history, Ky. But not the sort old Ollaron teaches us. Apparently, many years ago when Singers stopped the slave trade, they tested the rescued slaves and took those who could sing well enough back to the Isle to strengthen their breeding program. Among them were some dark-skinned women from the Quetzal Forest whose children turned out to be curiously resistant to the Songs. Although many of the children had good voices, they couldn't be safely trained, so they and their mothers were sent back home after having their memories wiped. But because our Songs didn't work properly on them, they couldn't have the standard treatment given to orderlies to protect the Songs, and were given *Yehn* to make sure they wouldn't remember. All record of the incident was suppressed. That's the shame."

"Given *Yehn*," she whispered.

Singer Rialle sighed. "Singer Ollaron thinks it's just possible Frazhin was one of those children — he was about the right age. I expect he was too scared to change the past once he found out he was born on the Isle himself, but we'll never know for sure. With the Xiancotl dead and all the Yellow Flowers gone from the forest, there can never be another Memory Trance, and what he foresaw in his final Trance only the quetzal will ever know. The forest people miss their holy man, but they're relieved, too. It was a terrible sacrifice to make — seeing the future had its price, as you witnessed. Yellow Flowers were never meant for human consumption."

"I remember now," Kyarra whispered. "My father's father was a Singer. So I *do* have Singer blood! Caell always said I did."

In the cave mouth, Yashra gave a small cough. Her mother must have loved Frazhin once, Kyarra realized. Still a little nervous of the dark quetzal, she went over to the Harai woman and put her arms around her waist. "I'm sorry," she said. To her own surprise, she burst into tears. Yashra stiffened, then hugged Kyarra back, stroking her faded blue hair.

"I know, Kyarra, I know," she murmured. "But it's best this way, believe me. You'll soon make new friends your own age, and when you're grown up the difference won't seem so great — it's only been five years for you. The Harai have a lot to make up for after the way we helped Frazhin back in the Mountains of Midnight before you were born. I've been helping Lord Zorahan put things right, and I'm looking forward to teaching you the duties of a Harai princess. But if you want to go back to the Isle and continue your studies, I'll understand that as well. Singer Renn says there's no reason why you shouldn't. You'd have to go down a few classes, though." She smiled.

Kyarra sniffed back her tears. She looked at the faces of her friends: Jilian turned into a beautiful young woman; Caell so handsome and grown-up looking; her mother still young enough to be mistaken for an older sister; Singer Rialle with her aged body but beautiful voice; the quetzal's unblinking black eyes . . . Strange to think a Half Creature could be her friend, but there was Lady Shaiala with her centaurs and Singer Rialle with her merlee. She had the weirdest feeling Night Plume had more to tell her and was simply waiting until they could be alone.

"Can I live as a Harai princess and still use the Songs?" she asked. "It would be good experience for when I'm old enough to be Second Singer."

Caell raised an eyebrow.

"A female Second Singer?" Singer Rialle said with a little smile. "That would involve changing a few things. But maybe it's about time we did."

THE LAST
MEMORY TRANCE

*We are in the Memory Trance. I have traveled back to the time before,
when the Dark One was young.*

*I see a boy born on an island of blue stone. His voice is strong, but he
sings the wrong songs. He drinks a potion that makes his head spin and
enters a place of midnight shadows where his head is filled with black
stars. The Singers send him away across the Misty Sea to a land where
dark crystal promises him power. He travels to the Karch where warlike
men live in smoky tunnels beneath the ice and snow, and they take him
in because he wields the dark crystal that fills their heads with black stars.
He forgets he has ever seen the island of blue stone. But he never forgets
his hatred of the Singers, and battles with them through three generations, until the time comes when he chews a Yellow Flower that makes his
head spin and enters a place of midnight shadows where his daughter
shows him what he could have been.*

*I see the Dark One, and he is dead because he dared not change the
truth that brought her into the world.*

*I see the Dark One's daughter, and she will live to become the most
powerful Second Singer the Echorium has ever known.*

*I see a future where Half Creatures and humans live in harmony as
they did long ago.*

I see all human history as an unbroken circle.

So it was. So it will be forevermore.

GUIDE TO
THE ECHORIUM SEQUENCE

Birthing House Attached to the Echorium, it is an ordinary slate house in which Singers give birth. Women who don't become Singers attend the Singer-mothers during childbirth and care for the next generation of novices until they're old enough to enter the Echorium. All Singers are expected to donate at least one child to the Birthing House. The mothers immediately return to their duties in the Echorium and the children grow up without family attachments.

bluestone Stone with magical properties, used by Singers to amplify the Songs and to transmit their voices across great distances.

Crazy Pallet slang for someone who is not right in the head and is brought to the Echorium for Song treatment and healing.

Dancing Canyons Steep-sided canyons in the foothills of the Mountains of Midnight. Site of an annual centaur ritual during which those foals ready to become adults crack the rock to find their herdstones.

death-braids Worn in the hair of a Karch warrior to show how many enemies he has slain; each braid is fastened with one of their finger bones.

Echorium Home of the Singers. Constructed entirely of bluestone, this ancient building stands on the highest point of the Isle of Echoes. There is no glass in the windows because it would be shattered by the power of the Songs.

Fane A hollow, many-faceted sphere constructed of semi-transparent panes of khiz-crystal, large enough to contain two people. When sealed by dark enchantments, it is virtually indestructible and only the Starmaker's Khiz-spear will open it.

First Singer   In charge of the Echorium, the First Singer always remains on the Isle of Echoes.

Five Thousand Steps   World-famous flight of steps, leading from the Isle harbor up to the main gates of the Echorium.

fohl   A very potent drink brewed from mare's milk by the nomadic tribes of the Purple Plains.

Great Sky Plain   Heavenly place where the tribes of the Purple Plains believe humans and horses go when they die.

Half Creatures   Ancient creatures — part human, part animal. Of limited intelligence and shy of adult humans, they sometimes communicate with children. There are four known breeds:

— *centaur*   Part human, part pony, they come in shades of blue from palest lilac to almost black. They live in herds, roam the Purple Plains, and use herdstones to conceal themselves from human eyes. They have developed lethal kicks for hunting and defense, including:
Snake: single strike with a foreleg.
Flying Snake: double strike with both forelegs.
Hare: single kick with hind leg.
Double Hare: double kick with both hind legs.
Dragonfly: sly sideways kick with any leg.
Canyon: downward strike with all four legs, used to crack rock to extract herdstones.

— *merlee*   Part human, part fish, merlee are found in the Western Sea and in the waters around the Isle of Echoes. Their Songs have power over the wind and the waves. They have short memories. Also known as fish-people.

— *naga*   Part human, part water snake, naga are very beautiful creatures that live in rivers. They breed in the flooded caverns under the Mountains of Midnight and have a weakness for sparkling objects, which they hoard. Also known as snake-people.

— *quetzal*   Part human, part bird, quetzal are found in the dense Quetzal Forest. They are perfect mimics with excellent memories and share a common ancestral memory called the *Memoryplace*.

Half Creature Treaty   Treaty drawn up between the Echorium and the world's leaders to protect Half Creatures from exploitation.

Harai   A renegade tribe of Purple Plains nomads who can be identified by their crimson-and-black striped *sharets*.

herdstone   Found in the Dancing Canyons, these green stones are used by centaurs to "bend the light" and thereby conceal the herd from human eyes. To make themselves fully invisible the centaurs' hooves must be in contact with the earth.

Horselord   Leader of one of the nomadic tribes that roam the Purple Plains. The tribes are always fighting one another but will band together if there is an external threat.

Isle of Echoes   Island in the Western Sea, about ten days' sail from Silvertown and thirty days' sail from Southport. The only place in the world where bluestone is found.

Kalerei   One of the most influential tribes of the Purple Plains, they can be identified by their green *sharets*.

Karchholder   A warrior who lives in the Karchhold, an underground system of tunnels and caves high in the mountains of the Karch, north of the Quetzal Forest.

Karchlord   Supreme ruler of the Karch, a hereditary position.

Khizalace   Palace constructed of black stone and khiz-crystal, which was destroyed in *Crystal Mask*, another title in "The Echorium Sequence."

khiz-crystal Black crystal with similar properties to blue-stone, found in the Sunless Valley deep in the Mountains of Midnight. If specially prepared, it can be used to control or steal people's memories. Masks made from khiz-crystal can be used to transfer thoughts from one wearer to another.

Khizpriest The chief priest of the Karch at the time of *Song Quest,* another title in "The Echorium Sequence."

Khiz-spear Spear made of black crystal that can be used to sort lies from truth and control people's thoughts. Also has the power to corrupt Half Creature memories. A symbol of office.

manhood braid Karch boy's first braid, to show he has completed his warrior training and is now old enough to fight. Normally fastened with the finger bone of a woman who has not died in battle, though there was a fashion for quetzal finger bones in the Khizpriest's day.

Memoryplace Ancestral memory of the quetzal. It is very accurate, and is the secret behind the quetzal ability to mimic and their gift of perfect recall. The Starmaker's quetzal have a false Memoryplace implanted in their heads by khiz-crystal. The quetzal Memoryplace can be accessed by the Xiancotl when he enters the Memory Trance.

Memory Trance Trance entered by the Xiancotl when he chews Yellow Flowers, enabling him to foretell the future. When he is not in the Trance, the Xiancotl is comatose because prolonged use of Yellow Flower poisons the human brain.

novice Child below the age of puberty who is training to become a Singer. Some gifted novices can hear and communicate with Half Creatures, an ability that is usually lost as they reach puberty.

Numbing Moss A moss with pain-killing properties that grows in the Quetzal Forest.

Orange Flower Lotion This extract from an orange flower that grows only in the Quetzal Forest is a cure for all ills. It is normally mixed with Numbing Moss because it stings if used on its own.

orderlies Men and (more rarely) women who don't become Singers. Employed in the Echorium as guards, cooks, servants, etc., they may also act as bodyguards to Singers who travel away from the Isle of Echoes.

painted people Dark-skinned people who live in nests high in the forest canopy beside the Red River. They have an extensive knowledge of the forest flora, and use the plants to make medicines and poisons. Their holy man, the Xiancotl, can foretell the future.

pallets Dormitories where novices sleep.

pallet-whisper An almost soundless, controlled whisper for the ears of one person only. Pallet-whispers are used by novices when they don't want their teachers to overhear.

Pass of Silence Narrow, unstable pass that avalanches at the slightest sound. It is the only land route into the Sunless Valley.

pentad Group of five orderlies who are trained to act as a bodyguard to protect the Second Singer while on official business.

Pentangle The heart of the Echorium where Songs of Power are given for healing, rehabilitation, or punishment. A large bluestone chamber with a five-pointed star (pentangle) engraved into the floor. The recipient sits on a spinning stool in the center. Singers stand on each of the five points. They wear gray silk and dye their hair blue so that bright colors do not interfere with the Songs.

Purple Flower Poison This extract from a purple flower that grows in the Quetzal Forest is a fast-acting and lethal poison.

Second Singer   The Singer who is in charge of Echorium business abroad and therefore travels a lot.

sharet   Wide scarf worn over the nose and mouth to keep out the dust when riding on the Plains.

Singer   One trained in the proper use of the Echorium Songs. A Singer has other, related skills such as:

— *farlistening*   *Listening* for vibrations over a distance greater than the normal range of the human ear. It is greatly enhanced by bluestone or water. Skilled Singers can also project their own voice (*farspeaking*).

Some young Singers can use this skill to communicate with Half Creatures but most of them lose this ability as they grow older.

— *truth listening*   Sorting truth from lies by *listening* carefully to a person's voice and body language.

Song Potion   Relaxant given to people before they are given Song treatment. It ensures the Song will have maximum effect. The recipe is a closely guarded secret.

Songs of Power   Five wordless songs that have the power to control emotions and memories:

— *Challa*   Dream Song. Most common form of healing. Puts people to sleep and helps them to forget their troubles.

— *Kashe*   Laughter Song. Wakes people up, cures depression.

— *Shi*   Pain Song. Forces people to confront their pain and heals through tears.

— *Aushan*   Fear Song. Gives life to inner fears. Makes people scream.

— *Yehn*   Death Song. Closes doors in the head. In extreme cases, leads to a form of *living death*.

Starmaker   Quetzal name for Frazhin, the Lord of the Forest, in *Dark Quetzal*. The quetzal hatched in Frazhin's nest of khiz-crystal believe he is a god because he has corrupted their ancestral memories.

Sunless Valley   Legendary valley deep within the Mountains of Midnight, where the sun never shines. It is believed to contain great treasure guarded by demons who swallow souls.

sunstep   An Isle of Echoes measurement, it is the length of time it takes the shadow of the Echorium's flagpole to move between two marks on the outer wall (about half an hour).

Trust-Gift   Bluestone jewelry, traditionally given to those who agree to let a Singer settle their dispute. It is worn as a sign they are willing to honor the terms of an Echorium treaty.

Two Hoofs   The centaur name for humans.

Wavesong   Echorium ship, used by Singers when they leave the Isle of Echoes on official business.

wild-speech   Quetzal name for telepathic speech. A true wild flock speaks as a single entity, finishing one another's sentences.

Xiancotl   Holy man of the painted people who live in nests in the canopy of the Quetzal Forest. When he chews Yellow Flower, he can access the quetzal Memoryplace and guide others into the Memory Trance with him in order to foretell their futures.

Yellow Flower   Rare golden cactus that grows only in the canopy of the Quetzal Forest. In excess, Yellow Flower is poisonous to humans, but it has the effect of breaking down barriers in the human mind to allow access to the quetzal Memoryplace.

ABOUT THE AUTHOR

Katherine Roberts is the author of *Song Quest* and *Crystal Mask,* the first two books in the *Echorium Sequence*. *Song Quest* won the Branford Boase Award for Best First Children's Novel, and *Booklist* called *Crystal Mask* "a novel of great depth as well as plenty of action and excitement." Ms. Roberts is also the author of *Spellfall*, which *The Book Report* called "an imaginative...believable and absorbing fantasy." She lives in Ross-on-Wye, England.